I0779750

PEGGY GODSON MUELLER

Third of May

By Peggy Godson Mueller

First and foremost, I'd like to thank God for giving me the inspiration and strength to complete this project. It's been a long process in which I have experienced as many personal twists and turns as the characters in this story, but He has been by my side throughout.

This book is dedicated to my mother, Ruth Godson, who was the first one to read my manuscript and for whom the book is titled *Third of May* (her birthday). She was the greatest cheerleader for my writing efforts. I miss her every day but know that I will see her again when my time on Earth is over.

A big "thank you" to my friends, Ann Williams and Gail Morgan, who offered their proofreading skills and spent their valuable time cleaning up my manuscript when my weary brain got careless with punctuation, grammar, verb tense, and so on and so forth. Wow—what a great job you did!

Next, a hug and kiss for my new husband, Steve Beaupre, who has been by my side through the editing process of this book; he patiently cooked, planted gardens, ran errands, and did whatever he needed so I could spend countless hours getting this story ready for publication.

Many thanks go to Cynthia Hickey and Winged Publications for taking a chance on me and making my dreams come true by publishing my works.

I want to thank you, my readers, for going on this journey

to Nantucket Island with me! I hope you enjoy your time spent reading my book, *Third of May;* please visit my Facebook page: *Write by Me – Peggy.* I would love to hear your comments.

I'm forever grateful to all of you!

-   Peggy

NANTUCKET ISLAND, MASSACHUSETTS

CHAPTER ONE

1989

A brief flash penetrated the dense morning fog catching Faith McCleary's attention. She walked to the ferry's upper deck rail on the starboard side and waited for the light to reappear. It teased her, darting in and out from behind the smoky, gray curtains of mist, becoming brighter until the faint outline of a lighthouse became visible.

Here I am drifting away from the gloom of my past, gliding on toward a beacon of light . . . my new life and home. She chuckled at the tired cliché. "Only in a cheesy movie," she whispered.

Faith was eager for the journey to end. Two taxis, one rental car trip, and now a ferry ride left her exhausted. But it was still early, and she had more of the morning to conquer. She smiled and silently congratulated herself for getting to Nantucket without losing her way—except for one minor mishap which she straightened out before traveling too far off course. Her decision to rent a car and drive from Rhode Island to Massachusetts was the second step she took in reclaiming her self-confidence. The first was to leave Providence and never look back. Faith felt she had no choice about the first step, but the second decision was a bold move. She never trusted her sense of direction when behind the wheel, and as of ten days ago her confidence was shaken in matters of the heart as well.

The rising sea mist dampened Faith's clothing, so she descended to the lower deck of the ferry in a vain attempt to warm herself. *I should've moved to Florida.* She shivered as she pulled a woolen scarf and gloves out of her oversized tote bag. After wrapping it tightly around her neck and throwing her jacket hood over her head, she decided to brave the cold and climbed back up the steps to the top deck.

Faith squinted her eyes against the chilly wind and scanned the approaching harbor, wondering if she would recognize The Scrimshaw Inn. *Is it even near the harbor?* Several buildings in sight looked similar to the photos she remembered seeing as a child – a large, gray-shingled house with a widow's walk high atop. The numerous wooden structures flanking the water's edge at the bottom of the hill struck a familiar chord. *Will I even remember Alice's face when I see it again?*

This was her new home. Life-changing experiences usually shook Faith to her core, but she relished the idea of being somewhere other than Rhode Island. When Faith's mother told her that her old friend, Alice Woodson, needed someone to assist her with the day-to-day duties of running her inn, she welcomed the thought of a new routine and receiving a free room, breakfast, and a modest paycheck in return.

Faith leaned over the side of the ferry not wanting to miss a thing as it docked. Souvenir shops lined the street leading from the water into the main part of town. Two older cars sat curbside while the young drivers shouted to the exiting passengers.

"Anyone need a ride?" One college-aged girl called and waved her arms wildly, then held up a sign which read "CHEAP TAXI".

Not knowing where on the island the Scrimshaw Inn was located, Faith decided to take the girl up on her offer. She walked a few steps in the direction of the taxi and waved back at the girl. Faith called to her, "Right here!" The car pulled closer to the dock and the driver immediately jumped out and approached Faith.

"Let me take those bags for you," the brawny girl said. Her long, black braid flopped from side to side as she lugged the bags to the car and loaded them into the back. "You're not what I'd call a light traveler!" She paused for a moment to catch her breath before grabbing another couple of bags. "You plannin' to be here for a while?"

"Sure am." Faith dug around in her tote bag. She'd written down Scrimshaw's address and now searched for the paper, finding it folded inside the tote's pocket.

"How long?"

"I suppose for as long as I'm needed. I'll be living and working at The Scrimshaw Inn."

"Nice place." The driver closed the back of the station wagon. "And a nice lady, Alice."

"Oh, you know her?"

"Sure. You get to know everyone on the island when you drive a taxi." She shaded her eyes from the low morning sun.

"I guess you would."

"So that's where you need to go right now? The Scrimshaw?"

"Yes, please. Is it far?" Faith shoved the piece of paper back into her tote.

"Nothing on this island is far. It's just down the street and around the corner. You'll have a good view of the harbor there."

The girl drove her recklessly, slamming the glove box closed with each bump she hit. Faith wondered if the vehicle would arrive at The Scrimshaw in one piece. When they reached the last turn, the car's headliner, held up by large safety pins, popped loose and flapped Faith in the face.

"Sorry," the driver said. "If you don't mind pinning that back for me?"

"Sure." Faith jammed the pins back into the foam lining above her head.

"These bumpy roads are pretty rough on cars. Not to mention the terrible things the salt air does to them. Tourists sure love this cobblestone. I'll admit that it does look pretty, but it's a killer." The girl came to a sudden stop in front of The Scrimshaw. She jumped out and popped the back hatch open. Her face reddened as she heaved the burdensome baggage into a sprawling pile on the sidewalk.

Faith handed her a bill. "Keep the change."

The girl's face lit up when she saw the folded-over twenty. "Hey, thanks. Have a nice stay. I'll probably be running into you sometime on the island. Well, not really running into you. You know what I mean. Just stay out of the road!" She laughed and drove off, leaving Faith at the front walk with a mountain of suitcases.

The inn was just as she recalled from the photographs. Weathered, gray shingles covered most of the two-story building; the white trim shone brilliantly in the morning sunlight. A dainty white picket fence promenaded around three sides of the property. Large chimneys rose regally from either side of the inn's weathered roof.

As Faith stood on the walkway admiring her new home, a woman about her mother's age stepped out of the front door and onto the portico.

"Faith McCleary!" the woman called out.

"That's me!" she replied, giving her a small wave. Alice had aged gracefully but her hair was now a soft shade of gray, a pair of glasses hung on a chain around her neck.

"You look like you could use a little help." Alice scurried down the walkway and stood in front of Faith, looked her over, and smiled. She shook her head slowly. "My, how you've changed. I believe you had braces and long hair down to your waist the last time you were here. And now look at you. All grown and so stylish." She gave Faith a big hug, leaned back, and smiled at her again. "You don't know how eager I've been for your arrival." Alice's eyes pooled with tears. "I see so much of your mother in you."

She knew she had changed a lot since Alice saw her as a teen. For the better, she believed since her acne had long passed. Now at thirty-two years old, she kept her naturally wavy hair sleekly pulled back into a ponytail and would never be caught wearing wrinkled clothing or without her trademark pearl stud earrings. Her slacks remained perfectly pressed, and her white boat shoes showed no sign of dirt on the toes which was a remarkable feat after riding the ferry from Hyannis.

"I'll show you to your room," Alice grabbed a suitcase and walked up the porch steps, holding the door open for Faith, who was carrying two of the most cumbersome bags. "Just follow me. I hope you don't mind not having a harbor view. We need to save those rooms for the guests. They always want a view. But you do have a private bath."

Alice took a right turn once they entered the hallway, past a large portrait of a woman. "You'll overlook the side gardens. In the summer it's quite beautiful."

"I can imagine it is. Everything's so gorgeous!"

Alice set the suitcase on the old wood floor and pointed to French doors. "There's a little patio out that door where you can sit and have some privacy." She led Faith around the bed. "Your closet is over there, and your bathroom is here." Alice took several steps and turned on the light in the delft blue bathroom; the blue and white border around the top of the wall matched the toile shower curtain.

Faith smiled as she admired the bathroom. "This is my favorite color. It's like it was designed just for me!"

"I'm so glad you like it." Alice patted Faith on the arm.

The floors throughout her suite were heart pine boards that had been varnished a multitude of times. The chenille throw rugs next to either side of the bed and in front of an antique dressing table were soft and inviting. On the long bedroom windows, blue floral drapes were pulled back and tied, ready to shut when the sun went down. Faith walked to a window and smiled admiringly as her gaze scanned the front lawn.

"There aren't any guests staying here at the moment. I'm only open for boarders the last week of May through the end of October. But I will make some exceptions," Alice explained. "I'll close for a week or two in the summer if I need time off for something important. Last summer we had a young girl who helped us with the cleaning, and, of course, I had Jim to help with other chores. This will be the first summer I haven't had Jim around. It'll be hard on me, I suppose."

"I'll be as much help as I can. I'm looking forward to it," Faith said. "I always thought running an inn like this would be so much fun."

"I think everyone dreams about owning a bed and breakfast, but it's not all fun and games," Alice headed out the door. "Let's go grab the rest of your bags." She motioned and walked down the hallway with Faith close behind. "Yeah, it's a lot of hard work keeping this place going, but the nice people you meet make it worthwhile. You can't be in this business unless you enjoy people." Alice turned around to face Faith when they reached the sidewalk. "You do like people, don't you? I forgot to ask you that on the phone." Alice handed Faith the two smallest overnight bags and grabbed a suitcase, letting out a grunt. Faith quickly took the heavy bag from Alice and insisted that she take a lighter load.

"Sure. I think people are great." Faith fibbed a little. She'd never been a sociable person but knew going into this job she'd have to hone her people skills. She was willing to put on a smile and be the perfect host when the job called for leaving her emotional baggage back in Providence where it belonged.

"When we get these bags to your room, I'll show you around the inn."

"I hope I didn't bring too much with me," Faith said, embarrassed about the number of suitcases and assorted other bags she'd packed.

"Just makes me believe you're taking this job seriously. It's encouraging to see that you brought so much stuff. If you'd shown up with one or two suitcases, I'd suspect this was just a trial thing for you."

The bags were deposited in Faith's room and the tour began. "This house was built in 1793 by a sea captain just before his marriage to a woman from Cape Cod." Alice led Faith over to a large, 18th century portrait of a woman. Chestnut brown hair framed the woman's pasty face as she stared ahead blankly.

"Her husband was gone many weeks out of the year sailing the seas. Whaling. His wife, Lauralee Dodd, would go to the widow's walk on top of the house with a telescope and look out over the water to see if she could spot him. This is Lauralee," Alice said as she lightly touched the portrait. "Some guests have told me she looks a little spooky. I hope you don't think so. I find her face to be comforting, in a strange way. She's like an old friend to me now. The house remained in the same family for one hundred and seventy-five years until the last surviving family member, Miss Adelaide Dodd, moved into a nursing home and sold the house to Jim and me. She has since passed on."

"How did you meet her?" Faith asked.

"We vacationed on Nantucket every year since we were married and stayed here at The Scrimshaw Inn whenever a room was available. Miss Dodd listened to us talk about our dream of running an inn and approached us when her health became bad. The house was never on the market. Miss Dodd had grown fond of us and felt the house needed to be kept in loving hands, so she made us an offer we couldn't refuse. As you can see, we didn't refuse. We spent all our retirement savings fixing the place up, paying special attention to keeping things as original as possible."

"It looks great. You did a wonderful job," Faith said, walking a few steps to the beautiful front hall staircase. The deep, dark mahogany had a warm patina which could only be acquired from many years of its existence. She ran her fingers across the handrail that felt as smooth as a polished river stone from numerous generations of use. The twisted balusters marched their way up the stairs from an intricately carved newel post and followed the staircase as it bent and continued up to the second floor. The center of each stair dipped slightly from years of wear only adding to the charm.

"This is the living room," Alice said as they made their way past the staircase into an airy, casual room filled with over-stuffed furniture. The sheer curtains floated gently in the breeze from the windows between a writing table and a large old bookcase. "Our guests are welcome to come in here and put their feet up, read a book, play the piano, or do anything they might do at home. We have such wonderful live theater on the island. We try to encourage our guests to catch a show while they're here. And, as you can see, we have a lot of books for them to read if they'd rather stay in."

"What a great idea!" Faith noticed several books she'd like to borrow.

"Now come and follow me this way." Alice turned and headed down the hallway to the kitchen. "You'll be spending a fair amount of time in here with me. But we'll discuss those duties after you get acclimated."

"There's going to be a lot to learn, I'm sure."

"I want you to take a few days and get to know the island. The guests will expect you to be an expert," Alice said. "But don't worry. I'll help you out as much as you need. It's quite fun to get to know the people who come here. Faith, I can't tell you how much it means to me to have you here. I've been looking forward to it so much. I know I've said that before, but I mean it. I think you'll come to love Nantucket as much as I have." Small creases formed around the corners of Alice's eyes as she smiled. Her face defied the sixty-eight years she'd seen come and go. "Why don't you take the day and explore the island. I'll point you in the direction of some interesting things to do."

"That sounds good. You don't want to come along with me?"

"You'll be able to see more without me. I don't move as quickly as I used to. Besides, I've seen all the sights a million times."

"Where do you suggest I start?"

"Take the island tour. Just go down the street and you'll see the information booth. That's where you buy the ticket. You'll see the whole island, then you can decide what you'd like to investigate further. We still have a couple of weeks before the guests start arriving. Well, I take that back. You'll have a little bit of practice next week. We have one couple coming to stay. I'll take care of them, and you can observe. Go have fun today and learn something."

"Good idea," Faith said as she started to walk out of the kitchen. "I'm going to change into something fresher."

"Let me get you a key so you can come and go as you please. When we have guests staying with us, the door is usually unlocked. Stay out as late as you like. The only concession I'll ask you to make to this little old lady," Alice said, pointing to herself, "is please don't bring home any overnight guests. You know what I mean. Now I'm not saying you would or anything, but I'm not that modern."

"Don't worry about me. I won't do that. I wouldn't care if I never saw another man for as long as I live." After she left, Faith realized she may have confused Alice with that remark, but she wasn't ready to explain.

She quickly changed and called "goodbye" to Alice who

was still puttering in the kitchen. When she reached the end of the sidewalk, Faith turned around to take another look at her new home.

"I think I'm going to like it here," she whispered to herself, admiring the delightful structure. With every breath of fresh salt air, she felt renewed. Her troubles were now three taxi rides and one ferry trip behind her. Things were definitely looking up.

CHAPTER TWO

Faith hopped off the last step of the tour bus and took out the list she'd compiled of places to visit. She read it and began planning the next few days. *First, I'll visit the Whaling Museum, then stroll around town, and then do a little window shopping.*

The walk to the museum was short. Faith was surprised by her newfound interest in Nantucket's whaling history and stayed longer than she intended. After leaving the museum, she rehearsed the facts she'd learned so she would be ready for any questions asked by the Scrimshaw Inn's guests.

Exploring the town of 'Sconset and spending time on the beach would be the plan for tomorrow, she decided. Faith looked over the list one more time to make sure she hadn't missed anything she wanted to see in the vicinity of the museum. Browsing through the quaint stores kept her occupied until late afternoon. At her last stop before leaving the Main Street shopping area she made her only purchase—a simple, yet pricey, straw hat with a rolled-up brim. She justified the purchase because the sun was bright and hitting her in the eyes while walking and her sunglasses were of little help, so she needed it to shade her face. Never mind the fact she had a cheap visor in her tote bag.

The aroma of seafood permeated the air around the harbor as restaurants began filling with hungry tourists. Temptation got the best of Faith, so she ducked into a lobster hut, grabbing the first available table she saw. She mentally ate every tasty morsel that passed by on the waiter's tray while waiting for her own meal to arrive. When her food came fifteen minutes later, she devoured the fried seafood platter as if food had not crossed her lips in days.

In Providence, Faith routinely took a walk after dinner to burn off some of the calories she'd consumed. Not being one to break tradition, she tucked her new hat under her arm, careful not to crush it, grabbed her tote bag and headed down a winding street past the Congregational Church close to the main part of town. She popped back into a couple of stores which remained open late to take a closer look at some items that caught her eye earlier in the day. Upon leaving, her curiosity took her down a picturesque side street. Being one who loved to look at old buildings, she couldn't pass it up.

The streets took on an even cozier personality in the evening. Soft, yellow light filtered through the ornate windows of several gorgeous old homes. Through the open window of one home, she saw a woman strumming a harp, oblivious to passers-by. The soft percussion of car tires on cobblestone leant rhythm to the harp's angelic chords. Faith stopped walking for a moment to listen. Couples strolled past her down the sidewalk, hand-in-hand, but she didn't care to watch them. She felt left out of the romance that pervaded the island.

A row of white mansions caught her eye, and she wondered what the stories were behind each house she passed. Perhaps this one was a sea captain's home? Or maybe a vacation retreat?

Faith squinted to read the time on her watch in the light from an overhead streetlamp. Ten o'clock already?! She had done enough sightseeing for one day. Best to head home and get some shut-eye, she decided. Faith rounded the corner and followed the cobblestone road back toward the harbor.

After passing several more houses, it became clear to her that she had taken a wrong turn. She recognized nothing she saw in the darkness except the faint light from the harbor.

She was lost.

"Good going," she mumbled as she looked around at her surroundings. Off, somewhere in the distance, she heard people laughing and talking. She walked in the direction of a large, three-storied inn. The voices got louder and clearer as she approached. She noticed light shining through an open side door situated below street level which turned out to be an entrance to a pub occupying the basement of the inn. Faith walked to the door and glanced inside. It looked safe enough to her. A couple of women sat amongst the men, so she entered and asked for directions to The Scrimshaw. The bartender told Faith where he thought The Scrimshaw was, but another patron corrected him.

"You're going to get her lost." The man who had spoken rose from his seat and Faith saw he was very tall—well over six feet. He was casually dressed in a tee shirt and warm-up pants. Large graying curls topped off his head and a couple of days' growth of stubble glistened on his cheeks.

"I'll take you to The Scrimshaw," he said as he took a couple of steps toward her.

"Oh, that's not necessary. If you can just tell me how to get there, I'll be fine." Faith hoped he wouldn't insist on following her home. The thought of being alone with him in the dark made her uncomfortable.

"Don't worry," the bartender chimed in. "He's safe. It's been several years since his conviction." The people sitting around the bar laughed. Faith did not.

"They're just pulling your leg. You know that, right?" The man's eyes pleaded with her to trust him, and when he smiled, his dimples took away some of her concern.

"If you're sure you're safe," Faith said warily. She looked around and everyone seemed to know him. She noticed he was drinking only coffee which made her feel better about the situation.

"Come on. I'll be happy to take you there. Never could resist a damsel in distress," he said. Against everything her mother ever taught her, she started toward the door following the man. A complete stranger.

"Bye, Novac. See you soon and take care," the bartender said as they left.

"Wait here while I grab my bike." He dashed off and came back pushing a bicycle to the door where she stood.

"I'm not going to have to—" Faith pointed at the bicycle.

He laughed, "No, no! I'll push it along as we walk. The Scrimshaw's just around the corner. I ride past it all the time. So how long are you here for?"

"Indefinitely."

"Is this a vacation?"

"No. I'll be working at The Scrimshaw."

"How long have you been here?"

"Just today," she said, not wanting to give him more information than necessary.

"Have you seen any of the sights?" he asked, as they walked along the sidewalk.

"I looked around town today. Guess I saw more than I really wanted to see tonight."

"I'm hurt," he said, laughing.

Realizing how her answer sounded, Faith covered her mouth with her hand and then pulled it away suddenly. "I'm sorry. I meant no offense!"

"No offense taken. By the way, my name's Novac."

"Faith."

"Nice to meet you, Faith. Well, there's The Scrimshaw." He pointed to the inn. "See? I really did know where it was. If you'd listened to Roy's directions back at the pub, no telling where you'd have ended up."

"Thanks a lot. I really appreciate your trouble."

"No trouble at all. I enjoyed the company. Besides, I was ready to leave. I have a seven-mile ride home."

"Where's home?" she asked, wishing she hadn't. She had no desire to engage him in conversation. She just wanted to get into the house safe and sound.

"'Sconset. It's a beach community on the east side of the island," he said.

"I saw it on my tour today."

"If you were on a tour bus, then you didn't really see it. You need to get out and walk around."

"Tomorrow. That's my plan tomorrow." *Why did I open my big mouth? What if he wants to come along?* She took her key out of her pocketbook and started toward the inn. "Thanks for your help."

"Well, have fun and don't get lost. Take care, okay?"

"Sure will. Thanks. You, too." Faith reached the inn's front door and felt relieved as Novac rode off on his bicycle. *I hope this doesn't end up like the time that strange fellow, Tom, kept showing up everywhere after he fixed my flat tire. Or what about the creepy guy who caught me when I tripped in front of the library? Wonder what his wife would've said if she knew he tried to get my phone number? Guess he didn't think I'd notice the ring on his finger.* "No wonder they always called me the weirdo magnet," she mumbled as she unlocked her bedroom door. "I won't tempt fate again."

The thumping of car tires on cobblestone woke Faith out of a sound sleep. Through an opening in the drapes, she could see the sky was beginning to brighten, painting the surrounding scenery in rich lavender light. She rose from bed, wrapped her bathrobe around her to keep the chill away, and opened the door that led to the small patio. The slate under her bare feet was cold and a gentle misty breeze blew across her face. She couldn't quite see the water or the boats at the harbor, so she decided to climb to the widow's walk and get a quick peek. After a minute, she went back inside and down to her room to throw on some clothes. Anything would do.

Alice was in the kitchen in her slippers and bathrobe, fixing coffee.

"Good morning, Faith," she called as Faith passed by.

"Good morning." Faith was sorry to have been spotted. She had not yet put on any make up, much less washed her face or brushed her teeth.

"Why are you up so early, honey? I don't mind if you sleep in this week. Might as well take advantage of it." Alice walked into the hallway where Faith stood.

"I thought I'd go up and see the sun rise over the harbor."

"It's a sight to see if the fog isn't too heavy. You can get up to the widow's walk through that door to your right. Why don't you take a cup of coffee with you? It's ready."

"I went up there for a second. It was a little chilly, so hot coffee is a great idea. I don't want to be any—"

"Don't be silly. Here's a mug. There should be a couple of chairs up there already. Take this rag to wipe the dew off," Alice handed Faith a dishtowel.

"You're too kind to me," Faith said, a little uncomfortable about being fussed over. She headed to the door on the right past the portrait of Lauralee.

Faith was sore from all the walking she had done the day before, so she felt every muscle in her legs as she climbed the stairs to the top floor. A crisp breeze greeted her when she opened the small door to the roof. After stepping over a short threshold, she noticed the two chairs just where Alice said they would be. A white metal table was placed between them. Faith set her coffee down and wiped off one chair.

Looking down, she could see scores of rooftops as the land made a slight dip to the harbor. She had never realized there were so many homes tucked away amongst the trees. As the fog lifted, she began to see the faint, ghostly images of faraway boats bobbing in the water. There were all types and sizes; some rested peacefully in the harbor, others slowly headed out to sea. A couple of cars drove along the road paralleling the water's edge. "What a way to start a day," she said as she sipped her coffee. "I could get used to this."

Faith thought about Phil as she looked out toward the harbor. The scenery reminded her of how much he loved boats and the ocean. More than he had loved her, she suspected. She was gone from his life now, but his boat remained. Faith felt sure of that. Loyal old "Bessie" he called it. "I hope they'll be very happy together," she muttered, shaking her head as if to clear away thoughts of him.

She collected her mug and dish towel, then descended the stairs. The warmth felt good. She washed the mug and went to her room to get ready for her day in Siasconset, or 'Sconset, as the natives call it. After showering, she put on her bathing suit and covered it with a pair of loose-fitting pants and a top. She slipped on some sandals, packed a tote bag, and grabbed her new hat.

In the daylight, she could see the path she traveled on the previous evening when she couldn't find her way back to the inn. Clearly, she had the harbor and church steeples as landmarks. *How could I have gotten lost?* The twisted roads must've thrown her off, she determined, as she walked to the corner where the shuttle bus made its morning pick-ups. Bells tolled the hour from a nearby church as she stood waiting at the curb.

The shuttle arrived on time. Faith climbed aboard with a few other tourists, paid her dollar, and took a place by the window. The bus bumped along the road, picking up a new passenger occasionally, as it cruised past scrubby trees and non-ending gray-shingled houses. Even the newer buildings and homes were covered in the island's drab, gray apparel, making it difficult to discern which were from a couple of centuries ago, and which were imposters. Some modern homes gave themselves away by having garages and driveways or a picture window, but most stayed true to the island's "whaling cottage" look. A cloudless sky dominated the scenery, and a bicycle path meandered alongside the road all the way to where the shuttle stopped in the village of 'Sconset. Faith gathered her belongings and exited the bus.

"You'll come back every half hour to pick up? Is that right?" Faith asked the driver through the open bus door.

"Right. Every half hour."

He drove away, leaving her standing in the middle of a charming little village full of more gray-shingled houses that were characteristic to the island. Many were so small they looked like playhouses children might have in their backyard. Vines climbed the sides and even on the roofs of a few cottages. Faith was enchanted, so she decided to walk down one of the roads and take a closer look. The paths between the cottages were so close to the structures, she felt voyeuristic as she passed by. Most had the curtains pulled closed. Beautiful, tiny gardens surrounded some of the homes, and there were larger homes intermingled with the tiny ones. One two-storied house perched on a small bluff boasting its view of the ocean, while its neighbors sat nestled, partially hidden behind scrubby trees. Faith reached the end of one short road and decided to turn and head down a sandy path that led her out to the pristine beach.

She slipped off her sandals and shoved them into the tote, shivering as the chilly wind whipped across the ivory sand. Faith burrowed her toes into the sand but quickly pulled them out, shocked by the coldness of the sand underneath. She stood still and tried to choose which direction looked best for exploration. Only a few people relaxed on the beach directly downhill from the cottages. The other way, the beach was completely deserted, and she noticed signs warning of the strong currents.

Faith proceeded toward the expanse of beach in the more populated area and positioned herself so she could people watch. She sat and watched a young man toss a Frisbee to a collie that obediently leaped into the air over and over. Several yards away, closer to the ocean, man and woman sat next to the water's edge building sandcastles with their young daughter. With each frigid wave that rolled in, the little girl let out a shrill, delighted squeal and jumped. Her round face grinned from ear to ear.

Faith pulled a beach towel out of her bag and spread it on the sand beside a small dune. She hoped the sandy mound would keep some of the chilling wind off her. After looking around to make sure no one was watching, she pulled off her pants and blouse, folded them neatly, and put them away. Faith shivered and rubbed her goose-bump-covered arms but was determined to not let the cool air stop her from getting some sun on her pasty skin. She popped her hat on her head, put on her sunglasses, and pulled out a magazine. Looking at her watch, she made a mental note to head back to the shuttle area at lunchtime. She gazed up at the robin's egg blue sky and determined the sun would not be too strong until afternoon. *I should be safe for a couple of hours.*

Drowsiness began to overcome her as she set the magazine down and listened to the ocean waves spilling over the sand. Reading always had that effect on her. She took off her hat and stretched out across the beach towel on her stomach hoping to warm the front side of her body which had grown very cold from the breeze. Before long, she was fast asleep, only to be awakened later by the sound of people talking as they walked past. She looked at her watch. One o'clock. She quickly gathered her things, put her hat on, and began walking across the sand.

"Gosh doggit!" she screeched. She let out another little yelp and sat to examine her foot. A nasty thorn was embedded in her heel. After sitting in the sand for a few minutes, mulling over the situation, Faith decided to pick at the spot with her fingernails, but to no avail. She held her throbbing foot and mentally measured the distance to the nearest beach exit. From the opposite direction, a small dog dashed to where she sat and looked at her curiously.

"Where'd you come from?" Faith asked the dog in an animated voice. The dog remained still, staring at her. He had a gross underbite and big, bugged eyes which wandered off in two different directions. *He must be the homeliest dog I've ever seen. Poor thing.*

"Why are you looking at me like that? You are looking at me, aren't you?" She noticed he was wearing tags, so she reached out and patted his head. His tail wagged fiercely. "You're a sweet doggie. Where are your Mommy and Daddy? And do you happen to have any tweezers?"

At that moment, Faith heard a male voice. "Doo! Come here!" The dog turned and ran to a man walking across the sand toward her. As he approached, there was no doubt in her mind. The tall, slender person approaching was Novac. Her heart sank.

"Oh, no," she whispered under her breath, looking down, hoping he wouldn't recognize her.

"Need some help?" Novac asked. She had no choice but to respond.

"Just a thorn or something stuck in my foot. Nothing big."

"Do you always get yourself in these situations or are you just trying your hardest to attract my attention?" He laughed. "You know I can't resist damsels in distress."

Faith could feel color creeping into her cheeks. She couldn't believe he had the gall to suggest she might be flirting with him. *Oh, no! Did he notice that my face turned red?!*

"I'm just kidding, okay? Lighten up!" He laughed again. "I really came down to see if I could help and to let Doo relieve himself in the bushes. I saw you from my yard." He pointed past the sand and scrubby bushes toward a few tiny cottages sitting atop a small bluff.

"You live up there?" she asked.

"Yeah. In the house with vines growing up it. I recognized you and came to see if I could help. You looked hurt."

"How did you recognize me?"

"Binoculars. And the hat. It was a dead giveaway. I saw you carrying it last night. Besides, you said you were coming this way today."

"Oh. I did, didn't I?"

"Let me take a look at your foot. I step on those things all the time. So does Doo." Faith stuck her foot up in the air. Novac brushed the sand off her foot and held it gently in his hand. He slipped his sunglasses off and took a close look. "Yeow! I do believe you found the biggest thorn on the whole beach. It's in there far. I can't catch hold of it. I'm afraid I'll need to operate," he announced.

"What do you mean?" She couldn't tell if he was serious or not.

"I mean I'll need to use a needle and some tweezers." The corners of his eyes crinkled as he smiled at her. "It won't hurt. I promise. I'm an expert."

"I'll be okay. I was heading home now anyway."

"Your heel will get pretty red and angry by this evening if it doesn't come out." She leaned forward and slipped her sandal on, determined not to spend any more time with Novac than necessary.

Remember strange Tom? He was helpful, too. "I can work on it when I get home." As Faith stood, she realized there was no way she could walk with that thorn in her foot. She hopped and tried to hobble, but in the sand it was impossible. Novac stood watching, shaking his head, smiling, looking amused.

"You're not going to get very far that way. Why don't you let me help you?"

She wouldn't look at him and continued trying to hop on her good foot. "I could leave you here. Or you could let me carry you up to my place and take care of that thorn."

"Carry? Can't you bring tweezers down to the beach?"

"Won't work. We need to clean your foot before surgery. Come on now. Time to quit being stubborn and let the doctor take care of it," he said, holding out his arms to her. She looked up at him, realizing she had no choice, and shrugged her shoulders in defeat. She became sensitive to the fact she was wearing nothing but her bathing suit, and it made her feel extremely uncomfortable knowing this strange man was seeing her in very little clothing. *No way he's gonna to carry me like this.*

"Wait a minute. I need to get dressed."

"You seem to forget I live at a beach. I see women in bathing suits all summer. I'm numb to it. I don't even notice it anymore. In fact, I didn't even look at your cute little black, two-piece suit with tiny white flowers all over it." He laughed.

She didn't appreciate his sense of humor. She looked at him as he laughed, realizing his hair was mostly gray. He had seemed so much younger to her the evening before. The way he dressed and moved had deceived her into thinking he was a man in his thirties. After seeing him in the bright sunlight, she realized he had to be forty-five or fifty years old. *Dirty old man.*

"Ready?" he asked, squatting down. "Piggyback or Scarlett O'Hara style?"

She knew she didn't want to ride on his back with her legs and arms wrapped around him. She wasn't crazy about being carried by him at all. He reached down to pick her up.

"I haven't decided yet!" she yelled. Before she could protest further, he scooped her up in his arms and carried her off with Doo trotting along behind them.

"I made your mind up for you, if you didn't notice."

She noticed. She also noticed how high up off the ground she was. *He's quite tall.*

"I'll take care of your foot and then release you so you can run away as I suspect you desire." He laughed. She wasn't sure if he was making fun of her or was just an odd person.

Strange Tom was helpful, too. So helpful he wouldn't leave you alone until you threatened to call the police. Faith silently said a quick prayer for protection as Novac reached the road and proceeded toward his cottage. She felt perspiration coming through his T-shirt at the base of his neck where she held on. It was odd to be touching a man she barely knew.

As they approached Novac's house, an elderly woman stood in front of one cottage, waving as she watered her potted plants.

"You caught yourself one, huh, Novac?" She laughed and kept on watering. Faith tried to hide her face. She felt like a fool and didn't want anyone to think she was enjoying it one bit. Especially Novac.

"Yeah. Gave me quite a struggle, but I reeled her in! Doing okay, Mrs. Graham?"

"Doing about as well as can be expected for an old lady," she answered back.

"I feel like an idiot," Faith mumbled under her breath as Novac made a right turn onto a short walkway.

"Ah, don't feel that way. Everyone's a little strange in this neighborhood."

"Including you?" she asked.

"Especially me. But that's for you to decide." She wasn't interested in getting to know him well enough to decide.

They reached Novac's front door. Faith was immediately struck by how cute his yard and cottage were. He had a neat, manicured row of bushes along one side of the yard and on the other was a vine-covered fence. In the yard next to the sidewalk was a circle of rocks surrounding an area that had been dug up and looked ready to be planted. A flat of pansies rested on the ground next to the hole. Two Adirondack-style chairs faced the ocean. The house itself was quite small. Rose vines climbed up the shingled walls. Window boxes hung from each window and a small plaque over the door read "HOUSE OF ALVIN". A brick chimney poked above the roof, and she spotted the familiar bicycle propped next to the front door.

Novac managed to free one hand to turn the doorknob. He pushed the door open with his foot, turned sideways and carried her through the door. "Over the threshold!" Novac goaded.

Faith was determined not to react to his chiding. This time she made no faces, offered no sarcastic remarks. Nothing.

He looked at her, puzzled. "Did you hear what I said?" She nodded.

"You're not even going to roll your eyes?"

"I'm pretending I didn't hear it." He carried her to his couch and set her down gently, then shoved a pile of books out of the way so he could sit down next to her.

"Come on in, Doolittle!" he yelled. The dog obediently did as he was ordered.

Faith looked in dismay at the interior of the small house. The outside had been so neat, but the inside was another story. Papers were everywhere and stacked on every flat surface. Legal pads, books, pens, coffee mugs, not to mention several pairs of beach shoes were scattered about. The place was trashed. Novac noticed the expression on her face as she looked around.

"I can read your mind. Sorry about the mess."

"Oh, no . . . no, it's not too . . . well actually, it's pretty awful."

He laughed, "Ah, now the truth comes out! You think I'm disgusting, don't you?"

"Well, I wouldn't say—"

Faith began laughing until tears rolled down her face. Novac watched as this continued for a long minute.

"What? Did I do something funny? What's going on? Tell me, huh?"

Faith managed to barely squeak out the words, "Your name" and held her side, laughing. "Do you have one? A vac?"

"You're gonna need to calm down now. Think you're the

only one to kid me about that?" He winked at her. "I'll go get the alcohol. Rubbing alcohol, that is. I don't want to scare you. I'm not a drunk. Or at least not this early in the day!" He chuckled and walked away. Faith sat very quietly and rolled her eyes, then took advantage of his absence and slipped on the rest of her clothing.

"I'm just kidding! You can smell my breath if you like," he called out, poking his head around the corner.

Novac came back with a cotton ball, rubbing alcohol, band aids, tweezers, and a needle. "Ah! The patient is dressed and ready to go! First, Dr. Novac's going to clean the patient's foot." He poured some alcohol onto a cotton ball and dabbed her sore heel. She let out a little yelp and withdrew her foot momentarily.

"Cold!"

"Would you like me to warm it up a little?" Once again, she couldn't tell if he was teasing her.

"That's not necessary. I'll be brave."

Novac looked up. "Now that you've made fun of my name, please refresh my memory. Faith, right?"

"Faith. That's right."

"I always remember pretty women with pretty names. Besides, I'm a smart guy," he said as he dabbed her foot a few more times.

"I'm glad to hear that, since you'll be operating on my foot. A gentleman and a scholar, eh?"

"Yeah. That's it. You hit the nail right on the head."

"What do you do? I mean besides rescuing women," Faith asked. "What do you do for a living? You do something, don't you?" she said looking at the mess.

"Yeah, smartie, I do something. Thank you." He smiled, put on a pair of reading glasses, and dug at the thorn with the needle.

"Ouch!"

"Now you know what I do. I bring women to my house and torture them! First I make them look at my mess, then I stick them with needles."

"No, really. What do you do for a living?"

"I write."

"You write what?"

"Novels mostly. A few short stories for magazines."

"I'm impressed. Any of them been published?"

"Yeah. A few of them."

"Do you have any of them here?"

"Yep."

"Guess that was a pretty silly question."

"Thorn's out," he said, holding it up with the tweezers. "The operation was a success. Let me put a band aid on the sore spot and then you're free to flee."

"I want to see them."

Novac carefully peeled the paper off the band aid and squinted to see the spot where the thorn had been. "You lost me. See what?"

"Your books!"

"Oh, yeah! When you get old, your mind drifts a little." He stood and walked over to the bookshelf and pulled off a couple of books. "Here are two of 'em," he said, handing them to her. "The others are around somewhere. Probably buried in this disgusting mess."

"New York Times bestseller list! Now I'm really impressed! You must be good, huh?"

"Either that, or I've got them really fooled." His eyes twinkled at her delight.

"I've actually seen these books in the stores! Wow!"

"You mean you didn't buy them?" he asked. "Just looking doesn't make me any money."

"I mostly read romances. Not suspense."

"I'm working on a love story now. It'll be my first crack at one of 'em. My publisher thought I had enough of a following to risk changing genres. If people like your first few books, they'll read anything you write."

"Novac Calvin," she read aloud from the front of the

book. "That's an odd name, Novac. Is it a family name?"

"Novac's my middle name. My real first name's Alvin." He waited for a reaction.

Faith scrunched her face and looked at him. "Alvin Calvin? Your parents really did that to you?"

"Sure did."

"Why, may I ask?"

"To keep me humble maybe. I really don't know. Are you gonna make fun of me again?" He shrugged and began digging under his fingernails with the tweezers.

"Now I understand why the sign over your door says "HOUSE OF ALVIN". I thought it had some historical meaning like the signs on some of the other cottages."

"Bingo! I'm making history here." He winked and smiled at Faith.

The front door opened and in walked a young woman dressed in a tank top with a sarong skirt tied around her waist. The multiple bangle bracelets jingled as she moved into the room where they were sitting.

"Hello, hello!" she sung out, looking Faith over very carefully. The woman's hair hung in two long braids which almost reached her waist. She wore no makeup and appeared to be in her mid-twenties at the most. Doolittle barked unceasingly.

Novac put the book he held down and turned toward the dog. "Quiet, Doo!" Doolittle obeyed. "Hey there, Venus." Faith couldn't tell whether Novac was happy to see the woman or not.

"The subject of your next book?" Faith said softly to him.

He turned his head toward Faith so Venus couldn't see. "Not hardly," he whispered.

"What're you two doing?" Venus inquired. As Venus approached more closely, Faith picked up a heavy floral fragrance on her clothing. It enveloped the small room's space, making it impossible to take a breath without inhaling the scent. She stopped in front of Faith, approaching closer than Faith liked.

"Venus, Faith. Faith, Venus," Novac introduced. "Faith had a thorn in her foot and I took it out." Faith could tell he wasn't pleased about explaining his actions to Venus.

"How's it going, Faith?" The young woman locked her eyes on Faith.

"Fine, thanks. Look, I'd better be going," Faith said as she looked at Novac.

"You just got here. Besides, the shuttle won't be around for another half hour. Venus just got off the shuttle. Right?" Novac asked.

"Right." Venus glared at Novac.

"So, it's gone now. Stay. Okay?" Novac asked.

"Novac, aren't we gonna talk about the play? That's why I came over. And I hoped you'd go with me to Fat Cat's later this evening and listen to the new group that's playing. I hear they're really great." Venus swished her hips as if she were dancing with an imaginary partner.

"Venus talked me into writing a play for the theater in town. They're doing an evening of one-acts this summer," Novac explained to Faith.

"Yeah. It's a shame to have a big-shot writer on the island and not put him to work. He needs to be involved in the community, don't you think, Faith?" Venus asked as she sashayed over close to Novac. The heavy cloying aroma of flowers curled its way around the room, invading Faith's nostrils. Venus plopped down next to Novac, nearly landing in his lap. He scooted away, rubbed his nose, and made a small coughing noise.

"Suppose you're right. Well, you two obviously have plans, so I think I will go. I'm going to grab a sandwich in town and wait for the shuttle." Faith picked up her tote bag and stood. "There is somewhere to eat over that way, isn't there?"

"Yeah, there is, but can't you stay a while?" Novac asked as he jumped to his feet. "You can go with us tonight. You haven't seen much of the island yet." Faith noticed the piercing look Venus shot at Novac. There was more to this than he admitted.

"Maybe some other time. You two have fun tonight." Faith approached the door and turned. "Nice to meet you, Venus. And Novac, thanks for taking care of my foot."

"Anytime."

Faith closed the door behind her and walked down the path which connected to the main road where the shuttle let her off earlier in the day. She stood in line and after placing her order at the small food stand, realized she had left her new hat at Novac's house. She liked that hat a lot and paid quite a bit of money for it, but there was no way she was going back and exposing herself to the daggers Venus had thrown at her. Furthermore, she didn't want to intrude on whatever might be happening back at the cottage.

Faith took her tuna sandwich to a bench, unwrapped it and took a bite. She chewed slowly as her mind wandered back to the little cottage and the scene that had played out before her. *What's up with that Venus? Novac's lover? Maybe he pretended not to be interested because she's so much younger. He is a dirty old man. Embarrassed, I guess. Whatever. None of my business. I'm glad the ordeal is over.*

My hat. I left my hat. Faith sighed and dropped her head forward.

CHAPTER THREE

Sorry I woke you. I tried to be quiet." Faith walked to the chair in the front yard where Alice lounged, covered with a small blanket. Alice sat up suddenly, sending her open book sailing off the arm of the white, wooden chair.

"I'm glad I woke up because I wanted to catch you before you made any plans for the evening. Would you like to go out for dinner with me so we can catch up on girl talk? I can tell you some things about the inn and go over your responsibilities. We haven't had a chance to talk about that much yet. How about it? It'll be fun. My treat." Alice waited a moment for Faith's response.

"Sounds good. I'll go clean up."

"Have you ever seen such a beautiful sunset?" Alice asked. "Look how the clouds are outlined in crimson. It's like God got out a big fiery paintbrush and traced the edges. I'm so glad we were able to sit out on the porch. And I'm glad they have a heater out here!"

Faith nodded her head, her mouth full of pie. "Mmm." She swallowed, "Gorgeous. Nothing like it in Providence."

"And how was your fish? Mine was sinfully delicious."

Alice said.

"Same here. Do you think it's still brain food with all that béarnaise sauce—or whatever it was called—on it?"

"Maybe a little bit brain food and a little bit hip food," Alice said with a chuckle. Her smile disappeared and she grew silent for a minute, fidgeting in her chair. After a moment, she broke her silence.

"Faith, dear, please tell me it's none of my business or if I'm prodding into something you don't want to talk about. But I don't understand why you decided to give up your life in Providence to help a lonely old lady at an inn. When I told your mother I needed someone to live and work here, she suggested I give you a call but didn't explain why. She only said that you'd had some difficulties and needed a change, and that you didn't want to talk about it to anyone."

Faith remained quiet and fidgeted with the charm bracelet around her wrist. Alice noticed her apprehension but continued questioning Faith.

"Now, honey, I'm not trying to pry. I just want to know where we're starting from in our work relationship. Are you here to stay? Are you in any trouble? Your Mom and I are dear friends, as you know, and I trusted her opinion when she said this job seemed like what the doctor ordered for you. I hope you'll forgive me for bringing it up."

"Nothing to forgive. In fact, I was surprised you allowed me to come live in your home without quizzing me more. It's painful to think about, but it's the past. I probably need to talk about it and move on with life."

"Only tell me what you feel comfortable telling me."

"It's nothing shocking. I was engaged to a man in Providence. Someone I'd known for quite a while. We dated off and on for several years. Being thirty-two, I suppose I was feeling my biological clock getting ready to go off. My parents loved Phil. I loved Phil. Phil loved me. Everything was wonderful. When he proposed, I was the happiest woman alive. I went right out and found a dress. Lined up bridesmaids. We set a date. It wasn't soon enough as far as I was concerned. Then he told me we would have to move to Seattle because of his job. The company he was a rep for wanted him to cover that region. It meant a lot more money," she sighed. "Not that he wasn't already making scads of money in Providence. He was. So, he moved out there ahead of time to find a place to live. Unfortunately, that wasn't all he found."

"Oh, no."

"Yeah, oh no. He had his boat there and most of his stuff. He just sorta forgot me. He kept pushing back the date of the wedding. I didn't understand why, so I flew out there to confront him about it face to face. Well, the reason was standing in his new apartment when I arrived unexpectedly. She even had the nerve to answer his door. She said, 'Can we help you?' I told her I must have the wrong apartment and left. I knew it was Phil's apartment because I heard his voice in another room asking who was at the door. She turned and yelled at him that someone had knocked on the door by mistake. I left him a message on a piece of paper stuck to his car telling him that she was right. I had made a big mistake." Faith stopped, dabbed her pooling eyes with the corner of her napkin.

"Excuse me a minute." Faith said as she rose from the table. She found the ladies' room inside the main dining area and stood in front of the mirror, fanning herself with her hands to cool her reddening face. She pulled a compact out of her purse and tried covering the blotches that now speckled her cheeks.

"Such an ugly crier," she said to her reflection. She took a deep cleansing breath. "You will stop being emotional," she demanded. "You're over him now and rid of him." Faith smoothed her hair and reapplied her lipstick before heading back.

Alice waited at the table with her head slightly bowed. Faith noticed sadness in her eyes and reached over to stroke her back softly as she passed to her own chair.

"Faith, I—"

"Don't say anything, Alice. I'm perfectly okay. I hadn't been able to cry about it before, so it's a good thing. Just a little embarrassing. Well, to continue my story—"

"Faith, don't feel like you have to."

"I want to. You know by now. The wedding was cancelled. It had already been postponed once, two weeks before the original date, thanks to him. Once again, I had to call everyone and tell them that the wedding was off. It was humiliating to say the least. He kept trying to reach me on the phone, but I wouldn't return any of his calls. He left endless messages on my voice mail, insisting there was nothing going on between him and that woman, telling me that we were better off apart if I didn't trust him."

"That must've been terrible."

Faith continued. "I think it was God's way of telling me we were unevenly yoked.

I don't know him, Faith, but it certainly seems like his morals aren't—"

"Christ-like?" Faith said.

"That's one way of putting it. So, what happened next?"

"I sent all the presents back. It was really humiliating to call all six of my bridesmaids to tell them they each had spent $250 on a dress they would never wear. Not to mention the cost of the dyed shoes. I swore to them I'd pay back every penny. A couple of them insisted they wouldn't take any money from me. The others were angry with me. You called shortly after all of that, so I decided to sell my car and pay back my so-called friends. That left me with enough money to live on for a short while."

"What happened to the other two girls? The ones who didn't ask for any money. Did they stick by you?"

"I gave them three hundred dollars each and never heard from them again. You'd think they'd call to see how I was doing, but they didn't."

"I'm so, so sorry. I remember being told the wedding was being postponed for a while, but that was right in the middle of all of Jim's surgeries. Please forgive me for not remembering."

"It's okay. Sounds like it was a bad year for both of us."

"It was the most difficult time I've ever gone through," Alice said.

"I second that. My husband didn't die, but in a sense, I did lose a husband. He was *going* to be my husband. All my dreams vanished after that knock on his door." Faith tried to hold back her tears by looking out toward the pitch-black ocean. She pulled her jacket around her shoulders to protect herself against the cool breeze.

"I know it's no consolation for you now, but there will be someone nice for you. And when he comes along, you won't give Phil another thought."

"I've sworn off men for a while. To tell you the truth, I'm in no hurry to find anyone. In fact, I don't care if no one ever comes along." She sat for a moment, deep in thought. "I would miss not having kids, though. I always thought by the time I was thirty I'd have a couple."

"You're too young to feel that way about love. Wait until you get to be my age before you start that kind of talk. When you're sixty-eight, the only reason to get married again is for companionship. But the guests at the inn are my companions now. And you, of course. You do plan on staying?"

"As long as you can stand having me around. I love it here already."

"I told your mother I'd take good care of you as if you were my own, so please don't mind me if I try to give you advice now and then."

"I don't mind." Faith scraped up the last bite of pie, chewing it slowly.

"Did you have fun at 'Sconset today?"

"Well . . . yes and no. The first part of the trip was fun. Then I overslept on the beach and got a little sunburned."

She reached up and touched the top of her shoulders lightly to see how sore they were. "Then I stepped on some kind of a thorn and got it embedded in my foot."

"Did you get it out, honey?"

"Yes. I had help from one of your locals. I gather he's a celebrity."

"Who's that?"

"Novac Calvin. He's an author. At least he says he is."

"Oh yeah! I went to one of his book signings here on the island. I've got all his books at home. How did you meet him?"

"He saw me on the beach and could tell that I was hurt. My hat was a dead giveaway, so he came down to help." Alice looked puzzled. "It's a long story."

Alice excitedly began to tell what she knew of him. "A reclusive man, or so I've heard. Doesn't come out much unless he must. When he first became famous, there was one reporter with the local newspaper who made it his mission to try to find Novac Calvin on the island. He would report Novac sightings in his paper. He got fired, I think, for invading Novac's privacy."

"He seemed very personable. A little strange. And a bit of a slob."

"You mean the way he looks. Ah, that's just from living a casual lifestyle at the beach. I think he's rather handsome in a free-spirited kind of way. But he's almost young enough to be my son." Alice said with a chuckle.

"His unkempt appearance carries over to his housekeeping, too."

"You mean his yard was a real mess or something?"

"His yard was actually quite pretty. The inside of his house was a disaster!"

"Inside of his house! You went inside?"

Faith was having fun teasing Alice with tidbits of information. "Yes. I didn't have much choice. He carried me there," she said with a straight face.

"Now you really have my interest. Tell me the whole story from the beginning. I think you've left out a few things." Alice giggled like a teenager as she listened to Faith recap her day and tell of how, twice, she was rescued by Novac.

Later at home, still stuffed from the delicious meal she had with Alice, Faith flopped on her bed and replayed the events of the day in her mind. She had become mildly intrigued by Novac. *What's this man all about and what's going on between Venus and him? Why am I even thinking about him? Am I just a little bit star-struck by him since I found out he's famous?* These things drifted through her mind until she fell asleep.

Faith sipped her morning coffee and resolved to keep her thoughts off Novac and concentrate entirely on the Scrimshaw. She told Alice she was ready to learn the process of checking in guests, preparing breakfast, cleaning rooms, and anything else necessary to know before the vacationers arrived. Only one couple was booked for next week. Since the inn wasn't officially open for business, Alice made an exception because it was their honeymoon. The bride's parents had spent their honeymoon at the inn twenty-five years prior.

About mid-morning, the ladies decided to take a break. There was a knock at the front door. Alice went to answer and found only Faith's new hat and a single red rose with a note attached. In the distance she saw someone on a bicycle riding off down the street.

Faith! You need to come here quickly and look!"

Faith walked to the open front door and peered outside. "My hat!" She snatched it up and looked it over carefully to see if her eyes deceived her. She then spotted the rose and picked it up. Her heart was beating a little faster as she opened the card and read the message:

"Faith, I know how much these hats cost and assumed you wanted it back. I also feared you'd never come back to 'Sconset to get it, so I rode my bicycle seven miles just to drop it off, and seven miles back home. You can show your appreciation by allowing me to take you to dinner tonight and for an evening stroll (without pushing my bicycle along, of course). I'll be very, very, very, very sad if you don't say 'yes.' I'll be by at six o'clock to pick you up. Fondly, Alvin."

Faith snickered as she read the note. She had mixed feelings about seeing him again and didn't want to encourage him. On the other hand, she wanted to continue the conversation they were having when Venus interrupted them. Yes, there was the issue of Venus. She didn't want to get in the middle of any strange situation. The young woman was without a doubt interested in Novac. Venus guarded him as a mother bear would guard her young.

Faith showed the note to Alice to get her reaction.

"That's so exciting! Are you going? Alvin? Who is that?"

"That's Novac's real first name. We had a chuckle over it. I wish I shared your enthusiasm. Doesn't seem like he gave me much choice. He does that a lot. I'll go if his oddball groupie isn't tagging along, but that'll be the end of it. I guess it's the least I can do since he brought back my hat."

Alice looked at her curiously. Faith sensed what she was thinking.

"No! I'm not interested in him. He's completely not my type. In fact, he makes me nervous. I never know when he's teasing me. He looks like he hasn't had a shave for several days, and his clothes look like he slept in them. Not to mention he lives like a slob and has a strange friend, Venus, who looks like she would sew a voodoo doll in my image and stick it full of pins."

"You've got to admit he might be a fascinating person to date," Alice said.

"There'll never be any interest on my part. Believe me!" Faith replied.

"Okay. I believe you. I think you should give him the benefit of the doubt, though. That was such a sweet gesture. He's trying so hard. He has been a gentleman, hasn't he?"

"Yes. I'll give him that. He has been a complete gentleman. I'm going to go rest a while if you don't mind."

"Sure. We're finished for the day. Have fun this evening."

Instead of resting, Faith headed straight to her closet to see what she should wear to dinner. After some pondering, she settled on a navy-blue dress and a nice pair of flats, figuring she would rather err in the direction of dressing up too much since she didn't know where he would be taking her. However, she couldn't imagine Novac in anything but those baggy shorts and a T-shirt, so logically speaking, she knew the chances were slim to none they would end up anywhere dressy.

When six o'clock came, there was a knock at the door. Faith was impressed with his promptness.

She opened the door and saw Novac. He was almost unrecognizable to her. His hair was combed . . . somewhat. He was smartly dressed in a pair of khaki pants and polo shirt. He had real shoes on his feet. Not beach shoes. She stared for a good ten seconds before letting him in. Without thinking, she exclaimed, "You shaved!" Her face reddened.

"You're right!" He laughed. She had come to appreciate his ability to laugh off things that would have bothered her.

"What I meant to say is that you look nice."

"I return the compliment. I'm glad you got my note. I expected you to be gone when I arrived, or feigning an illness."

"Did you ride your bicycle in those shoes?"

"No, I borrowed Mrs. Graham's car. She likes me to use

it now and then. She says it keeps the battery charged. I didn't want to get dressed up and ride my bike for fourteen miles, only to be stood up. If you don't want to go, I'll take in a show or something."

"I'm not that mean. I appreciate your returning my hat. And the rose. That was unnecessary, but sweet. You can be a sweet person, can't you?"

"Shhhh! I don't let many people know the real me."

"Why's that?"

Novac shrugged. "Basically, I'm a private person. And it's a bit of a game I play. Keeps people more interested in my books. You know—the reclusive writer. What makes him tick? That sort of thing. Well, are you about ready to go? You are going with me, aren't you?"

"Yeah, I suppose so. After all, you did go to the trouble of shaving." She smiled and couldn't believe she was flirting with this man. Only a couple of days ago, she was revolted by the sight of him. Yesterday, she began trusting him but was still not interested in seeing him again. Now, there he was. Standing inside her new home, looking handsome, and acting charming.

They got into Mrs. Graham's old blue car and started their trip to the other side of the island. Faith kept thinking about Venus and wondered exactly what her relationship with Novac was. She got up her nerve to begin the inquisition.

"So, where's Venus tonight?"

"She's probably at the theater. They're rehearsing a play. Opening night is in a week or two. Why?"

"Just wondered why you weren't out doing something with her tonight." Faith tried to sound casual.

"We're not joined at the hip."

"Didn't say you were. Where are we going, by the way? She said, changing the subject.

"I thought we'd go over to this restaurant near my house and get take-out. It has a reputation for being the best on the island."

"Are we not dressed well enough to eat there?"

"Actually, I'm not. I mean you are, but I don't have a jacket on. No, I thought we could have a little more privacy if we went elsewhere."

When they arrived at the restaurant, Faith was delighted by the picturesque setting and was disappointed not to be eating there. She noticed the lovely courtyard patio, surrounded by flower beds bursting with red and yellow blooms, sitting atop a small bluff overlooking the ocean. The main building had the same type of rose vines growing on the walls and roof as many other homes in 'Sconset.

"Come on in with me. It's worth seeing inside," Novac said, opening the car door for Faith. "They probably have our food ready."

"This place has take-out?"

"Not exactly. But they do for me. They make exceptions for celebrities," Novac said with a wink and a grin. "I always give them a sob story about not wanting to be bothered while I eat, so they fix something to go. I offer to bring my own dishes, so they won't be seen handing out those tacky Styrofoam containers. It's bad for their reputation. And mine." He laughed.

"You don't have any dishes with you." Faith observed.

"I dropped them off on my way to pick you up."

"So, you knew I'd agree to join you tonight. You were pulling my leg about taking in a show by yourself." Novac smiled at the comment.

She was struck by how confident he always seemed to be. As they reached the front door, he opened it and gestured for her to enter the restaurant. She looked around and admired the colorful furnishings and beamed ceilings which gave the place a charming French country feel.

"Good evening, Mr. Calvin," the maître' d said, nodding also to Faith. "Ma'am."

"Good evening, Harold," Novac replied.

"We have your dinner ready. I think you're really going to enjoy what Jean-Pierre has created for you tonight. He was feeling quite imaginative, so you should be pleased, Mr. Calvin. It's simply fabulous."

"Sounds great. He's never failed me yet." A waiter walked to the front podium with a couple of covered dishes in a large basket.

"Enjoy, sir," he said, handing the basket to the maître' d. Novac reached into his pockets and pulled out his wallet. Faith was dying of curiosity to know how much this dinner was setting him back. She tried to look inconspicuous as he opened the small, black leather folder containing the bill for the meal. Novac handed the grateful maître' d three $100 bills, took the basket, and extended his arm to Faith.

"May I escort you to the limo?" Novac gently tucked her hand in the crook of his arm. "Goodnight, Harold. Thanks!"

"Goodnight, Mr. Calvin. Ma'am. Have a good evening."

Novac propped the basket on the back seat of the car, driving carefully and slowly the short distance to 'Sconset to prevent anything from tipping over. He pulled in front of his house and stopped.

"I'll be out in just a second. Stay here a moment." He went to the door and opened it. Doolittle charged out and ran to the open car door where Faith sat.

"Hey there little fellow," she said as she rubbed his head. He stood on his hind legs to get close to her.

"Okay. We can go now," Novac said.

"Go where?"

"You'll see. Follow me." Faith got out of the car while Novac pulled the basket off the back seat. "Come on." He led the way down the little road toward the beach. As they started across the beach, sand got into her sandals, so she was glad they didn't have far to go. Spread out before her on the beach was a blanket. On top of the blanket was a small, short table with a candle on it, two glasses and a pair of binoculars. A wine bucket sat partially buried in the sand next to the blanket. Doolittle ran over to the table and began to lift his leg.

"Hey! Do it and you're dead meat!" Novac yelled at the dog. Doolittle stopped cold in his tracks and minded his master, curling up on one corner of the blanket. "Good boy, Doo." Novac patted him as he set the basket down.

"I can't believe you did all this!" Faith was flabbergasted. No one had ever gone to such trouble for her before.

"You'll find that writers have good imaginations," Novac said, pulling the dishes out of the basket and setting them on the table.

"So, you do this often?" Faith hoped the answer was 'no'.

"I'm embarrassed to say that I do eat take-out pretty regularly. Usually, it's just me and Doo. If he's been a good boy, I pick up some bones from the restaurant while I'm there."

"I noticed that they knew your name," Faith said.

"It's all part of the image. Makes them wonder what I'm up to. Who my flavor of the week is. Sorry. That was in bad taste."

"Ooooooo . . . so mysterious . . ." Faith joked.

Novac lifted the lids off the silver dishes. The smell of garlic and seafood rose from the table.

"Let's see what Chef Jean-Pierre has done for us tonight. Um. Looks like some kind of shrimp scampi-like dish over linguine with truffles maybe, a pate', and a medley of sauteed vegetables. I asked him to give us two different meals. I hope you like seafood. That's what I asked for."

"Love it!"

"Let's see. Under door number two, there seems to be sesame-crusted salmon and a stuffed artichoke. Looks like some sort of crabmeat stuff inside. Smells like a cheese souffle on the side, possibly. I'm not exactly sure what it is, but it sure smells good. He uses all kinds of exotic ingredients, so I need to describe it in layman's terms. Wanna just swap around and share some of each?"

"Sounds great, smells great, and looks great!" Faith said. She couldn't wait to dive in, but used restraint while Novac struggled to open a bottle of wine. "Grabbed this at the store. I don't know much about wine. Just figured we needed it for our picnic. Ripple, I think the man told me it is."

Faith laughed at his joke. "They probably don't even have Ripple on Nantucket," she said.

"Probably right. Would you like some? I also have a bottle of water stuck down in the ice just in case you or Doo preferred that."

"I don't usually indulge, but since you went to the trouble to find Ripple just for me, I'll have a small glass."

"Cheers," Novac said, holding his glass up in the air. "Welcome to Nantucket."

"Thanks."

"Go ahead and get started on the food."

"I think I will. Thank you. It smells absolutely wonderful." They scooped sections of each item and traded plates until everything had been tested and met with their approval.

"It is wonderful," Faith said with a rapturous look on her face. Novac was pleased to see her content with the arrangements he had worked hard making.

"What made you so sure no one would mess with your stuff here at the beach?" Faith asked.

"My secret. You know. Mysterious." Novac took a bite of pasta and licked sauce off his fork. "So, what brought you to the island?" he asked.

"A ferry." Faith grinned.

"I had that one coming to me," Novac responded with a chuckle.

"It's a long story. And a downer, so not sure you want to hear it."

"I like long stories. Remember, I write for a living?"

"What about you?" she said, trying to change the subject.

"You're not going to get off that easily, but I'll begin and break the ice. After I'm finished, it's your turn. Fair enough?"

"We'll see." She really had no desire to divulge private information to him now. She barely knew the man.

"I rented the cottage from a man one summer to finish writing my first book. I'd saved money so I could have plenty of undisturbed time without the hassles of working at a real job. The man who owned the cottage was also a writer and decided to travel and do a little research for a book." Novac paused. "Wait. Let me back my story up a bit. I met him at a writer's conference and happened to mention I'd like to get away and work on my book. He told me about his plans to be away and asked me if I'd like to rent his cottage. Said he'd give me a fair price on it. We struck a deal and it turns out he was gone longer than anticipated. The book was sold to a publisher right away, thanks to a great agent, so I ended up living here off the money earned from my advance and articles I'd written for magazines. When my book hit the best-seller list, that allowed me a chance to write full time and become a beach bum."

"What did you do before writing?"

"I was a journalism professor at a small college in Vermont. I expected to go back but the writing bug hit me big time. I liked writing better than teaching it."

"Are you still renting the cottage from that guy?"

"No. He decided to live in France. That was where he did his research. He met a French woman and the rest is history. He called and asked me if I had any interest in buying the cottage. By that time, I had two books that were successful, so I could actually afford to live here."

"Sounds like the cottage has helped launch a couple of successful writing careers?"

"I guess you could put it that way. There may have been another writer who lived in it before Frank; I just don't know. There are lots of artsy types in 'Sconset." Novac poured a little more wine into Faith's glass. "Now it's your turn to talk."

Still trying to avoid telling him her story, Faith said, "Have you ever been married?"

"Well, kind of."

"How can you be kind of married?"

"Do you count two weeks?"

"I suppose. You said 'I do'. What happened?"

"I met Madeline at the college. She worked in the admissions office. We dated for a couple of years, off and on. She stuck with me through some challenging times, which I appreciated. We got along great until a day or two before the wedding. I thought she just had cold feet. We got married and went on a short honeymoon, then came over to Nantucket so I could begin writing. She was miserable. Before we got married, she wanted to come here and live but didn't realize how isolated she'd be. While I was holed up writing, Madeline just flipped. She told me she never should've married me, didn't love me. She missed her family, missed her job, and on and on. Next thing I knew, her bags were packed, and she told me she was leaving.

"That's terrible."

"I begged her to stay. I even promised her I'd quit writing and go back to the college to teach. I loved her so much. My marriage meant everything to me. I believe marriage is forever, but I couldn't force her to stay. Her mind was made up and she took off. She told me not to follow her. I tried to contact her every day, but her parents wouldn't let me speak to her."

Faith dropped her head and let out a sigh.

"A few weeks later, I received papers to sign. I signed them. It broke my heart, but I did it. I'll never go through that again."

Faith could see his eyes tearing up as he spoke. He obviously had never gotten over the hurt. She knew some of his pain.

"Okay." Faith said. "Since you told me your story, I suppose I can reciprocate. I had a similar situation, only I never made it down the aisle. After hearing what happened to you, I should feel glad I never did."

"Go ahead, I'm listening."

"You weren't spinning a story to get me to open up, were you?"

"Scout's honor," he said, lifting his fingers into the scout salute.

"Don't try to get me to believe you were ever really a—"

"Oops. You caught me in a fib. Sorry. But you can trust that my story is true."

She believed him. Faith told him the whole story about her broken engagement. His concerned look made her feel comfortable letting him in on this part of her life.

"Unevenly yoked," Faith said.

"Huh?"

"Unevenly yoked. Me and Phil. You know how the Bible tells us we shouldn't be unevenly yoked? We were."

"You lost me somewhere."

"The Bible. You do know the Bible, right?" Faith teased.

"Yeah. I've seen it around once or twice." He winked.

"Sorry. That sounded rude."

"That's okay. I like a girl with a little spunk. I need to be put in my place sometimes." Novac sighed. "So, I guess we're both on guard when it comes to love."

"We were unevenly yoked. You know, different morals, beliefs, values. I had them, he didn't. Obviously. I don't ever care to go through that again." She reached over to rub Doolittle, who was still curled up on the blanket. Dinner was finished and the candle on the table was burning down close to the base it sat in. "No, never. Not marriage material I suppose," she said so softly it was barely audible.

"Sounds like the beginning of a beautiful friendship to me," Novac said in a bad Humphrey Bogart voice. "To staying single." He raised his glass.

"To staying single," she repeated, touching his glass with her nearly full one. "Now, I have one more question I've been wanting to ask you." She was suddenly feeling brave, not sure if it was from the two or three sips of wine she'd had or from the revelation of their similar backgrounds. "What's up between you and Venus?"

"Venus? Why would you ask that?"

"She seemed to be very familiar with you," she said, prying a little.

"With me?"

"Yeah. She walked right through your door without even knocking. Kinda like she owned the place."

"That's her style. She's very open and free. You know the type."

"Not really," Faith said. "She was checking me out pretty good."

"Are you sure? I didn't notice." Faith noticed the discomfort in his voice.

"Yeah. I think she has a thing for you," Faith pried further.

"Me? We work on some projects together from time to time. That's about all. Let's take this stuff back and go for a walk. What do you say?"

"Sounds fine to me." They gathered as much as they could carry in their arms, leaving the blanket.

"Don't worry about that," Novac said, "I can come back and get that in the morning."

When they reached Novac's house with Doolittle following close behind, they dumped the things and Doolittle off and grabbed a flashlight for the walk. Novac placed one of his jackets around Faith's shoulders. The binoculars still hung around his neck. "Beach or road?" he asked.

"I was having a little problem walking in the sand," she said as she pointed to her feet. "But it would be more fun to walk on the beach."

"I'll tell you what. When we get down there let me carry you until the sand gets packed down closer to the water.

Then you're on your own. Nobody will see." When they reached the loose sand, Novac turned to her and pointed the flashlight's beam toward the ground so she could see. "Time for a lift?"

"Yep. Guess it's time. Scarlett O'Hara, please." He reached down and scooped her up, taking careful pains to keep her legs covered with her dress. When they reached the wetter sand, he lowered her gently until her feet touched the ground. The tide was out and the sound of far-off waves crashing gave away the fact there was a black ocean hiding in the night's darkness. A three-quarter moon suddenly appeared from behind some clouds, creating sparkles on the rippled surface of the water. Novac held his binoculars up to his eyes.

"I love looking at boats on the water at night. Here, take a look." He handed the binoculars to Faith. She adjusted them to fit her eyes. "Nantucket is notorious for having fog," he said. "But we lucked out tonight."

They walked along the edge of the water for a while without saying a word. Novac broke the silence. "Have you heard from him?"

"Who?"

"Phil. Have you heard from him since?"

"He tried to reach me several times, but I didn't speak to him. I let him leave messages. Now that I'm here, I doubt I'll ever hear from him again. I certainly didn't tell him where to find me."

"Do you miss him?"

"I'd never admit this to anyone else; I hate him, and I miss him. Crazy, right?"

"Not crazy at all."

"Have you heard from Madeline?"

"Not a peep. She was my friend. I hate not having contact with her anymore. I don't let too many people get close to me."

"I don't believe that. You're so outgoing."

"Not really. You may think I am, but I don't open up much."

"You're opening up to me," Faith said.

"That's true. I know it sounds corny, but when I first met you, I felt comfortable. You seemed different than most people on this island. There are a lot of fakes and kooks here. There are nice, solid people, too. Don't get me wrong. But most of the single people are either college kids, elderly spinsters, or, well, way out there like Venus. The art community is very active on Nantucket."

"But you're part of the art community, aren't you?"

"To a certain degree, but when you write, you spend a lot of time alone. Madeline had problems with that. I started writing when we were dating, and she wasn't comfortable with my quiet moods. When I wanted to be left alone, she took it personally."

Faith and Novac continued walking along the cold, wet sand near the water's edge. The beach made a bend and became rocky.

"Let's head back in the other direction," he said, taking Faith gently by the arm.

"You mentioned that Madeline went through some hard times with you. I hope you don't mind me getting kinda personal, but what did you mean by that? You don't have to tell me if you don't want to. It's really none of my business."

"I don't mind. While we were dating, I had surgery for colon cancer. Chemotherapy was terrible. It was rough on both of us. She rallied when I was sick but seemed to cool off some once I was in the clear. She said she felt needed by me while I was recovering, but when I began living my life again, she felt rejected. I couldn't convince her that I still wanted and needed her."

"Why did she go through with the marriage if she felt that way?"

"My powers of persuasion were pretty good."

"Yeah. They are. I'll testify to that," Faith said. They

stopped walking for a moment. Faith looked up at Novac's head full of graying curls in the faint light from the flashlight. "Wow. Cancer and chemotherapy . . ." Her voice drifted off.

"I can tell what you're thinking. You're imagining me without hair!"

"Did you lose your hair?"

"Every last strand of it. Bald as a billiard ball! When it grew back, I looked like an old man. My hair was brown before the cancer. Now look at it!" He pointed the beam of light at his head and grinned, baring all his teeth. "Scary, isn't it?"

"You have a nice head of hair. Well, it's a little scary when you don't comb it!" she joked back. "Are you okay now?"

"Far as I know. If it doesn't reappear within five years, you're considered cured. I'll just have to watch myself carefully and get checked out more often. Colonoscopies." Novac shivered. "Bleh! Men are real babies, huh?"

"Never known one who wasn't," she agreed. "What time do you have?"

Novac shined the flashlight on his watch. "Eleven o'clock. You need to get back?"

"I guess so. I'm pretty tired."

When they reached the loose sand, Novac instinctively bent down and picked Faith up in his long arms. As he stepped onto the paved road, he set her down softly.

"Now slip your sandals on." He took the sandals from her hand and brushed the sand from her right foot. He slid her sandal on while she held onto his shoulder. She held her left foot up and he repeated the process. As they walked down the road to the parked car, Novac wrapped a protective arm loosely around her shoulder. He unlocked the car and they both climbed in and headed back to town.

Aside from briefly discussing the beautiful, clear night, the remainder of the ride back to the Scrimshaw was silent.

There was no need for idle chatter; no need to try to impress.

Have I told him too much? She also wondered if his silence was indicative of similar thoughts. As the car made the final left-hand turn onto her street, she felt a bit sad about the evening being over and wondered if she would ever see him again.

A lamp post and front porch light offered the only illumination as they silently walked up to the house. Faith fished around in her purse for her key, then remembered Alice kept the door unlocked. She reached to turn the knob, but not before Novac reached out gently and held her arm. She turned to face him, removed his jacket from her shoulders, and handed it to him. His eyes sparkled in the soft light.

"Faith, thank you for joining me this evening," He whispered. His intense gaze made her feel uncomfortable.

"Thank you," she said. "I'm touched by the trouble you went to. It didn't go unappreciated." He cocked his head to one side and smiled at her.

"It wasn't just for you. I enjoyed it too."

"I hope I didn't depress you too much with my sob story," Faith said.

"Your sob story? What about mine? I think I have you beat. But you know what?"

"What?" she asked. Novac's smile had disappeared and was replaced by a tender look that caused her to stir a little inside.

"Oh. Never mind. See you again soon, huh?" he asked.

"Yep. See you soon, I hope."

"Good. I look forward to it. Goodnight." He squeezed her arm a little and walked away. After he opened the car door, he paused and waved, still smiling. Faith wondered how long it would be before she would see him again. She hadn't left anything at his house this time. No. All her belongings were accounted for, she noted disappointedly. She tiptoed to her room and closed the door behind her quietly.

Later, as she lay in bed, her mind kept going back to their toast, "to staying single." *Had she really meant it?* Until a few hours ago, her answer would've been an unequivocal and resounding yes. After spending the evening with Novac, she now realized she wasn't the only one in the world who had suffered because of love. And maybe someday, she might give it another chance.

CHAPTER FOUR

In the morning, Faith attended a church down the road from the inn and had a tough time concentrating on the service, knowing she would begin her duties at the inn early the next day. One couple would be arriving to celebrate their new marriage. Alice declared Faith ready to face the public, so she decided to let her practice her assistant inn-keeping skills on the honeymooners before the main tourist season began in earnest.

After church, Faith sat on the patio enjoying the soft breeze and sunshine. She leaned back in her chair and mentally ran through the checklist of duties she would be performing over the next few days. The much-anticipated newlywed couple would be arriving soon, full of joy and expectations for their new life together. It saddened her to realize that if life had gone as planned, she would now be married to the man she once loved. She would be living in her own home, making plans for her future and naming future children together with her husband. Instead, she was thirty-two years old and starting over.

She wondered what Phil was doing right now. *Is he still seeing that woman? Does he still live in Seattle? Does he ever think about me? Why do I think about him? No stinkin' fair. He gets to go on living his life happily, while I waste time thinking about him! No more. He's not worth it. He's hurt me for the last time.*

Alice met Faith on the patio with a cup of tea. "I didn't

have a chance to ask you about last night before you left for church." Faith cleared the depressing thoughts out of her head and smiled.

"Did you have a good time?"

"Yes. Real nice."

"What time did you get in? Not that it matters. I just didn't hear you come in."

Faith noticed that Alice was giving her that "worried mother" look.

"Oh, it must've been about eleven or eleven-thirty."

"Then I guess you did have a good time." Her eyes studied Faith's face. Small lines between her brows contradicted her smile. "Are you glad you went?"

"Yeah. I think so. Novac surprised me. He really is a nice man. Not like I thought in the beginning. I mean he was nice from the beginning, but I thought it was an act."

"You thought he was just trying to impress you."

"Exactly. Like a wolf being charming so he could devour the little bunny."

"And he's not like that?" Alice wanted to hear more.

"No. I think he's genuinely a nice person. Thoughtful too."

"Is he a Christian? I know that's important to you."

"I don't get that impression, but I don't know for sure." Faith didn't want to confess that her heart was ninety percent sure he was not. She wanted to cling to the ten percent hope she had. "Maybe there's hope if he's not," her voice trailed off.

"Honey, be careful about that situation," Alice warned. "I'm afraid it didn't work out well for you before. And I want you to find your happily ever after." She stroked Faith's arm gently. "So where did you two go on your date? If you don't mind me asking."

Faith was a little hesitant to speak. She knew Alice would jump to all kinds of romantic conclusions if she didn't word her answer exactly right.

"He got take-out food."

"You mean like chicken and hamburgers?" Alice seemed disappointed as she continued. "I thought he'd really wine and dine you. Sending you that rose was such a romantic gesture. And he was a little bit dressed up."

Faith realized Alice must've peeked out the front library window as they left. She enjoyed telling Alice about the picnic on the beach. After the story was finished, she feared she may have sounded like an eager sixteen-year-old glowing over her first date.

"Oh, honey, I'm so happy for you. But go slowly. You don't need to get your heart broken again," Alice said.

"Don't worry. It's not like that at all. I think he just wants a friend, and that's fine with me. He made it quite clear he never wanted to get serious with anyone ever again. I seconded the motion." Faith said it with conviction, but her words defied what was in her heart. Just a little.

"Are you going to be seeing him again?"

"Yeah. I think so. We didn't set a time or anything, but I have a feeling I'll be seeing him again."

Alice stood holding her cup of tea. "I'll go and let you have your quiet time to do whatever you need. Let's get together tonight. Maybe go grab a quick dinner and make our plans for tomorrow's honeymooners."

At six o'clock that evening Alice and Faith headed to the corner pub to grab a sandwich and talk. From their window seat they could see taxis taking people back toward the harbor to catch the evening ferry to Hyannis. Alice chatted about how busy the island will become once school lets out for the summer then waved through the window at someone she recognized. Faith tried to listen to everything Alice said but found herself mesmerized by the variety of tourists busily coming and going from the shops, wanting to make their last-minute purchases before departing the island.

A familiar face caught Faith's eye as she looked at the passers-by. Unmistakably it was Venus. Her hair was pulled up off her face in a small French knot. She was wearing a long, gauzy dress in a paisley print and lots of bangle bracelets. Faith watched curiously as Venus stood at the door of a pottery shop and motioned for someone to hurry up. A tall man walked around a crowd of people who were standing on the sidewalk. It was Novac! Venus took a few steps toward him, took his arm, and dragged him into the shop under protest.

Faith was motionless as she stared at the door of the shop. Alice kept the conversation up between bites of her sandwich, unaware of what was going on outside.

"I thought I would let you make the coffee and set the table in the morning when you . . . Faith? What's wrong?"

Faith focused completely on the two figures emerging from the shop. Alice recognized Novac immediately. His height and curly hair made him stand out. They watched as the two walked down the sidewalk. Novac's arm draped over Venus' shoulder. Venus chattered away as she looked up at Novac while dramatically gesturing with her arms.

Alice remained quiet, waiting for Faith's attention. When Faith turned back toward her, she realized Alice had witnessed the scene on the sidewalk.

"Well, guess we need to talk about tomorrow, huh?" Faith said to a still watchful Alice.

"Do you want to talk about that?" Alice said, nodding toward the window.

"There's not really anything to talk about. He certainly has a right to do whatever he wants with whomever he desires."

"Yes, I guess he does. But how does it make you feel?"

"How's it supposed to make me feel?" Faith's voice had a defensive edge to it.

"I suspect it makes you sad and even a little bit curious. But after all, honey, he did tell you he didn't want a committed relationship with anyone, right?"

"Yep."

"You have to take him at his word."

"I suppose. How do I know he doesn't have something more serious going on with Venus? Now I'm feeling a little foolish for going out with him."

"Please don't feel that way. You won't know what their situation is unless you ask him. Then you have to believe him."

"I did ask him."

"What did he say?"

"He sounded like it was nothing more than a professional relationship. I don't even know why I care. That's what's worrying me most. He's not my boyfriend."

"No woman likes to have competition paraded around in front of her no matter what the relationship. Friends included."

"I guess it wouldn't bother me so much if Venus hadn't looked at me with such disdain. Like I was intruding on her territory. I think there's more to it than he cares to admit," Faith said.

"What has Novac admitted?"

"He just brushes it off like it's nothing. I told him I thought Venus had a thing for him, and he almost laughed."

"You told him that?"

"Maybe I shouldn't have, but I wanted to know what was up. Do you think I encouraged him to make a move on Venus?"

"Could be. Men are sometimes slow on the uptake about women. A woman can flirt like crazy and there are some men who would never notice. That happened to Jim once. We were at a party at a friend's house when we were younger. Now Jim was a very handsome man. I don't think he realized how nice looking he was when he dressed up in a dark suit. I walked away to go to the restroom and left Jim by himself for a couple of minutes. I can't even remember what kind of a gathering it was but there were a lot of pretty women around. When I came out, I spotted a beautiful blonde standing next to him. It was obvious to me from her body language that she was interested in getting to know Jim better. I walked over to him, and she stood there looking at me, giving me a hateful look for interrupting their conversation. He introduced me as his wife, and she quickly left. When I mentioned to him how she was flirting, he said he hadn't noticed. I think he was telling the truth. He said he didn't even recall what the woman was saying to him. All he could think about was how he wished I'd hurry up using the restroom because he needed to go, too! He was clueless!"

Faith laughed. "I guess you do have to knock them over the head sometimes!"

"Should I believe you when you tell me your feelings toward him are only friendly?" Alice asked, her head cocked. "It almost sounds like the old green-eyed monster has reared its ugly head."

"You can believe me. We barely know each other. Even if I wanted to be interested in him, I'm not ready to get involved with anyone again for a long, long time. And I'll need to be certain about his principles." Faith was trying to convince herself. "I'm looking forward to getting back to work. I really am. It'll help take my mind off my past few months."

"And you know what's so good about working at the inn? When you're serving other people, it's hard to think about yourself. It'll be fun. You'll see."

Monday morning crept in with a foggy, misty rain. Alice and Faith straightened the inn one last time and put finishing touches on the honeymooners' room. A small bouquet of flowers in a cut glass vase graced the front of their window. Alice loved this room with its view of the harbor and a small balcony, perfect for breathing in the fresh ocean air. The bride's parents stayed in this room twenty-five years ago while they were honeymooning.

Faith put a bottle of champagne in the wine chiller, carried it upstairs, and set it on a small round table next to the bed. The table had a beautiful lace overlay on it and a small porcelain lamp. An old, intricately carved armoire sat against one wall serving as extra closet space, for the house was incredibly old and closets were scarce. She looked around the room and admired all the thoughtful appointments: binoculars by the window, lilac-scented candles placed next to the claw foot bathtub, daintily embroidered hand towels by the pedestal sink. A wistful feeling came over Faith as she imagined the newlywed couple, toasting each other with champagne, staring lovingly at each other as they stood on the balcony.

This is exactly the way I wanted things to turn out for me, she thought with a smidgen of envy. *At least I wasn't married to him when I found out about that woman,* she rationalized.

Faith joined Alice in the lobby as they waited for the couple's arrival. "Anything else I can do?"

"No, honey. I only wish Jim could be here. He loved greeting the guests so much and talking sports with the men."

Faith reached over and put her arm around Alice. "I know I can't take Jim's place, but I'll do the best I can. However, I know nothing about sports." She smiled at Alice.

Alice wiped a tear from her eye with the corner of her apron. "I know you will. And I already feel like you're family. Like the daughter I never had. That's what I call you sometimes when I talk to my friends. My long-lost daughter. All through your life your mom has kept me up on the news about you. When you were small, I'd babysit you while your folks went out. That was before we moved apart, of course. You probably don't even remember that."

"Oh, I do. I can remember sitting in your den with a big bowl of beads on the floor. You'd give me some string and we'd sit and string the beads for hours. I thought that was so much fun. And Jim would take me on a walk around the neighborhood, telling me the names of the dogs living at each house we passed by. If one was standing at a backyard fence, he'd bark at it and get it started barking. I'd laugh all the way back to your house! You were my favorite babysitters."

"He could be such a clown. It's nice to know we entertained you so well! Not having had any daughters, we always wondered if—" Alice stopped and listened for a moment. "They must be here! Someone's at the front door. Let's go see!"

Faith slipped easily into the routine at the inn, thoroughly enjoying every minute of her new job. The week flew by and left her eagerly anticipating the tourist season.

"Are you sure you haven't worked at an inn before? You're a natural!" Alice said to Faith as they watched the honeymoon couple ride off in their cab toward the pier.

Faith reached over and grabbed the telephone next to her as it rang.

"Hello. The Scrimshaw Inn. This is Faith. May I help you?"

"You sure may," the male voice said, then fell silent.

"Yes?"

"I need a date for tonight. Are you available?" the voice asked.

"Who are you trying to reach?"

"It's Novac! You didn't recognize my voice?"

"No. I've never spoken to you on the phone before. I was afraid I was about to hear heavy breathing."

"I'm serious. I need a date for tonight."

"What about Venus? She's probably available." Faith hated the way the words came out. *So high-schoolish,* she thought. After all, Novac was free to do as he pleased.

"Who said anything about Venus? I'm asking you. Not her."

"Sorry. What did you have in mind?"

"This is opening night for the play I wrote, and I'd like you to go with me to the grand premiere. Please!" Faith thought for a minute. *Hadn't Venus said she was acting in one of those plays tonight? Or was she directing Novac's play?*

"I don't think I can make it tonight. I mean I'd love to see the play you wrote, but I don't think I should go. Do you?" she asked. Venus was sure to see her with Novac. That was a situation best avoided in her opinion.

"Ah, come on, Faith. There's nothing going on between Venus and me. I promise. She's just a friend. If she feels anything more than that, she'll just have to deal with it and learn to get over it."

Faith was silent. *Am I that transparent? Sometimes I could kick myself!*

He continued, "She's not my type. She's just someone I go out with occasionally and have fun with. She's a little odd, but she can be fun, too. You need to get to know her. You'd balance each other out well as friends. You could teach her how to be a little grounded. She could get you to let your hair down."

So that's what he thinks about me? Uptight? She wanted to tell him that she cared nothing about getting to know Venus, but she bit her tongue. "Okay. I'll go," she said.

"And you'll make yourself have a good time whether you want to or not!" He laughed.

"That's not exactly what I meant." *But pretty darn close,* she thought. "What time?"

"The show starts at eight o'clock. Let's go grab a bite to eat beforehand. I'll be by around six. That way we'll have time to visit."

Faith had an hour and a half to get ready for the date. She walked over to her closet and selected a tan shift dress and a pair of high-heeled sandals. "My legs always look great in these," she mumbled to herself as she held them up for inspection. "If I do say so myself."

Alice looked her over as she waited in the library for Novac. "My, my! You're snappy looking! He won't be able to take his eyes off you tonight!"

"Thanks. But I don't want to look terribly excited to go.

If you know what I mean," Faith said.

"Well honey, go and have a good time. You've worked hard this week. You deserve it." She understood Faith's apprehension about seeing Novac. "If that girl meant anything to him, he wouldn't have asked you to the show. Why would he want to mess up things with her if he cared about her?"

"I really couldn't care less. I mean it. Friends only," Faith replied.

The ladies stood by the front window and watched Novac drive up and park the car. Alice gave Faith a small hug and a pat on the back.

"Now go and have a good time. Don't let him get to you. Remember, there are a lot of other fish in the sea." Faith grabbed her jacket and went to the door to let Novac in. Alice and Novac shook hands as Faith briefly introduced them.

"Take good care of my adopted daughter, Novac," Alice said, patting his extended hand.

"I will guard her with my life," he said as he turned to help Faith put on her jacket. "Good night, ma'am." Novac pulled the front door closed behind them.

"Don't hurt that girl," Alice said under her breath as she watched them hop into the car and drive off.

The small theater was already packed when Novac and Faith arrived. Two seats were reserved for him along with seats for the actors' families. Friday evenings were normally busy at each of the live theaters in town, but because this was opening night, all the seats were filled.

Novac's play was the last one performed. It was a short historical drama depicting a voyage of Captain Obed Starbuck, the legendary hunter of whales. The scene took place entirely on board the ship "Hero" which was captured by the Spanish pirate, Benevedes, off the coast of Chile, only to be retaken by Starbuck and sailed to freedom. Faith admired the dreamy feel of the set. Blue lights and a flowing, filmy scrim hung from the back of the stage to simulate the famous Nantucket fog.

After the final act of the evening, the actors took their bows to the warm applause of the audience. When the lights came up in the house, the director of the play walked onto the stage. He asked Novac to stand up and take a bow. Novac hesitated but stood and gave the audience an uncomfortable wave, sat down, then slumped into his seat like an awkward teenage boy.

As the theater began emptying, Venus bolted around the stage curtain and spotted the two of them as they rose from their seats to leave. She ran across the stage to the center front edge and gave a shout, "Novac! Well? What did you think?"

"Great! You did a fantastic job!" He walked over to where she stood. She bent down and hugged him, nearly falling a short distance off the stage.

"Wait there just a minute!" she told him as she ran backstage. A moment later Venus came running back, carrying a bag full of her clothes and assorted things she'd brought with her to the theater. "Will you give me a ride back to my house? I don't want to walk home."

"Sure," Novac replied. He looked at Faith and shrugged.

"You're a doll! And can you take me by the grocery store so I can pick up a few things I need for the morning? I didn't have a chance to do that today because of rehearsals." Venus had now come down from the stage and was standing next to Novac. She wrapped her arms around his neck in a possessive gesture.

"Venus, you remember Faith?" He said, shaking Venus loose.

"Yeah. Hi, Faith. How's it going?"

"Fine, I suppose." Faith felt horribly uncomfortable once more. Venus completely took over Novac and as they walked out of the theater and commanded the position by his side, leaving Faith to follow behind, fuming.

As they reached the parked car, Novac opened the front

passenger side door and motioned for Faith to get in. Venus hopped in the back seat behind Faith so she could see Novac better.

"Just go ahead and drop me off first so you can go shopping," Faith said, still upset by the intrusion.

"I have a better idea. Why don't we drop Venus off at the store and let her do her shopping? We can go hang out somewhere, then pick her up in a half-hour or so. What do you think?" Novac suggested.

"The Scrimshaw is so close. Just go ahead and take me there."

"Is that where you work?" Venus asked with a lilt in her voice.

"Yeah."

Novac pulled up in front of the inn and parked the car. "I'll be back in a minute," he told Venus. They had only walked a few steps up the sidewalk when Novac turned around to make sure Venus wasn't following. He saw her climb over the center console of the car and into the front passenger seat.

"Faith, I'm very sorry she did this."

"It's okay. I'm tired anyway. Oh, I didn't have a chance to tell you it was a great play. I thoroughly enjoyed it." Faith turned to walk inside, but Novac grabbed her arm gently, bent over, and kissed her cheek lightly. Faith figured that Venus' eyes were riveted to them. *Oh Novac! You've done it now! She'll get even with me for this,* Faith thought.

As Faith entered the inn, the portrait of Lauralee Dodd gazed down at her. "I don't need you staring at me, too!" she growled. The darkened hallway looked eerie to her, so she quickly walked to her room, not looking back.

That night in bed, Faith glanced through a couple of books about the history of Nantucket. Novac had given them to her to read so she could familiarize herself with the lore, thus being a more informative host at the inn. She fell asleep with the book still by her side. Moonlight filtered softly through sheer curtains over the patio door.

It was eight o'clock in the morning when she awoke. She had forgotten to set the alarm. At first, she panicked, then realized there were no guests currently staying at the inn, nor were any expected until The Scrimshaw officially opened for business on Monday.

Faith threw on some clothes and went to the kitchen to grab a cup of coffee. There was always a pot ready and available any time of day. That was one of the unwritten rules of running a bed and breakfast inn.

She was finishing her coffee on the patio as a van pulled up in front of the inn. The company's name printed on its side was not distinguishable from a distance. The van's door slid open. Alice must have ordered supplies, she deduced. Faith walked back into her room, closing the door behind her. She was soon surprised by a gentle tapping on her door.

"Honey. Are you up?" Faith unlocked the door and was greeted by Alice who was holding a bouquet of yellow tulips, purple iris, and red carnations. "These just arrived for you. I have this phone message as well. This gentleman called while you were out last night and said it was important. I hope nothing's wrong. It was a long-distance number. I would've left it for you, but he asked me to please deliver it in person, so you'd be sure to get it. I was in bed when you came in."

Faith took the scrap of paper and looked at it. Bill St. John, it said. Alice had misunderstood his name over the phone. Her hand shook as she looked at the number. Her face reflected the shock she felt.

"How did he find me here?"

"Who is he, honey?" Alice asked. She had not made the connection.

"Phil. This is Phil. How did he know where to reach me?"

"Maybe he called your home?"

"Mom would never give him my number."

"Oh, honey. I'm sorry. I didn't mean to upset you. Are

you going to call him?"

Faith didn't answer. She took the bouquet from Alice and set it down on a table. Reluctantly, she pulled the card off and tore the small envelope open. She was still thinking about Phil as she opened the card on the flowers and read the message aloud: "Oops! I've done it again! I'll make it up to you. - Novac"

"I'll put the flowers in water for you." Alice smiled as she took the bouquet leaving Faith to ponder Novac's gesture and the phone call from Phil. When she returned, she noticed that Faith had snapped out of her trance.

"What should I do?" she asked Alice. "I don't know if I can deal with Phil."

"Only you can answer that. He sounded desperate to speak to you, but you certainly don't have to call him back if you don't want to. You owe him nothing. What does your heart tell you to do? That always seems to be the best gauge."

"My heart tells me it was just beginning to heal a little."

"My experience tells me that scars can be rather tough."

"What are you trying to say?"

"Nothing in particular. Just that maybe after you give yourself a little more time the hurt will be healed, and you'll be able to talk to him with your head clear."

"What did you say to him when he called?"

"I told him you'd gone to a show and would be back later in the evening. I'm sorry, honey. If I'd recognized the name, I would've thought twice about the whole thing. Maybe I would have told him he had the wrong number or something."

"It's not your fault. Can I use the phone for a minute? I'm going to call Mom and see if she knows anything about this." Alice walked away and left Faith by herself in her room to make the phone call.

The phone rang and rang before someone finally answered.

"Hello?" the woman's voice said.

"Mom. It's me. Did Phil call you for my new number?"

"Faith, please don't be upset with me. He'd already found out you worked at The Scrimshaw and would've just looked up the number if I hadn't given it to him. Faith, he's called over and over pouring his heart out about how sorry he is about what happened. I never would've encouraged his calls if I hadn't thought he was sincere."

"But Mom . . ."

"It's almost like he needed to get it all off his chest or something. Why don't you just call him up and let him explain."

"Mom, there's nothing to explain. He ruined my life and now it's time to move on. I've gotta go." Faith ended the call, feeling deceived by her own mother. Nothing good could possibly come out of calling Phil. He didn't deserve a chance to explain himself after what he'd done. The phone rang and Faith sat petrified as she waited to see if the call was for her.

Alice tapped on the door. "Telephone, Faith. It's Novac."

"Are you sure?"

"I'm sure. He told me his name."

Faith picked up the receiver in her room. "Hello?"

"Faith, I wanted to apologize about Venus. She isn't the most considerate person you'll ever meet."

"She's not. I'll agree with you there."

"Do you forgive me?"

"Yes. I guess I do. The flowers are beautiful."

"I asked them to deliver them as early as possible. I couldn't stand the thought of you fuming at me any longer than necessary."

"How long is necessary?"

"No fumes is good fumes." He said, getting a laugh from her. "I never intended to hurt your feelings. Your friendship is important to me. Look, I was going to ask you to go cycling with me around the island today, but I woke up feeling kind of blah."

"What's wrong?"

"I don't know. Something I ate or maybe the flu. I hope I didn't pass any germs to you."

"I'm not afraid of germs. Can I get you anything?"

"Nah. I'm just gonna stay in bed and see if I can get my gut to feel better. It feels like I ate rocks for supper last night."

"If there's anything I can do . . ."

"I'll call. Glad you're not sore at me. See you soon I hope?"

"Yep. See you soon." She got off the phone and wondered if she should insist on helping him out in some way. He didn't seem like the type to be sick, so she decided he must really be feeling poorly. Or was he faking an illness because he had other plans? Whether he needed her help or not, he was going to get it. It would be the perfect excuse to be unavailable if Phil decided to call again.

"May I borrow your car, Alice? Novac's sick and I want to take him a few things. If Phil calls back, don't tell him where I am." Alice nodded.

Faith packed a tote bag with some snacks, in case she got hungry, and a few magazines to read if she ended up sitting around his house with little to do. She threw it on the front seat of the car then drove down the cobblestone road toward town. She wanted to be anywhere other than the inn where Phil could find her.

Having been to 'Sconset twice before, she was fairly certain she could remember the way. A small convenience mart was open on the east side of town, so she decided to stop and was surprised at the number of people there for a Saturday morning. She found the Nantucket/Martha's Vineyard paper which usually contained theater and movie reviews but decided she'd wait until she got to Novac's house to read it. As she waited in line, the cashier joked with one customer about the hordes of frantic people who had come in buying milk, bread, and water. Faith didn't understand the cashier's story, nor did she care about it. Phil's call was on her mind.

She paid little attention to the weather warning being broadcast over the store's small television set. "Take cover and prepare for the worst."

From the windows of the borrowed car, she could see dark, billowy clouds stacking up thicker and thicker in the distance like black exhaust from an old steam locomotive.

Faith entered the town of 'Sconset and took a left turn at the stop sign beyond the bus stop in the center of the community. Relief swept over her when she saw Novac's cottage five houses down the tiny road. She parked Alice's car along the curb in front of the cottage and reached over to gather up the things she brought with her. The ominous-looking sky was creeping closer, so she grabbed an umbrella out of the back seat. "Might need this," she said as she slammed the door shut and headed up the short sidewalk to his front door.

CHAPTER FIVE

Novac's front door was slightly ajar when Faith arrived. She tapped lightly on the door, gently pushed it open, then stuck her head in to see if he was in sight. She saw him asleep on the couch and called his name softly so she wouldn't startle him with her sudden appearance. At the sound of her voice, he woke from his nap and grinned. "Am I dreaming?"

"I'm sorry. I didn't want to wake you," she whispered.

"Then you shouldn't have walked in." He winked and smiled. "Quite alright. I'm glad you're here. Why are you here?" he asked. Now that he was fully awake, it dawned on him how unusual it was to see Faith standing in his house unexpectedly. "Don't get me wrong! It's a pleasant surprise."

"You said you were sick, so I . . ."

"Thought I was faking? Am I right?" Novac said.

"No. The thought didn't even cross my mind," she lied. "I thought you might need help with a few things. Also, I stopped and picked up the paper so we could read the review of your play." She held the folded paper out to him.

"That'll either make me feel better or worse."

"I never thought about it that way." She glanced down at the paper in her hands. "Are you really worried the review might be bad?"

"Nah. I don't care about them. They always feel obligated to give the local celebrity a good review."

"Then you don't mind if I look through the paper to find

it?"

"Go right ahead."

Faith thumbed through the paper a couple of times and found the entertainment section. Novac sat on the couch watching as she read the columnist's words to herself; her face was totally void of any expression.

"You'd make a great poker player," he stated as Faith handed the paper over to him.

He read for a minute and began thumping the paper with his fingers. "See! There it is! Local writer does a splendid job with his first play. Blah, blah, blah, oh, give me a break. Says they hope they'll be seeing more of my plays performed in the future, yeah, yeah, yeah . . ."

"What's wrong with that? It sounds pretty good to me."

"They're such sycophants, those critics."

"They're what?"

"Brown-nosers. They think if they give you a complimentary review, they're sure to get plenty of free tickets, nice interviews, whatever they want. He didn't mention one word about why he liked the play. He didn't say one thing about the plot or the quality of writing, but he did mention that he thought it was well acted out."

"Maybe you should be the critic for the paper. Then you could just criticize or sycophant all you wanted. I don't think I've ever seen you in such a bad mood before. I didn't mean to get you all stirred up."

"Oh, sweetheart, it's not you. I feel lousy. That makes me cranky."

"What can I do for you? Walk Doo? Clean your house?" She laughed.

"Yeah, that'd be great. Walk Doo. He hasn't been out much today. I left the door open so he could do his business, but he doesn't like to go out without me. Now about cleaning my house, I wouldn't ask that of my worst enemy."

"Come on Doolittle! Come on doggy, doggy, doggy!" Doo followed Faith out the door, his tail wagging. She walked him down to the end of the road and back before returning to the cottage. "He didn't seem too interested in walking. He kept trying to turn around and head back," Faith said to Novac as she walked back in, shutting the door behind her. "Have you seen the sky? It looks ugly."

"I'm surprised you ventured out today. They've been saying bad storms are headed this way."

"I didn't have the car radio on. Real bad storms or just kinda bad storms?"

"Really bad. They've caused some damage down the coast already. Maybe you'd better start back home." Novac groaned loudly as he changed positions on the couch.

Faith remembered the message from Phil and wished to delay leaving as long as she could. "I'll be okay. I needed some company."

"What's up? You seemed a little down when you came in," Novac asked.

Faith was eager to get Novac's opinion.

"I had a message from Phil last night."

"Oh. Did he say what he was calling about?" Novac asked.

"No. He told Alice it was very important and that I should call him back immediately."

"So did you?"

"No. I don't have anything to say to him. Or maybe I'm afraid I'll get so angry at him and say something I'll regret."

"You need closure. You never confronted him about that woman in his apartment, did you? The jerk."

"No. I didn't want to talk to him. He tried to reach me, but I made myself unavailable. I didn't want to hear his lame story." She sat down on the couch next to Novac.

"Precisely my point. It's cathartic to talk to someone after an experience like that. When you face up to them, it puts you in a position of power. You need to get it off your chest and give him a chance to tell his side of the story. I know that's hard, but it'll eat you alive if you don't put it behind you."

"So, you think I should call him?"

"Yep. Sure do. Have a good cry. Throw something at the wall. Beat your fists on your chest. Scream your head off at him. Whatever you need to do to get him out of your system. Probably best if there aren't guests around at the inn when you do it, though." He smiled.

"How did you handle things when Madeline ran off?"

"You don't want to know. It wasn't a pretty sight. I did some things I never should've done. But the only thing that allowed me to get on with my life was speaking to her on the phone and telling her just what I thought. It was all a learning process for me. I learned not to be so selfish, to try to figure out what's best for the other person before thinking about my own needs. It straightened me out in a lot of ways I don't care to go into. Might tarnish my reputation."

Faith pondered the things Novac was telling her.

"My advice is to do it and get it over with. I'd do it for you if I could. But I can't," he said. Novac picked up his bottle of Maalox and took a swig. Faith noticed the pallor of his face. This was the only time she thought he looked fifty years of age. When he told her his age the week before, she believed he was pulling her leg. Other than his predominantly gray hair, only a couple of "laugh lines" around his eyes gave any hint he was a day over forty.

"Poor thing. You really got a hold of some kind of bug, did ya?"

"Yeah. This happened to me last week too. I've been eating a lot of fried things lately. I should know better. They never agree with me. What was that noise? Could you go out and check? Sounded like something blew over."

Faith went out the back door and walked around until she found the source of the bang. "Your watering can took flight off the table. The wind's really picking up. Anything I can take care of before the storm hits? The sky over the ocean is black and eerie looking."

"Well, shiver me timbers, we've weathered many a storm before, so I think we'll make it this time. But if you'd like to go out and make sure loose things are brought in, I'd appreciate it."

Faith walked back outside and took down a birdfeeder which dangled from a post. She propped chairs up against the house to keep them from blowing around and latched his gate down tightly, as the wind was causing it to swing open and slam shut repeatedly.

"I've battened down the hatches. Why don't we turn on the television and see what's happening?" she said as she wiped rain from her face with the back of her hand. Novac was in a lot of pain now, so Faith got the remote control herself and found a local station on the small television in the living room.

The announcers reported that gale force winds and severe thunderstorms were headed toward the island from the southeast. A strong storm had traveled up the coast past North Carolina and toward the New England area where it was expected to weaken as it made landfall. Everyone on Nantucket must have heard the news earlier in the day, except for Faith and Alice. They were so involved getting the inn ready that they hadn't had time for the television or radio in the past week.

"I'd better call Alice and make sure she knows how bad this storm is going to be. Do you mind if I use your phone?" Novac pointed to the phone on the coffee table. Faith glanced over at Novac to see if he was watching her. He wasn't, so she wiped the telephone off with the tail of her shirt. "Hey, Alice, did you know a big storm is coming? It's supposed to be a bad one."

"If it gets too bad, honey, don't try to drive home. Those streets are difficult to navigate in hard rain. Just stay put and be safe. Okay?"

"Okay. I will. Have I gotten any phone calls?"

"None yet. What do you want me to tell him if he calls?"

"Tell him I'm taking care of a sick friend, and I'll call him as soon as I get home."

"Oh, really? So, you've had a change of mind?"

"I'll talk to you about it when I get home." Faith was getting nervous about the lightning flashing outside. As she hung up the phone, the lights in the house flickered. Novac ran to the bathroom and slammed the door. He hobbled back out after a few minutes, looking pasty, and flopped down on the couch.

"Do you have any candles or flashlights? We may need them soon."

"Try looking in that drawer by the stove in the kitchen. Should be some in there. Matches too."

Faith carried a handful of candles into the living room and set them on the table, then grabbed a flashlight from the kitchen counter. As soon as she sat on the couch next to Novac, the lights blinked out completely. Only dim illumination from the overcast sky streamed through the windows, making the inside of the cottage barely visible until her eyes adjusted to the darkness. A bright flash and loud crack made Faith jump to her feet.

"Sounds like lightning hit something pretty close." Novac said as he roused himself from the couch to look out the back window. "Don't see anything. Just sheets of rain and trees bending over. Come here and look!"

The surf was splashing onto the sand and close to the bushes behind Novac's house. "I've never seen the water up that far before." Rain blew in pulsing waves against the window. When a gust of wind would shift momentarily, blowing the rain in the opposite direction, they could catch glimpses of the battered beach. In a couple of hours, daylight would completely disappear, and they would be left in the cottage with no electricity. "Guess you're stuck with me for a while."

"What's this? It looks old," Faith said as she fingered a wooden object sitting on a desk in Novac's small living room. She started to open the lid, but Novac called out to her.

"Don't open it! That's a lap desk that belonged to my grandfather. I keep personal papers and manuscripts I'm working on in it." She noticed he was watching her intently making sure she didn't intrude on his privacy.

"Sorry. I wasn't trying to see what was in it. I was curious to see if it opened. Don't worry. I'm not the snoopy type."

"Do you keep a diary?" Novac asked Faith, who was now looking at photographs in the faint light from the windows.

"I think I did when I was young. I have scrapbooks."

"You may feel like it's silly, but I keep a journal. It's a good way to keep in touch with my feminine side." He grinned and looked at Faith for a reaction. "When I have creative feelings or thoughts, I don't like for them to get away from me. I may need to draw from them for a future book."

"I don't think it's silly. Sounds like a clever idea. And it's kind of sweet." She walked over to him and pinched him lightly on the cheek. He brushed her hand away.

"I never should've told you."

"Don't worry. Your secret's safe with me." Faith pretended like she was locking her lips and throwing away the key. "How are you feeling?"

"Pretty lousy, but I'll live."

"Do you want anything to eat?" Novac let out a moan. "I'm guessing that means no. I'm getting rather hungry."

"You can't exactly cook anything in the kitchen. And I suppose the restaurants are all closed. Probably can't get a pizza delivery in this kind of weather." He waited for a reaction from Faith. "Go look in the pantry. I think there's some bread in there. I don't know how old it is. There might be something you could make a sandwich out of."

Faith walked over to the pantry and noticed a partial loaf of bread. She got the flashlight and inspected it. Just as she suspected: mold. And not just a little bit either. She tossed that in the trash and continued looking through the pantry.

Mostly jars of spaghetti sauce. An empty jar of peanut butter. Cookies, left open of course. Boxes of assorted pasta and a can of sardines. *Revolting,* she thought. *You wouldn't catch me eating anything out of this kitchen.*

"I'll just munch on some of the snacks I brought with me." She ripped into a package of Fig Newtons. Novac leaped up and dashed to the bathroom. After he settled back on the couch, he reached for his glasses which were on the end table next to him. "Have you ever thought it might be food poisoning?" she asked, thinking about his pantry.

"Heh, heh, heh. Will you do me a favor and hand the lap desk to me? Please." She walked over to the desk and lifted the flat wooden box and carried it over to him, curious to know what he was going to do. He opened it up and pulled out a pad. "Time to work," he said, smiling at her.

Faith walked over to her tote, retrieved the magazines she brought and sat by the window. Novac slipped his reading glasses on and began writing on a legal pad. "Your new book?" Faith asked, trying to make conversation.

"Yeah. I guess you could say that. Thought I'd better get a few lines written down before we completely lose the light. I try to write at least three pages every day, no matter what." Doolittle, who had been making himself scarce until now, jumped up on the couch next to Novac. "He doesn't leave my side during storms," Novac commented. "Stop shaking little fellow. Daddy's keeping you safe."

"Hurricanes, illness . . . nothing stops you from writing, huh? Like Superman!" She smiled at him as he continued to write.

Looking up from his pad with a frown, Novac tapped his pen on the edge of the lap desk, then spoke, "She was totally disgusted by his surroundings. Then, she realized, everything about him repulsed her as she watched him run to the bathroom, sick as a dog,"

"You're not really gonna write that! Are you?"

"It's a love story I'm writing, remember? This situation is

hardly inspiration for me."

For the next hour, the rain beat down at a constant pace while thunder rumbled continuously off in the distance.

"Seems like it's never going to let up," Faith mumbled to herself as she peered toward the window. The setting sun was completely obscured by a solid mass of storm clouds. She rose and lit a candle, putting it on the table in front of Novac. "You looked like you needed more light."

"Thanks, sweetie. Now you see why I need to wear glasses. I get so engrossed in my writing. I'll sit on the couch working, not even realizing I'm practically in the dark. Eye strain. I give myself headaches all the time," he said, barely looking up at her as he continued to write.

Time passed slowly as the wind continued battering the cottage. She walked over and picked up the phone to give Alice a call to see how she was doing, but realized there was no dial tone.

"Novac. The phones are out," she said, slamming the phone down. "How am I going to get home?" She knew she wasn't going to be able to get there but wanted to see if Novac had realized that fact.

"You're not. I would never let you go out in weather like this. Not in a million years. You can have my room for the night. I'll stay on the couch. There are some clean sheets in the bedroom closet."

"This is SO frustrating. I don't have any supplies with me, not even a toothbrush. No clean clothes to put on tomorrow. And I can't even let Alice know not to expect me home."

"She'll figure it out."

Faith let out a long sigh and threw up her arms in surrender. "Okay. You convinced me, but Novac, you're sick. I'll be happy to sleep on the couch."

"We can't both fit on the couch, so take the bed, okay?"

The sound of glass breaking came from another part of the cottage. Faith lit a candle and walked down the short hall to look around. Wind and rain were blowing into the bathroom through a broken window.

"Novac!" Faith yelled out over the sound of the roaring wind. "Come here quick!" Novac jumped up off the couch to find her. He immediately ran to a utility closet and came back with a small piece of plywood. He handed it to her, telling her to hold it up against the window to keep out some of the rain as he ran back to the closet. With a hammer and a handful of nails he boarded up the window as best he could, but small amounts of wind and rain still came through the crack around the board.

"These old windows aren't exactly square," Novac said. "Hand me that!" he pointed to something just out of his reach. Faith grabbed Novac's towel off the shower door, then she took the bathmat and mopped up water on the floor. After they'd gotten most of the mess cleaned, they returned to the living room. Novac let himself drop back onto the couch.

"Whew! What a time to get sick! I'm gonna call it a day and get some sleep while I can. Do you mind?" He stretched on the couch and pulled a throw blanket over his legs.

"You need plenty of sleep so you can get well." Faith stood still, looking toward the windows. She bowed her head, "Heavenly Father, please protect us. Keep us safe and Alice, too," she whispered.

"What's the matter, sweetie?" Novac said, sensing something was wrong.

"Oh, nothing much."

"Aren't you sleepy yet?" She made no comment. "Come over here," he said tenderly as if speaking to a small child. "What's up? Thinking about Phil?"

"No. You'll think I'm silly."

"Hey, I told you about my journal."

She smiled as she stood in front of him. "I'm scared. I don't want to go back there and sleep."

"Then come over here," he said as he sat up and patted

the cushion on the couch. "Sit down." Faith obeyed. "You can stay here as long as you like." He took the blanket and wrapped part of it around her shoulders to keep her warm. They sat silently, shoulder-to-shoulder, for a long time, listening to the wind and rain. The flickering candle on the coffee table offered their only light in the drafty room.

Novac looked at Faith and realized she'd fallen asleep propped up against him. He gently laid her down on the couch and covered her. He went to the bedroom and pulled the blankets off his bed and dragged them back to the living room next to the couch. After spreading them on the floor he walked around and checked the windows and doors one last time. In the beam of the flashlight, Novac could see that Doolittle left a puddle on the kitchen floor. He cleaned it up and went back to the living room, blew out the candle, and stretched out on the blankets. Doolittle curled up near his feet, spinning around a few times before settling.

"Goodnight, sweetheart," he whispered as he gazed over at Faith's sleeping face on the couch. "Don't be frightened. I'll take care of you." Still looking at her he sang softly, "Hush a-bye, don't you cry . . ." The storm raged outside, but inside they rested, safely and securely.

Daylight brought with it a massive cleanup for the entire neighborhood. Debris was scattered over the beach for as far as the eye could see. Limbs, seaweed, lawn furniture, trash cans had been tossed about, turning the once pristine sand into the storm's dumping site.

Because he was feeling a little better, Novac took Doolittle out for a walk to prevent another potty accident. When he opened the front door, he was met with a horrible sight; one side of Mrs. Graham's small house lay crushed beneath the weight of a tree, an unhealthy tree he had just warned Mrs. Graham could cause some destruction.

He ran across the street and pounded on her door. No answer. When he tried to open the front door, it was locked. Grabbing a rock from beside her walkway, Novac shattered a tiny window in her door, reached in, and turned the knob. Mrs. Graham was nowhere in sight. He knew she'd been at home the evening before because he called her to make sure she knew about the upcoming storm.

Dashing to the crushed back portion of the house, he found Mrs. Graham lying silently on the floor under a pile of rubble which had fallen from the ceiling. A beam pinned down her torso and her face was speckled with blood from shattered glass. Novac knelt next to her and lifted her slightly warm wrist. Her pulse was weak but present. He gently set her arm down and dashed across the street to get Faith's help.

"I'm going to run down the street and flag down that emergency vehicle I see. Mrs. Graham's badly hurt! I don't have time to tell you about it!" Novac shouted the words to Faith as he poked his head inside the door. "Keep Doo with you."

After paramedics arrived and transported Mrs. Graham to the island's small hospital, Faith and Novac followed them to the hospital, driving over the muddy streets, dodging fallen trees and limbs along their way. On their way, they saw people milling around their homes, surveying the damage from the evening before. The buzzing chainsaws sounded like an invasion of locusts in the neighborhood.

The hospital was frenzied with activity; a generator had kept it up and running. People were lined up in hopes of having their wounds cared for or to inquire about other patients. Some had been cut by shattered glass; others had been hit by flying objects. Most of the patients Novac and Faith saw in the emergency waiting room appeared to be there with superficial cuts and bruises. The hospital was the only place on the island people could go to have such injuries looked at, since all other clinics closed and sent their patients there when the power went out.

"Faith, don't judge me for what I'm about to do," Novac said as he walked to the registration desk.

"May I help you?" The assistant at the desk was clearly overwhelmed and peered over her readers at him.

"My mother, Mary Graham, was just brought here. She was trapped under debris at her home. Will the doctor give me a report when he knows something?"

"Let me see your ID."

Novac handed her his license and waited for her to question him.

"Novac Calvin, the author?"

"Yes. That's right," he replied. "She remarried, so we have different last names."

"I'll let him know that you're waiting for a report on your mom. I love your books! Wish I had one here so you could autograph it."

Novac walked back to their seats with Faith. She remained quiet, holding back a grin.

"Guess you're right that it helps to be a celebrity," she teased. "And a liar."

After thirty minutes, a doctor came out to the waiting room.

"Your mother has suffered a moderate concussion and severe bruising to her torso area. She'll need to remain hospitalized for a couple of days until the swelling goes down and to make sure there are no internal injuries. She's still unconscious because we have her sedated. We don't want her trying to move around right now. We'll wean her off the meds soon and assess her further. If you'd like to go home, someone will give you a call and keep you apprised of her condition," the doctor told Novac. "Assuming phone service is restored soon. Or feel free to come by and check on her if that's preferable."

They shook hands and Novac thanked the doctor.

"Let's go back and do a little clean-up. Or rest. I'm still feeling a little rough."

Upon arrival at the cottage, Faith walked around the yard with him, picking up trash and shingles. A section of fence had blown over to the neighbor's property. Repair and debris removal would keep Novac busy for a while. Faith would have liked to stay longer and lend a hand, but she remembered Alice remained home by herself.

"Go back and make sure Alice is okay. I'll be alright. She needs you more than I do right now. I'll keep you posted about Mrs. Graham."

The trip home was treacherous with many detours along the way due to fallen trees. Alice was walking through the yard when Faith pulled up to the inn. Amazingly, it suffered no severe damage—just a shingle missing here and there; one section of gutter had come loose from the house. Power was still out on other parts of the island, but repair trucks could be seen around town, so it wouldn't be long before electricity would be restored to the north and east sides of the island.

Unfortunately for Faith, the inn never lost phone service, so Alice relayed a message to her upon her return.

"Phil called in the middle of the storm and asked for you. I told him you'd gone to check on a sick friend. That made him worried. He said he saw on the news that remnants of a hurricane were moving over the island. He made me promise to have you call as soon as you got in," Alice said.

"Hm. Did you tell him I'd consider it?"

"I told him I couldn't make you call. That was your decision."

"Who does he think he is fooling, pretending like he cares so much for my wellbeing? He never gave it that much regard when we were engaged!"

"So, you're not going to call?"

"After talking to Novac, I decided to call Phil. Novac made a good point. He said I needed some closure so I could get on with my life."

"Wise words."

"Where's that number? I'll call it right now and get it over with." Alice handed Faith the piece of paper with the scrawled message and number.

"Wish me luck." Faith walked to her room and reached for the phone. The number, she noticed, was not the same one she called many times when he lived in Seattle. It had an area code that seemed vaguely familiar to her. Massachusetts perhaps? *Hmm . . . Sunday morning*, she thought. *Where would Phil be right now?* She tried to think of every reason she could not to call him. Maybe he would be at church? Probably not. Out on his boat? "Don't put it off any longer," she told herself as she lifted the phone and called his number.

"Faith. Is that you?"

"Yep. It's me." She took a deep breath.

"I'm so glad you called me back. I was worried when that lady said you were out in the storm. Was there much damage?"

"Yeah. Some. Phil, I'm sure you didn't call to discuss the weather so let's just get on with it. Okay?"

"I called to apologize for being such a jerk the past two months. You didn't deserve any of it. If there's any way I can make it up to you, just tell me."

"You can quit calling me," Faith replied.

"You have every right to be angry. Go ahead and tell me what you think of me and get it off your chest. I mean it. It'd make me feel better too. But let me tell you my thoughts first. Then if you want me to leave you alone, so be it."

"Phil, I've already screamed at you so many times over and over in my mind. I'd just rather try to forget it and get on with my life. Okay? Apology accepted."

"Faith. That woman you saw was someone I worked with. I admit, I let things get a little out of hand there, but after you came to the door that day, I told her to leave and never come back. Honest."

"That's so wonderful of you. Now let's drop it."

"I never would've intentionally hurt you. You're the woman I love."

"You mean loved."

"No, Faith. I still love you. I don't expect you to feel the same."

"That's good because I don't. Do you know how humiliating it was to cancel a wedding and send gifts back? No, you don't because you never even bothered to help me take care of the mess."

"Faith, I didn't even know you'd cancelled the wedding until I called, and your mother told me. By that time, you'd already contacted everyone."

"Did you really think I'd go through with a marriage to someone who was fooling around with his business associate? Get real, Phil! All you've ever been able to think about is yourself. Yourself, your boat, your job. In that order!"

"You're right. I realized that and I've changed."

"I've heard that from you before."

"I sold Bessie. I'm not living in Seattle anymore. I've taken a position with a company in Hyannis."

"Whatever for?"

"I knew you'd never move out to Seattle away from your family. In Hyannis, I'm close to you. I could court you properly, and you could keep your eye on me although that's not needed anymore. You could even keep your job on Nantucket if you wanted to. Just ride the ferry over on days you work. I was really hoping you'd give me another chance, Faith."

"Chance to ruin my life?"

"Chance to show you how much I really do love you and how much I've changed. I need you, Faith. You keep me grounded. You make me happy." Faith was silent as Phil continued trying to convince her he was a changed man. She remained quiet as he spoke of his new home in Hyannis; a home he hoped she'd share with him someday.

Faith's hands were trembling, and her lips were hesitant to respond lest they'd give away some feelings of warmth she still had for him buried deep inside. She had to remain level headed with feet firmly planted on the ground. He wouldn't get the best of her ever again.

"Well, what do you think? Can we give it another try?" He waited for her answer.

"I need to think about it, Phil." Her heart wanted to cry out "Yes!" much to her surprise, but her mind threw up red flags in all directions.

"That's wonderful! At least you didn't tell me 'No.'"

"I didn't say 'yes' either."

"But you haven't closed me out completely. I'll accept that as an answer."

"Phil, I need to get off the phone now. This is Alice's business line."

"Okay. I'll let you go. But promise me you'll give me another chance?"

"I'll think about it. Bye."

"Goodbye. Call me when you make up your mind, okay? Promise me you won't keep me in suspense long."

Faith hung up the phone, wondering what had just taken place. A few hours ago, she was ready to wipe Phil out of her life for good; now she was considering taking another chance with him. *Once again, has he pulled the wool over my innocent eyes? Is he at home laughing about how easy it is to persuade me that he has honorable intentions?* These things came to Faith's mind as she looked for Alice. She'd know what to do. She'd heard most of the story and cared about her as if she were her own daughter.

Since church services had been cancelled due to the power outage, Alice was sitting outside on her deck chair, her sneaker-clad feet propped up on a table. She was tired from sweeping the sidewalks and cleaning storm-blown rubbish out of her gardens. Faith took a deep breath as she approached her. Alice smiled at her, shading her blue eyes from the sun that was now trying to peek out from behind puffy clouds.

"Did you talk to him?"

"Yes. I sure did."

"Did you get things straightened out?"

"Nope. I'm more confused now than ever." Faith hoped Alice would offer to listen to her thoughts.

"Would you like to talk about it?" Alice asked.

"Phil wants me back. Gave me all this junk about how he's changed and how much he loves me. I don't know what to believe."

"What's your heart telling you?"

"My heart hasn't been too reliable in the past, but I think I do still love him. Even after what he did, it's hard to let go of all the good things wc had together."

"Do you believe him? Do you think he's really changed?"

"There's no way to tell from one conversation. He said he sold the boat." Alice raised her eyebrows. Faith continued, "And he's bought a house in Hyannis. He said he did it so he could be near me."

"Seems that's a mighty risky reason to relocate, don't you think?" Alice turned to look Faith straight in the eyes. "Honey, what're you going to do? Does he want to see you?"

"He didn't say anything about that but I'm sure it's coming. What would you do?"

"Suppose I'd have to consider the person's past track record. Was that the only time he did anything like that to you?"

"Far as I know," Faith said.

"Well, I would advise you to go very slowly and make him prove he's changed. That is, if you even want to see him again. But you're an adult, so you must decide for yourself the right thing to do. I'd hate to see you get hurt again. Sounds like you need to spend time in prayer over this. What about Novac?"

"Novac's not a factor here. He still stands firm that he wants to remain a bachelor forever, no matter what. He was hurt worse than I was. We'll be good friends. That's all. I'm okay with that."

Faith sat on a piece of plastic Alice had laid on the grass next to her, staring at the sky. The bright white clouds glided across the now blue sky carrying with them no hint of the devastation brought to the tiny island the previous evening. They remained quiet, enjoying the warmth of the sun, wishing for an answer to the situation with Phil. Faith jumped up and stretched her legs.

"I need to make a phone call."

Faith had never known friendship like the kind Novac offered her— unconditional and true. Never had she had someone to spill the contents of her heart out to who would not be judgmental. Besides, she wanted to give him one more chance to change her mind.

She thought about calling her mother first. Her mother could be a good listener at times. However, she could not be impartial when it came to her daughter's affairs of the heart. Her mother, naturally, wanted her daughter to have the finest things in life: a nice stable man who could provide a home, children, financial security, all the things she had in her own marriage. Love was only secondary to security, according to her mother—it comes and goes. In her parents' marriage, it left ages ago, leaving behind a cold, yet secure life that satisfied her mother enough but not completely. Faith had always held on to the hope that both love and security were obtainable and could be permanent. Phil represented those things to her not so long ago. Was his indiscretion so great that it could not be overcome? After all, she had known couples who had overcome the unfaithfulness of one partner, only to become stronger for it. No. She won't tell her mother now, she decided. That was a battle she'd face later.

"Hey, Novac," she said over the phone. "I'm thinking about doing something and need to know if I'm being stupid or naive."

"Shoot," he said. "What's up?" he asked apprehensively.

"I'm thinking about seeing Phil again."

She heard Novac sigh and take a deep breath, "You mean see, as in physically see him in person so you can tell him off, or see him as in dating?"

"I mean physically see him and date him. Am I being really, really stupid? Please tell me if I am. I trust your opinion."

Novac thought for a moment before answering. "My initial gut feeling is to tell you not to see him. But I figure you must've talked to him on the phone? Am I right?"

"Yes. We spoke."

"Pretty convincing, huh? I don't want to probe too much into your private conversation, but why the change of heart? Did the ox decide to pull his weight?" Novac asked.

"What?"

"Sorry, that sounded rude."

"Yes, it did," Faith said. She stuck her tongue out at the phone.

"You once told me you and Phil were unevenly yoked. Isn't that what you called it? That drums up an image of oxen to me. So, I'm wondering if the yoke is even now?"

"I don't know yet. You may be a smart alec, but you're also my friend, so I value your input. But I honestly believe Phil has changed. Before you scoff, I'll tell you why." Faith rehashed the entire phone conversation for Novac's assessment.

"I'm not completely persuaded about Phil's intention," Novac said, "but I also can't judge him because I've never met the guy. Sweetheart, you know I just want you to be happy, right?"

"Right."

"You loved him, and I suspect you still do. I wish I could look into the future and protect you from any pain that might be around the corner. But all I can offer you is my support, whatever you decide to do. I care about you and want you to do what you feel is right in your heart."

"Thanks."

"Give it some thought. It won't hurt anything to take it very slowly and carefully. Promise me one thing, though."

"What?"

"Make ole Phil do the chasing this time. Keep him at arm's length and see how he reacts."

"Don't act too eager. Is that what you mean?"

"Exactly. Men don't like women who are too eager. That's something we don't like to admit. We like to be fawned over, but once the woman is in our pocket, she's not so interesting anymore. We're just a bunch of cads. Make him prove he's worthy of your affections. You're worth too much to have to settle for less. You know that, don't you?"

"You think?"

"I think you're worthy of the love of a man who will do right by you. If you believe Phil's that man, then he's a very lucky man to have you. You just remember that."

"That's the nicest thing anyone has ever said to me. I'm glad I called you, Novac. You're a good friend, and I love you for it."

"I feel the same, Sweetheart. I feel the same. Don't get yourself hurt. Okay?"

She hung up the phone, realizing that Novac's approval meant more to her than anyone else's in the world. Faith decided to take Novac's advice and wait for Phil to call her. If he was serious about wanting her back in his life, he should be prepared to go the extra mile to win her over. Novac said she was worth it. *Why couldn't it be Novac wanting me, loving me, pledging his devotion to me, wanting to make me happy the rest of my life? Face it. He's not that interested romantically and doesn't want to hurt my feelings.* She flopped back on her bed. She wanted Novac to always be in her life, no matter what. She knew that to be true. If Phil wanted her back so much, he'd have to accept that fact.

Novac already occupied a special place in her heart. A place no one—not even Phil—could inhabit.

CHAPTER SIX

Guests arrived Monday morning and the inn was alive again with voices and faces—some new, some from years past who were seeking refuge from their daily ho-hum lives. Alice had a natural knack for rousing the guests' sense of adventure while staying at The Scrimshaw and for making them feel completely at home. For some, this would be a first bed and breakfast experience. Often, the first timers came through the door feeling a bit like intruders in a stranger's home, but those feelings soon passed after meeting Alice. She could instinctively tell which guests like to be fussed over, who liked to be left alone, and which ones needed to be entertained. Repeat visitors often coaxed Alice into playing the piano for them, which she did happily as she sang along in her off-pitch voice. By the time their trip was over, her guests felt like they were leaving the home of a close relative.

After her two-week training period, Faith fell into the role of inn assistant without a hitch. She anticipated Alice's needs beautifully. If Alice was entertaining guests with music or tales of Nantucket, Faith would busy herself in the kitchen cleaning dishes and getting things ready for the next morning. At the end of the day, it gave the women a good feeling knowing their guests slept comfortably and happily.

Most evenings, Novac came by the inn to pick up Faith for an evening stroll. They spoke of their day's accomplishments, their hopes and dreams. But there was one subject they seemed to always ignore: Phil. Novac had politely skipped over the subject. Faith appreciated his lack of intrusion regarding Phil but wondered if he even cared about knowing what was going on.

The fact remained: it had been two weeks since Phil called Faith. He hadn't made any further efforts to reach her, leaving her to wonder if he'd moved on to greener pastures. She had predicted that if Phil did not receive an answer from her within a couple of days, he would be burning up the phone lines trying to convince her to give him another chance. Her prediction was proving to be wrong. In her heart she was glad she had taken Novac's advice by not appearing eager.

After the evening walk, as he had done every other evening, Novac escorted Faith to the inn and into the foyer. He kissed her lightly on the cheek and bid his farewell.

Alice had taped a note to her bedroom door: "There's something for you on the guest table." A tall, bright bouquet of flowers sat regally in a cut glass vase like a beacon in the darkened hallway. A card hung from the puffy yellow bow.

"I can't wait much longer without self-destructing. I really meant what I said. I love you and want to make it up to you. Phil"

She carried the flowers into her room and placed them on the table next to her bed. Faith read the card again two more times and reached for the piece of paper containing Phil's telephone number. *Ten-thirty,* she thought as she glanced at her watch. *He'll still be up.* Feeling confident about what she was doing, she dialed.

"Phil," she said after he answered in his familiar low-pitched voice. "Thanks for the flowers. I love them!"

"I love you," he replied. Faith didn't know how to answer. There was a long silence. "You don't have to answer me. You called. That's what's important. Does this mean you've reconsidered?"

"I suppose there's no harm in seeing each other again.

Now don't get me wrong, we can never be at the same point where we were before. A lot of things have changed for both of us. I need to know I can trust you again before it advances beyond anything more than casual dating. I'll need to get to know you again. Start over."

"I understand. Believe me, no one is as sorry as I am for what happened. It was a mistake. You won't be sorry if you give me another chance."

"So, what do we do now?" Faith asked as she lightly stroked the telephone with her finger.

"I want to see you as soon as I can," Phil said. Faith's heart pounded a little. She wasn't sure how ready she was to see him face to face. "What about tomorrow?" he asked.

"Give me more time than that."

"The day after tomorrow then. I won't take 'no' for an answer," Phil insisted.

Faith hesitated and took a deep breath. "Okay." She wondered if she would regret this decision.

Plans were set. Phil would be staying in a room at The Scrimshaw Inn for a couple of days. Alice had a cancellation on one upstairs room due to a death in the guest's family, so Phil's name was written in the reservation book.

"Why don't you take those two days off?" Alice suggested as they stripped the sheets off the bed Phil would be using.

"Oh, no. I would never do that. Phil can just work around my schedule. He's the one who made the plans, so he can be flexible."

"Good! Sounds like you have the right idea! Don't look too eager."

"That's what Novac told me," Faith said.

"He's right. Too bad you and Novac—" Alice began.

"Alice!"

"I know. I just think he's such a nice man. So thoughtful and kind to you. I'm sure he wishes you would fall head over heels for him like he has for you."

"He's not head over heels for me! Whoever told you that?" Faith said, letting her end of the fresh sheet drop to the floor in surprise.

"I can tell. When you've been around as long as I have, you just know these things."

"Well, he certainly hasn't made any moves in that direction. He calls himself a confirmed bachelor every time the subject of love or marriage comes up." She picked up the end of the sheet and tucked it under the mattress.

"I'd try to change his mind if I were you."

"What makes you think I want to?" Faith asked.

"Remember. I can tell." Alice winked at Faith and walked out of the room with the soiled sheets and towels in her arms. Faith remained in the room, pondering what Alice had said.

Am I that obvious? Does Novac really feel the same way? Well, whatever he feels, he has no intention of making a commitment to me or anybody else.

She had always dreamed of settling down and having a family. *The only family Novac wants is of the canine variety.* Her mind was made up. Phil had finally come to his senses, and it felt good to be wanted in a permanent way.

Faith looked at her watch. Time for the evening ferry to be leaving Hyannis headed toward Nantucket. Faith had to keep telling herself over and over she was doing the right thing by seeing Phil again. Anxiety got the best of her, however. She had tried to dial his phone before he left home to tell him it was a big mistake, but to no avail. The calls would not go through. So, she resigned herself to the fact that soon the man who had broken her heart so desperately would be blending with her new life. A life that had become comfortable. People she now cared for tremendously would be facing a piece of her past and passing judgment on him. She admired Phil's courage to meet her on her turf. He had to realize that her new friends knew every gruesome detail about his "other woman."

All of Faith's fear dissolved the instant she saw Phil standing at the front door of The Scrimshaw. His familiar smile, his nervous, stuffy body language, all brought back memories of Providence, good and bad. Oddly, she felt empowered. He had come to her. Now the fate of their relationship was in her hands; she could either reject him or accept him. It felt good.

She followed Phil into the inn's library where Alice sat, pretending to read the open book in her hands.

Has he always had that balding spot on the back of his head?

Alice stood. They shook hands and exchanged all the proper pleasantries. Faith noticed that Phil was trying his best to charm Alice.

"Beautiful blouse, Alice. My favorite shade of green," Phil said.

"I love green, too. My late husband gave this to me on my last birthday." Alice smoothed the hem of the silk blouse. "We're glad to have you here. I'll go and let you get settled. I have a million things to do in the kitchen."

Faith led Phil up the aged staircase toward his guest room. They stopped two times along the way up to admire portraits hanging in the stairwell. She couldn't tell by Phil's "hmm" if he was genuinely interested or not as she explained the inn's history. At least he was trying.

After Phil freshened up, he came downstairs and found Faith sitting in the library. "Let's go grab a cup of coffee down the road and catch up. We have a lot to talk about," He suggested.

"Sounds like a good idea." A pit formed in Faith's stomach as she silently gave herself a pep talk, going over a list of subjects not to bring up on this first time together. He had made an effort to reconcile with her, so she needed to hear him out.

The conversation was polite on the short walk and no mention was made of the broken engagement. They spoke of the weather and several other "safe" subjects over coffee, which relieved Faith, until Phil took his last sip from the cup. She noticed a change in his facial expression as he dabbed the corners of his mouth with his napkin. He reached across the table and tapped Faith's saucer with his index finger, his eyes fixed on hers. "I'm sorry."

Faith turned her eyes away. Even though these were words she yearned to hear, she didn't want to smile, nor did she want to cry. She felt either response would diminish her dominant position. Phil had always been able to tease her emotions with words, drawing from her any response he desired to suit the situation. Faith made no sound and raised her coffee to take a sip, peering at him over the barrier of the cup's rim.

"It's water under the bridge," she finally said, hoping she sounded sincere.

"You're beautiful," Phil whispered to her, still getting only a polite smile from her.

Feeling the need to break the tension, Faith said, "Tomorrow, after I'm finished with my morning chores, we'll head out to the other side of the island for lunch. I want you to meet a good friend of mine." Phil raised his eyebrows.

"Is she someone you met here or knew before you came?"

"Someone I met here," she responded without feeling the need to clear up the confusion over the friend's gender.

They walked back to the inn and sat with Alice for a few minutes before parting to their separate rooms. Faith took her shoes off and reclined on her bed as she rehearsed the next day's plans in her mind. They would meet Novac for lunch at Fat Cat's. Novac said he would be very hurt if she didn't introduce Phil to him. After all, she often reminded Novac that he was her absolute best friend in the world, so she wanted to give him a chance to scrutinize the man who desired to spend the rest of his life with her.

Faith laughed at the thought of Phil dining on burgers at Fat Cat's. Sand on the floor, waiters in flip-flops. Yes, Phil was about to experience life as he'd never seen it before. To Phil, casual dining meant taking off his tie. He'd always been the button-down collar type. Even when he sailed on Bessie, his clothes were immaculate. He'd take a change of clothes along with him just in case he got the slightest bit dirty or wet. His shoes were always lined up in his closet perfectly straight, complete with shoe trees placed inside to prevent them from getting misshapen. The clothing in his closet was separated according to color. Shirts on the top row, pants on the bottom. White shirts on the left, dark shirts on the right. Once upon a time, Faith had been as fussy about her clothes. The casual atmosphere of Nantucket changed that.

Novac arrived at Fat Cat's a little early and reserved a table far from the kitchen so they wouldn't be disturbed by the noise. While he was waiting, Venus happened by, making her way to the back of the restaurant, carrying a small brown paper sack.

"Thought I'd find you here! I went by your house and Doolittle told me where you were," she said, lightly scratching the back of Novac's neck with her frosty pink nails.

"Good ole Doo. I'm meeting Faith and her boyfriend for lunch. They should be here any time now." He motioned for her to scat.

"I didn't know she had a boyfriend. Cool. I thought she

liked you," Venus said, plopping the sack down in front of Novac, raising her eyebrows, hoping to get a response from him. He didn't take the bait.

"What's this?" Novac picked up the small brown sack and squeezed it.

"Oh, I was down at that candy store in town and picked up some of those jellybeans we like so much. Thought I'd be nice and share them with you."

"Thanks, Venus. You're so thoughtful." Novac reached into the bag and grabbed several pieces of the candy and tossed them into his mouth, but never once looking at her. His eyes were fixed on the entrance of the restaurant, awaiting Faith's arrival.

"Can I stay and hang out with you guys? Think anyone will mind?" Venus asked as she pulled up a chair and sat down.

"Does it matter?" Novac asked sarcastically. Venus completely ignored him and motioned for the waiter to get her some water. Just as the waiter left, Faith walked in followed by Phil, who was wearing an uncomfortable smile.

Venus bent over and whispered in Novac's ear. "What do ya think about those legs? They haven't seen daylight since he was three, I bet. He's a piece of work. A perfect match for her. "

Phil's clothing choice caused him to stand out as he passed through the casually hip Fat Cat's crowd. Bermuda shorts. Red, white, and yellow plaid. Probably bought a decade ago for playing golf. A white oxford button-down shirt, sleeves rolled up, and black loafers finished look.

Faith was surprised to see Venus. *What was Novac thinking? Totally inappropriate of him.*

"Phil, this is Novac and his friend, Venus. Guys, this is Phil," Faith said as she and Phil stood in front of the table. Phil reached out and shook hands with Novac, who was now standing, towering over Phil by a good four or five inches.

"Nice to meet you," Novac said cordially.

"Same here," Phil replied. Venus, however, remained seated and watched with interest.

"Venus happened to stop by and found me here," Novac said, casting a frown toward Venus. Faith could read Novac well and sensed he was not happy about her presence.

"I have sort of a Novac radar," Venus said. "I always know where he is and who he's with." She cut her eyes over at Faith.

The statement gave Faith a chill. She always suspected Venus kept close tabs on him. She glanced at Novac to see his reaction. None that she detected. *Didn't he hear what she said? Does she know that Novac and I spend almost every evening together? Was this a threat or is she marking her territory?*

"When Faith told me we were meeting her good friend, I thought it was a girl," Phil chuckled and brushed Faith's arm with the back of his hand. "But you're not!"

Venus rolled her eyes and turned her face away so they wouldn't see her grin at Phil's remark. "So observant," she murmured under her breath.

"Nope. Not a girl. Never have been," Novac said.

"I can attest to that," Venus added.

Faith ignored her comment and pretended to follow what Phil said as he rattled on about his sales job. She thought it odd that he never inquired about Novac's line of work. But with Phil not being an artsy person, that conversation would have been one-sided and awkward for Novac. Seeing the two men together made one thing clear—they were complete opposites in every way aside from their mutual concern about her.

Venus lingered throughout lunch, getting up frequently to talk to the young man playing guitar in the bar. Each time she came back to the table, she had a new drink in her hand. Her eyes were getting sleepy and her actions slowed down. Venus said nothing at all as the other three finished their salads; she lit a cigarette and sipped her drink, swaying to the tunes coming from the bar, which relieved Faith. She knew Phil would be forming strong opinions about the people she knew on the island, and she knew she had some explanation regarding Venus' eccentricities.

"We need to be leaving," Faith said as she rose from her seat. Phil grabbed the bill away from her. Novac rose, shook Phil's hand, and pulled the bill away from him.

"My treat. Glad we could have lunch together. I need to tell you before you leave that it's an island tradition to toss a penny into the water as your ferry exits past the lighthouse. That's supposed to ensure that you'll make a return trip to Nantucket soon!" Novac winked at Faith.

Phil shrugged and cocked his head. "I thank you. And I'll make sure to have a penny on me so I can toss it. I want to come back very soon." Phil took Faith's hand in his.

Novac's eyes followed Faith and Phil as they walked out of the restaurant. Venus shook her head lazily as she took a deep drag off her cigarette.

"Perfect for each other, don't you think?"

Novac ignored her comment and snatched the bag of jellybeans off the table.

"You can have 'em," she said, rising from her stool, motioning with the short stub of cigarette between her fingers. "See ya."

Hand in hand, Faith led Phil around the bustling shopping area, past old churches, and sea captains' homes. He seemed mildly interested in the sights and mostly interested in winning back Faith's affections. His attention was completely on her; something she hadn't experienced previously.

By the time he left the following morning, the two behaved as if nothing had ever gone wrong between them in the past. His parting words to Faith were, "I'll be back every other weekend. I can't stay away for longer than that."

The trip was a success. It pleased Faith when Alice said Phil seemed like a nice, sincere young man. Faith couldn't wait to call Novac and ask his opinion of Phil even though she suspected she'd have to endure some ribbing about the shorts.

When Novac picked up the phone, Faith thought he sounded irritated, which wasn't normal for him. "Did I catch you at a bad time?"

"Oh! Hi there. No. You didn't catch me doing anything. What's up? Phil gone home?"

"Yep. Sent him back on the ferry yesterday." Faith paused and drew a deep breath. "So?"

"So what?" Novac was afraid of what she was going to ask.

"So, what did you think?"

"Think about what?" he teased.

"Phil! You nincompoop!"

"Oh, Phil! Well, he seemed like a nice enough guy."

"That's all?"

"What did you want me to say? You're the one who's in love with him. Not me."

"Did I say I was in love with him?" Faith giggled.

"You don't need to say it. It's the way you smiled at him during lunch even though he was wearing those shorts. Didn't seem to bother you at all. Now that's love!"

"Novac! You're so mean!" Faith laughed. "I thought it was sweet. He just wanted to be casual. I suppose he stuck out like a sore thumb, huh?" Faith laughed again. "But you have to admit, it was sweet of him to try to fit in."

"Yeah. Real sweet. He's just a regular honey bun. But I need to know. How did those shorts make him fit in?" Novac said teasingly.

"Okay. That's enough. Did you like him at all? I want to know what you think." Faith was serious now.

"Do you like him?"

"I like him," Faith answered.

"Well then I like him. I want you to be happy. I'm being serious. That's all that matters," Novac replied.

"I love you. You're the best friend anyone could ever have."

"I love you, too, Sweetie. See you tonight? Wanna ride bikes? I'll show you a new path I found past Jetties Beach."

"Sounds great. You want to grab a sandwich out somewhere before?"

"Yep. See you at the usual time."

Alice kept bicycles at the inn for guests to use during their stay on the island. They weren't in the best shape, but they did the job. Their tires were slightly worn, and they'd been exposed to some harsh weather and salt water which caused rust spots on the fenders. Faith borrowed one each time she and Novac rode in the evenings. When Novac first began this nightly tradition, she had to take it easy; it had been many years since she'd been on a bike. But now it was something she enjoyed doing with him when the weather permitted. Little by little she was working up to her goal of making it all the way out to 'Sconset by the end of the month if she kept up with her riding.

That evening, as they rode out past the Whaling Museum and on toward Jetties Beach, Novac slowed down and waved at a small group of women who stood in front of a surf shop, talking and gesturing with their hands as though in a lively conversation. One woman jumped up and down and waved both hands back at him. When Faith neared the group, she recognized the woman's relaxed posture and long blond hair. Venus fixed her gaze on Faith as they rode by. Faith waved and smiled at her, hoping to elicit a friendly acknowledgement in return. Instead, Venus stood frozen, a repugnant look on her face as if she were a stone gargoyle guarding her territory against the enemy. The other women in the group looked at Venus, waiting to see what her response would be to Novac as he rode by with "another woman." In her peripheral vision, Faith saw one woman lightly stroking Venus on the back to calm her down.

When Novac and Faith reached their destination just

beyond Jetties beach, he motioned for her to pull over to a large rock next to the path. The sun was just beginning to set over the ocean. High, wispy clouds were outlined in fluorescent pink. They parked their bicycles and sat on the rock, admiring the beauty God created.

"Did Venus seem odd to you?" Novac asked.

Faith just raised her eyebrows and peered over her sunglasses at Novac.

"Okay. I know she's always odd. But did she seem a little hostile or something?"

She sighed, pulled off her sunglasses, and stowed them inside the small pack hooked to the bicycle.

"She certainly did," Faith replied. "I thought she'd start throwing rocks at me any moment. Novac, face the music. Venus is very hot for you."

"You think so? Nah. I think you're mistaken."

"Are you blind or are you just playing games with me?" Faith giggled and sighed again. "Hello? Earth to Novac. Can you read me? Or should I say Venus to Novac?" She slapped him lightly on the arm. "Did you see the way she looked at me?"

"I tried to ignore her, but she did seem miffed a little, huh?"

"She was staring holes through me. Do you think she's been doing some kind of witchcraft spell or voodoo thing on me? Didn't you tell me she believed that junk?"

"Yeah, she believes in it, but I don't think she practices it. It's your imagination. Women can be so catty!" Novac hissed and clawed at Faith. She wasn't amused. She turned toward him and pushed him off the rock they were sitting on.

"That was uncalled for!" Novac barked as he pulled himself to his feet.

"Serves you right. I haven't done anything to that woman. I resent being called catty."

"I mean some of the things you women say about each other sound catty."

"If I didn't know better, I'd swear you've got a thing for Venus. You're always defending her. And besides, what do you mean by 'you women'? I haven't said anything out of line. What has she said about me?"

"Nothing much." Novac brushed himself off and sat back on the rock.

"Nothing much? So, she *has* said something? I want details." Faith put her hands back on Novac, threatening to push him again if he didn't answer.

"She accuses you of being crazy about me. She speaks the truth. We all know you are, so that's not much of a secret." He laughed as she started to push him again. He grabbed her and held on around her waist to keep from falling over. "If I go, you go, too!"

"She really says that about me? Doesn't she know we're just friends?" Faith asked as Novac loosened his hold on her.

"I've told her that a thousand times."

"And she doesn't believe you?"

"Not a bit. She keeps telling me there's a lot more going on than I'm admitting. The same sort of things you accuse me of concerning her."

Faith sat with her mouth hanging open, feigning surprise.

"It's so wonderful to have two women fighting over me!" Novac laughed. Faith punched his arm with a balled-up fist.

"She can have you! You're nothing but trouble," Faith said, smiling to make sure he knew she was just kidding. "And conceited, I might add."

"Are we back in high school?" Novac asked. "Because it sure sounds like the two of us are arguing over who will take us to prom."

"Well, I have to say that Venus is not far from her high school years," Faith said, giving Novac the "side eye". They laughed over her comment, then sat quietly, silhouetted against the last bit of orange glow in the sky. She had always appreciated the fact she could sit and be silent with Novac. He understood her need to be left alone with her thoughts sometimes. Faith's left foot twirled round and round as her legs dangled over the side of the large rock, signaling to Novac that she was uneasy about whatever thoughts were going through her mind. "Does she know you're a C.B.?"

"What do you mean, C.B.? Who? Venus?" Novac asked.

"C.B.," Faith said. "You know. Confirmed bachelor."

"Oh! Yeah, she knows." Novac stared straight ahead toward the ocean.

"What does she think about that?"

"Not that it makes that much difference to her, but she doesn't believe in marriage anyway. She's more the living together type."

"Has she suggested it?"

"Yeah, once."

"Really! When was this?" Faith's heart pounded as she waited for the answer.

"Okay. I'll confess, but I'm not proud of it." Novac took a deep breath and let out a sigh. "Venus and I dated briefly when she first came to the island, oh, maybe about a year and a half ago. She started trying to push things along a little further, and I didn't want to get serious. We began seeing less and less of each other after that. That's all. Okay. Now you know." Novac looked out at the ocean, not making eye contact with Faith.

"Wow! I had no idea! Why didn't you tell me?"

"It's embarrassing."

"Why?" Faith asked.

"Well, because she's, uh . . . Venus! She's a bit strange, don't you think?"

"Yeah. I think. And young. You dirty old man."

"Okay. Let me have it. Make your comments and get it over with."

Faith put her arm around Novac. "Why?" she said with a curious smile on her face.

"You mean why did I go out with Venus? Let me get this straight. She approached me. I didn't approach her. She was too young for me. But she was persistent, and I finally gave in because she was charming—in a Venus sort of way. She could be cute and funny. Then she became interested in peace, love, and rock & roll, and everything that goes along with that. She turned into a sixties flower child. I went through all that in the sixties and I didn't care to relive any part of it. She's changed lately. The Venus you see isn't the same Venus I had a relationship with. I suppose I was flattered that she found me attractive. Maybe I was going through a mid-life crisis?"

"Like 'em young, do ya?" Faith joked. It disturbed her to think of Novac and Venus together. *Why did he take a chance with Venus and won't with me?* "Now I understand why she hates me."

"She doesn't hate you."

"Oh, yeah. She hates me. Women don't like to have competition paraded around in their faces. And she still likes you."

"Is that what you are? Competition?" Novac smiled and winked.

"You know what I mean. In her mind I am."

"I know. You're right. You're always right. Let's head back. It's getting dark." They hopped on their bicycles and rode back into town. Novac led the way, with Faith following close behind. No further words were spoken until they arrived at the Scrimshaw and Novac walked her to the front door.

"I'll talk to you tomorrow," Novac said as he bent over and kissed her on the cheek. "Sleep tight."

"You, too." As usual, the front door was unlocked until all the guests were in for the night. Faith stepped into the hallway of the inn, trying not to make any noise as she walked across the wooden floor. A lamp cast a soft, welcoming glow on the wall where Lauralee stared down from her portrait. As Faith approached the door to her room she paused and walked a few steps back to where Lauralee's likeness hung. "What do you think, Lauralee? You've seen a lot of people come and go. Is he a hopeless cause? Just what I thought," she mumbled to the somber-faced woman dressed in late eighteenth century clothing,

Faith unlocked her bedroom door and walked to the phone to call Phil. Maybe speaking with him would erase any jealousy she felt over Venus and Novac's past life together. *There's no reason for me to have feelings for any man but Phil. He's my future. My permanent future. Novac's fascinating because he's unobtainable. He's only a wonderful friend.* She rationalized.

Hearing Phil's voice cleared away her feelings of melancholia.

"Please come again soon," She begged. He reminded her of his promise to visit often and it pleased Faith to be pursued.

She excitedly chatted on and on about the itinerary for his next visit. "We'll take a ferry across to Martha's Vineyard," she explained. Phil had always been interested in Victorian and gothic architecture. "I can't wait to show you Oak Bluffs! You'll love it!" She told of how they would work their way around the island to the other five towns, each with their own personality. Faith read to Phil about Martha's Vineyard from a guidebook she purchased the day before.

"Listen to this: the Campground in Oak Bluffs is home to three hundred fancy little cottages, each trying to outdo the other with their variety of colors and elaborate gingerbread trim."

Her conversation with Phil lasted an hour and proved to be the dose of medicine that cured the blues and gave her something to look forward to the next weekend.

Once in her favorite flannel pajamas, she curled up under the covers with a book, The Great Whale Hunters, she had grabbed from Alice's library. She opened the cover, licked her finger, and turned to the first chapter. *I really must learn a little more about the history of the island,* she told herself as she read the first paragraph over and over, not really comprehending any of it. No matter how hard she tried, Faith could not take her mind off the revelation Novac divulged to her as they sat on the rock. "I should've known," she mumbled as she slammed the book closed and tossed it on the bed beside her. "I knew that chick didn't like me for some reason. Now I know why."

She picked the book up and put it on the bedside table. "I don't get him at all. What's wrong with him? I'm cute. I'm smart. Not crazy like some people. Guess I must not be young enough. He's probably *still* going through that mid-life thing men go through," she told herself. She turned off the lamp next to her bed and settled under the covers. Only a stream of pale light from the full moon shone through the patio door into her room. She closed her eyes and drifted into a light slumber.

Close to midnight, Faith opened her eyes, not knowing why she was jarred awake. Perhaps because a soft, cool breeze brushed across her face? Possibly one of the guests accidentally opened her door looking for the library or kitchen. No. She was sure she had locked her bedroom door after she came in. She sat up in bed and groped for the lamp's chain. Her fingers reached it, and she pulled. There was a momentary, intense flash of light from the lamp. "Blast it!" she exclaimed over the blown-out bulb. She thought she detected a slight movement over toward her door.

"Hello?" she said, praying not to receive a reply. Her heart thumped hard in her chest. *It was my imagination. A bad dream. Yes, that's it.* Her eyes strained to adjust to the room's darkness, then she noticed the door to the patio slightly ajar. As the breeze blew outside, the door opened a couple of inches and then slowly closed back with the cross draft, creaking a little as it moved. She had the eerie feeling of a presence in her room.

Faith sat up and draped her feet over the side of the bed

and felt around for her slippers using her toes. She walked over to the patio door, peeked outside briefly, and pulled it shut, latching it tightly. Before she had a chance to turn around, her bedroom door opened and shut suddenly. Faith froze for a moment, collecting her racing thoughts. Mustering every bit of courage she could, she picked up a heavy vase and approached the bedroom door, opening it quietly. She cautiously poked her head out, walked down the dark hallway past Lauralee's portrait and glanced in the direction of the kitchen doorway. A figure swept out of sight toward the inn's back exit, pausing briefly before turning to the right and disappearing into the darkness behind the back staircase. A woman, she was sure. Barefooted, perhaps, as there was no sound of shoes. She was certain she saw the outline of a long skirt in the small amount of light streaming through the front door sidelights. She had noticed the slender build and graceful gait of the person. She relaxed once she realized it had not been a man in her room. It had to be someone who was lost. After all, the hall was very dark.

A woman took a wrong turn in the hallway, and I must've forgotten to lock my door, she reasoned, as she went back into her room and flipped on the ceiling light. Faith made sure the door was locked this time and went over and double-checked the patio door latch. She was struck by the sweet smell of flowers as she walked across the room to her bed. *Are gardenias blooming in the garden this early in the season? Did anyone even grow gardenias on Nantucket?* She didn't recall seeing any around the patio. Alice could answer that question in the morning. *Could it be Alice's roses along the fence I caught the fragrance of?* They were ready to bloom when Faith last noticed. Anyway, she was too tired to worry about it now. Time to go back to bed.

Still a little shaken, she apprehensively walked back over to the switch and turned off the overhead light. Faith felt her way over to the bed and stretched out under the covers. With the lights off, she didn't feel so brave anymore and lay there stiffly, her eyes darting back and forth across the room trying hard to detect anything out of the ordinary. Exhaustion finally won out and Faith, once again, drifted off to sleep. She woke up several times throughout the night in response to every car that went down the street, every breeze that rattled the windows, and every thought of that mysterious figure who had invaded the privacy of her room.

CHAPTER SEVEN

By six o'clock the next morning, Alice was already busying herself in the kitchen teaching a guest, Mrs. Shepherd, how to make her almost-famous three cheese omelet.

"Now fold it over gently," Alice told Mrs. Shepherd, looking up and smiling at Faith as she entered the room.

Faith walked over to the hot stove, put on her oven mitts, and pulled out a tin of baked muffins. The sweet aroma filled the air.

"Good morning, Faith. Sleep well last night?" Faith shrugged. "Mrs. Shepherd begged for a cooking lesson, so I told her to meet me in the kitchen at 6:00 AM. She surprised me by showing up so early, but I'm glad she did!" Alice turned her attention back to Mrs. Shepherd. "Now flip it out of the pan onto the plate. Good!"

After serving the guests, Faith returned to the kitchen where Alice and Mrs. Shepherd were discussing garden mulch as they ate their omelets. Faith hated to interrupt but jumped in as the women paused between sentences.

"Before I forget, I was wondering if there are gardenias in the garden. I smelled something extremely sweet drifting through my room last night, but I couldn't find the bushes when I looked this morning." She was determined to find the underlying source of this mystery.

"Well, honey, I don't have any. I can't imagine what you smelled blooming at this time of year. It won't be too long before the roses start appearing." She thought for a moment, tapping her cheek with her finger. "I don't believe the neighbors grow anything that smells sweet. They don't enjoy gardening like I do."

"That's funny," Faith said. "I know I smelled gardenias. My grandmother grew them, so I'm familiar with the fragrance."

"Sorry to disappoint you, honey."

"Oh. One more thing. You're going to think I'm crazy, but were you in my room after I went to bed?" Alice shook her head. "I saw a slender woman walking through the hallway late last night. It was dark so I couldn't make out her features. She'd been in my room and scared me half to death!"

"It wasn't me. But I appreciate you thinking I'm a slender woman." Alice chuckled. "I went to bed early last night and slept like a rock. Didn't you lock your door?"

"I thought I did, but I could've been mistaken."

"Didn't you turn on your light to see who it was?"

"My bulb blew out when I flicked it on. I noticed my patio door was open and when I went over to shut it, someone ran out of my room while my back was turned."

"Oh my!" Alice put her hand up to her mouth.

"I went out into the hall to see who it was. It must've been after midnight because the hall light was out. But I did see the figure of a woman in a long, dark skirt walking out toward the back. I could tell she was slender. That's about all."

"The only woman we have staying at the inn right now is Mrs. Shepherd." Alice motioned to the woman sitting next to her at the kitchen counter. Faith realized immediately that Mrs. Shepherd wasn't the woman she saw in the hall last night. Mrs. Shepherd was about as wide as she was tall, and she was a tall woman.

"I wasn't up walking around last night," the rosy-cheeked woman said to Faith. "And I hardly fit the description of a slender woman!" Mrs. Shepherd laughed heartily and picked up her coffee cup and took a sip. "Do you have any ghosts around here?" She smiled, but her face showed she was dead serious about the subject. "These old whalers' houses are chocked full of them."

Alice thought for a moment, squinting her eyes. "Well, one or two past guests claimed they saw someone walking up and down the halls and they heard odd noises. Babies crying, shoes clomping on the wood floors. The usual ghostly noises." Alice turned toward Faith and shrugged her shoulders. "I haven't seen any, but who knows?" Faith felt the hairs on her arms stand straight up.

"I'll really sleep well now," Faith said, peering, wide-eyed, around at the ancient kitchen.

"Sorry. Didn't mean to bring it up if it scares you," Mrs. Shepherd said matter-of-factly. "Ghosts don't hurt people. They're just lost souls. In fact, most people who've seen them say they're helpful. Warning them of danger. I'm sure you've heard the stories." Mrs. Shepherd took another sip of her coffee. "I've done a lot of reading on the subject. It's intriguing. You ought to have one of those ghost hunters come to the house and check it out," she added as she looked over at Alice. "You'd probably get written about in a book."

"There's got to be a better explanation for it than that. Personally, I don't believe in ghosts," Faith said. Alice smiled and winked at her behind Mrs. Shepherd's back. Faith's mouth may have bravely stated her disbelief in ghosts, but it was far from convincing the rest of her.

After completing the morning duties, Faith wanted to get out of the house to clear her mind. She immediately thought of Novac and how he'd mentioned wanting to go to the Brant Point Lighthouse sometime when the weather was nice. The sky couldn't be more crystal blue, and she had no immediate obligation, so she called him from the phone in her room.

Seven, eight, nine rings and he still hadn't answered. *This isn't like him. He always hangs around his house in the mornings. Maybe he's taking Doolittle out for a walk on the beach.*

"Doesn't he ever stay in and write?" Faith grumbled.

She picked up the book she had attempted to start reading the night before. *Might as well make my time useful while I wait for Novac to get back to the house.* Glancing at her watch, she realized fifteen minutes had passed. Enough time to walk the dog, she resolved. She let the phone ring and ring. At first, she was mildly worried. After a couple of minutes of worrying, she began to get nervous, but for another reason. *Did Venus contact him after seeing us together? Did they have a long talk and resolve the differences between them, and he was so flattered by her jealous rage that he flew back into her arms and begged forgiveness for foolishly letting her go. Now I'm being a little bit ridiculous. Or am I? Phil is my man, not Novac.*

The doubt still lingered in her mind when she made the third attempt to reach Novac. "This will be the last time I'll try to call him today," she grumbled as the phone rang six, seven and eight times. She was about to hang up when Novac answered.

"Hello?" His voice sounded tired.

"Novac? Are you okay?" Faith asked. "Did I wake you up?" *Please be alone, please be alone,* she thought again and again as she waited for his reply.

"Uh, no. I don't think you woke me up." There was a pause. "I don't feel so well today. Maybe I dozed off for a minute."

"Are you sick?"

"Same old, same old, you know," he slurred.

"Novac? Don't you think you need to get checked out?" Faith asked, now concerned for her friend.

"Yeah. I have an appointment later this week on the mainland."

"You don't think . . ." She was afraid to finish her sentence.

"Maybe. Maybe not. It sure seems like I've traveled down this path before," he answered.

"Oh, Novac." She didn't exactly know what to say. Her stomach felt tense and nervous. "Can I do anything? I'll come right over if you need me to."

"I know, baby. But if it's all the same to you, I'd rather not have anyone see me like this. It's not a pretty sight. And besides, I don't feel like entertaining."

"Understood. But you'll call me if you need anything, right?"

"Right."

"Will you need help getting to your appointment? Alice won't mind if I take a morning off," Faith said.

"Uh, yeah. I might. It's on Friday. Call me Thursday night and I'll let you know."

"I'll call you before then to see how you feel. Okay?"

"That's more than okay," Novac replied. "In fact, I'm sure I'll feel better if you do."

"Go get some sleep and I'll be checking on you."

"Thanks, Babe. I love you."

"I love you too, Novac. Take care." An ominous feeling came over Faith as she sat on the bed replaying the conversation. Her hand was shaking as she pulled a Kleenex out of the box on her dresser. "Don't die, Novac. I need you," she spoke through gasping sobs. "I don't know what I'd do without you." Mental pictures of him lying in a hospital bed whirled through her mind. Watching him waste away to nothing. The pain. Attending his funeral. There was no way on earth she could ever go through that. She suddenly realized he could be the most important person in her life right now, and she was behaving like a coward. Just when he might need her most, she wanted to wimp out on him. She knew this was no way to treat a man who had helped her through the most difficult time in her life. No. She would have to be strong for him, no matter what. She prayed this was a false alarm. Just because he'd had colon cancer once before didn't mean every time he got an upset stomach it was cancer. He had told her the doctors declared a person cured of cancer if it hadn't reoccurred within five years. It was five years now. Almost to the day.

Faith was glad the inn was busy. Her many chores made the week fly by and kept her mind off Novac's health concerns. Alice requested her assistance in the mornings for the coming weekend, but the afternoons and evenings would be free if she finished her work in time, which would be ideal for Phil's impending visit. It pleasantly surprised her when Phil offered to help her make up beds or whatever else he could do to lessen her load. She found herself daydreaming about a life together with him, a life with the new, improved Phil. Not the Phil of old, but a Phil who would love and cherish her and had learned his lessons. A Phil who found her worthy to be loved, just as Novac said she was. A Phil who would not only love her in a romantic way but love her deeply as a best friend. A Phil who would protect her and take care of her, carry her when she needed to be carried both physically and emotionally, the way she once thought Novac would.

Faith quickly cleared those confusing thoughts out of her head. It wasn't healthy and right of her to make comparisons when Phil was making a valiant effort to prove himself worthy. If she was going to find her happy ending, she needed to give him a chance and remain focused on him, and him alone.

Faith was setting the table for Friday morning's breakfast, which was her Thursday night routine, when Alice called for her to pick up the kitchen phone.

"Hello!" she said in her sweetest voice. "I'm counting the

hours until I see you tomorrow! I have so many fun things planned."

"Wow! Absence really does make the heart grow fonder!" It was not Phil's voice on the other end. Faith felt her face grow red and hot with embarrassment. "I skipped seeing you for one day, and you're a tiger! I'll be over in fifteen minutes!"

"Put a lid on it, Novac. Okay? I thought you were Phil." Faith was not amused.

"Lucky Phil!"

"Okay. Enough already. What do you need?" she said curtly.

"I'm calling about tomorrow. You remember? I told you I'd call tonight about going to the doctor tomorrow."

"Oh my gosh! Novac, I'm sorry! It slipped my mind. I am so, so sorry! What did we say I was going to do?"

"You offered to take me to my doctor's appointment." He chuckled at her absentmindedness.

"Now what time do you need to go? I'll be meeting Phil at the morning ferry but can—"

"Hold on before you get too worried. I was calling to say that I feel well enough to make it to the appointment without needing you to go along. I can borrow Mrs. Graham's car. Besides, they may need to keep me overnight for tests or something."

"Are you sure? I can call Phil and—"

"I'm sure. You need to get ready for Phil's visit. You have a busy weekend planned. Don't worry about me. Have some fun. I mean it. I'm not trying to sound like a martyr."

"If you're sure."

"I'm sure," Novac replied.

"You'll call me with any news as soon as you get back?"

"I'll call. You'll be the first on my list. Now go and finish up whatever I caught you in the middle of and, Faith, have a great weekend. You deserve it."

"You're wonderful, Novac. I'll be praying for you and

your doctor's visit. I hope it all turns out well. I'll wait for your call. And I really am sorry about forgetting. I had so many things on my mind with Phil's visit and—"

"Love ya, Sweetie."

"Love you, too, Novac."

Faith hung up the phone feeling so ashamed about forgetting her best friend's appointment. He weighed so heavily on her mind the evening before, but since that time, all her thoughts had been on Phil's impending visit. At that moment she resolved never to let selfish desires get in the way of her friendship with Novac. Phil was important to her and Novac was important to her—but in diverse ways. Nothing's wrong with that. There was room in her life for both.

Alice released Faith from her early Friday duties to meet Phil at the harbor. The parking area was uncharacteristically crammed full of cars for such an early hour. So, Faith drove around the square three times in search of an empty space, but seeing none she pulled the car into a small area along a curb marked "No Parking Anytime". It was worth the risk of getting a ticket to be on time. She couldn't leave Phil waiting and wondering if she had second thoughts about seeing him. With a slam of the car door, she took off dashing toward the dock just in time to see Phil disembark.

When she met up with him, she flashed a smile as wide as Nantucket Sound and embraced him warmer than she ever had in the past. Her heart had forgiven him for his past indiscretions and she was, once again, deeply in love. Phil handed her a single red rose. It had made a long, hot trip over from Hyannis and was beginning to wilt, but Faith didn't care. She admired it and stroked its soft, velvety petals. His arm around her waist felt good to her as they walked toward Alice's illegally parked car. She let out a "yippee!" as they got closer.

"What a great beginning to the weekend! No ticket, and only fun ahead!" Faith said excitedly, as they drove off toward The Scrimshaw Inn, leaving the crowded harbor behind them.

The weekend was as wonderful as Faith hoped it would be. Phil was on his best behavior. He couldn't have been more attentive. They explored the architecture of Martha's Vineyard on Saturday, taking many pictures and keeping a log so they would not forget the names of the various houses and inns. Faith had never ventured to Martha's Vineyard and had wanted to wait until she and Phil could see it together. "Let's come here on our honeymoon," Phil said as they strolled through the streets of Edgartown. Faith smiled and shrugged off the comment not knowing how seriously to take it. They walked through the campground section of Oak Bluffs, making up stories about the various cottages which were painted a variety of pastel shades and rivaled the "Painted Ladies" of San Francisco in the imaginative use of gingerbread trim and color.

The next day, after her Sunday morning duties at the inn, Phil suggested they take the inn's bicycles out for a ride around town. The entire time they were out, Faith had an uneasy feeling as she followed Phil's lead. Since this was an activity she had participated in often with Novac, she had to stop herself from talking about him whenever they stopped at a point of interest she had already visited. She couldn't help but notice how awkward and stiff Phil looked as he peddled his way down the twisting roads. *He must not have ridden a bicycle since he was a kid.*

A couple of times he turned around to smile at her and came close to hitting parked cars and pedestrians as his bicycle wobbled. She winced and hated that she felt so turned off by his lack of athleticism.

Novac had always ridden his bicycle with such ease, gracefully skimming down streets unfamiliar to her, able to point out places of interest as they rode along. With Novac leading the way, every road, every beach, every sunset, was an adventure. *Stop comparing! Phil was wonderful in his own way. He's quirky. That's all.* She watched him clumsily use hand signals, sometimes forgetting which meant a left turn and which signaled a right turn. *Security. That's what Phil represents,* Faith thought, keeping her eyes on him as he led her off onto a road she recognized—the road on which she got lost the night she met Novac.

They approached the inn with the basement lounge. It looked completely different in the daylight. She couldn't help but glance over as they passed it to see if his bicycle was parked anywhere around the entrance. No bike in sight. She felt something tug in her heart as they headed off further down the street. Novac had not called her Friday night as he said he would. He knew Phil was in town, so he didn't want to disturb her, she figured. They circled around and ended up heading down the same street again. Phil was lost. She pulled up next to him and motioned for him to stop.

"Are you ready to go back?" she asked.

"Yeah. Let's go get cleaned up. I want to take you out for an early dinner if that's okay."

"Sure. Follow me. I know the way back." Faith took the lead and headed down the familiar road toward The Scrimshaw Inn. She and Novac had laughed many times about the evening he escorted her home from the bar.

The entire way home, Phil remained uncharacteristically silent and unresponsive, almost absent-minded. She didn't understand his change in mood. Phil? Absent-minded? No way. Phil was the most clear-headed person she'd ever known. She was constantly amazed by how quickly he could come up with information pulled from the depths of his memory. He never forgot anything. Nothing ever went unnoticed by him. He was always keenly aware of his surroundings and quick to take control when an opportunity presented itself. This afternoon was different, however. Only one other time could Faith remember Phil acting in a far-away, "not with it" manner; only one other time did he act this preoccupied with something other than his boat. An uncomfortable feeling of déjà vu enveloped Faith as she remembered how Phil conducted himself just after his move to Seattle.

This time, Faith knew for certain he didn't have his mind on his boat. Bessie had sailed off into the sunset, or so he said. No, there was something on his mind and it was sure to come out at dinner tonight. *If he's getting ready to break my heart again,* she thought, *I only have myself to blame for trusting him.*

Faith was putting the finishing touches on her makeup when Phil knocked on her door.

"Are you about ready? We need to get on the road soon," he called out to her. She walked across the room from the bathroom and let him in. His dark blue wool suit was accented by a burgundy paisley tie; a burgundy pocket square was neatly tucked into his suit jacket. He looked as proud as a young boy donning his first "big boy" Sunday suit.

"Wow! You clean up nicely!" she said, circling him, inspecting him up and down.

"That goes double for you! I don't think I've ever seen you looking so beautiful. No—ravishing!"

Phil had told her to dress in her finest for the evening. She settled on wearing an above the knee black dress which dipped down low in the back, showing off her tan. A delicate, lightweight shawl draped across her shoulders and was tied loosely in front. She took advantage of the natural curl in her hair and piled it up on top of her head, allowing a couple of curls to dangle down her neck. The shoes she wore raised her height almost three inches, making her just shy of Phil's height.

"Have I told you that I have a fondness for tall women?" Phil said jokingly. Faith, however, didn't find his comments comical. She remembered arriving at Phil's apartment in Seattle for the first and only time and being met at the door by a barefooted woman who had to be close to six feet tall.

Faith dipped her head and let out a sigh.

"I'm sorry," Phil whispered, stroking her back softly. "You're the only woman I find attractive, Faith. I really mean that." She timidly looked up at him. His gaze met hers and she read sincerity in his eyes.

"I apologize for how that comment sounded. I should've thought before I opened my mouth. Do you forgive me?" Faith nodded slowly. Phil reached over to her, pulling her close to him, wrapping his arms around her. "Ahhhh, Honey."

He reached into his breast pocket, pulled something out and shoved another thing back in. He handed a small brush to Faith and turned around with his back toward her. "Could you please brush off the back of my suit? I think I leaned up against something." Faith obliged, taking the brush from his hand.

"What time's our reservation?" she asked as she handed him his lint brush.

"Uh, 5:45." He looked at his watch nervously.

"Don't you think we'd better be going? Alice's car is gassed up and ready." Phil put his arm around Faith's back and led her out of her bedroom, locking the door behind them.

Conversation was sparse all the way to 'Sconset. Phil kept his eyes straight ahead on the road barely turning his face toward Faith the whole trip. As they pulled into the driveway of the restaurant, she recognized it. This was where Novac bought their beach picnic dinner.

"They tell me this is the best restaurant on the entire island," Phil stated as he opened his car door. "Priciest, too. So, it'd better be good." He walked around and opened the door for Faith. She drew in a deep breath as she looked at the arched wooden door she once walked through with Novac. The striped awning was half-way obscured by the twisting rose vines. It just didn't seem right to be here with someone other than Novac. She took another slow, deep breath as they entered.

"Two for St. John. Five-forty-five," he told the maître d'. Faith recognized him as the gentleman who had packed the picnic basket for Novac. Of course, he didn't remember her from their one meeting.

"Come this way to the patio," the maître d' said as he stiffly strolled down a short hallway to the outside patio dining area. The roses were in full bloom, climbing their way across the walls and roof of the restaurant.

"This is just beautiful!" Faith exclaimed as they took their seat at a table overlooking the ocean. The last time she saw this patio, the flowers were not yet in bloom and the outside area was not officially open for the season.

"I thought you'd like this better than sitting inside," Phil said, perusing the wine list. He shut the notebook and frowned.

"Is there something wrong?" Faith asked.

"No, no . . ."

"Are you sure? You've been so quiet since the bike ride. Did I do something to upset you?" Faith needed to get to the point and not let her fears fester.

"Uh, no, honey. It's just that . . . well, it can wait. We'll talk about it later."

"Phil, now you've got me worried."

"Don't be. There's just something I wanted to tell you about and I'm just not sure how to bring up the subject."

"Something that will upset me?" Faith was worried. She had a bad feeling about the evening, and now her fears were coming true.

"I hope not, but I can't be sure. Let's not talk about it now. We'll discuss it later before I leave."

Oh great, she thought, *right before he leaves. Yep, he has a real bombshell to hurl at me and is waiting until right before he leaves. Just as I suspected.*

Despite her churning stomach, Faith managed to eat most of her food. After Phil's comment about the cost, she didn't want to waste anything. She was terrified to hear what Phil needed to say but she was determined not to show it. He'd gotten the best of her once. This time she would pretend to be strong and unmoved by his hurtful words.

When they were finished with dinner, Phil suggested a walk on the beach. The setting sun cast orange sparkles on the ocean's ripples. Faith slipped off her shoes and squinted hard trying to find any familiar landmarks in the direction of Novac's beach. It would be comforting to know he was close enough to swoop down and rescue her just as Phil broke her heart.

When they got to the water's edge, Phil stood quietly, then took his shoes and socks off and rolled up his suit pants, bracing himself on Faith's shoulder. He folded his socks and stuffed them into the toes of his shoes, placing the shoes gently on the sand.

"I don't exactly know how to say this," he said, taking Faith's hands into his, "so here goes." Phil dropped down on one knee in the wet sand. Faith was astonished that Phil, the man who was so persnickety about his clothes would dare get salty, wet sand on his $1,000 suit.

"Faith, I've been doing a lot of thinking lately about what we've been through this past year. I want to make it up to you. I don't know how you feel about me, but I know that I get a hole in my heart every time I must leave you here to go back home. I'll get back to my house and it's dark and lonely, and all I can think about is you. I realize it's not home without you. It's just a dark, empty, lonely house. Faith, what I'm trying to say is this," he rose from his knee, switched knees, and continued.

"Faith, I want you to come back with me and stay. I don't

want to leave you here anymore. You belong with me, or at least I know I belong with you." He let out a deep sigh. "Oh boy, Faith. This is difficult because I know what I put you through once before. But I'm just going to say it. Faith, I'd be honored if you'd live with me forever as my wife. Give me one more chance. I need you. I want you. I can't live without you." He looked up at Faith, who had tears dribbling down her cheeks. She cocked her head and looked at him, both smiling and crying at the same time. Removing her right hand from his grip, she wiped her eyes with her shawl. Phil gallantly pulled his pocket square out of his jacket breast pocket and handed it to her to use.

"Happy tears or sad tears?" he asked as he rose and held her tightly.

They gently rocked in each other's arms. Phil pulled away slightly, holding her away from him as if to read her expression.

"What do you think?"

Faith looked down at her feet for a few seconds, then back up, still not answering.

"I'm serious, honey. Please give me some kind of answer. You're killing me!"

Faith shrugged her shoulders slightly, staring at Phil's eyes for some sort of reassurance. "I'm afraid to give you an answer. I . . . I just wasn't expecting anything like this."

"Maybe this will convince you." Phil reached into his suit's breast pocket and pulled out a tiny, black, heart-shaped box. He handed it to Faith. He couldn't hide his anticipation. The expression on his face clearly showed he was enormously proud of the bauble hidden inside the wee box. Faith tossed her shoes on the sand and opened the box, gasping softly as she viewed the sparkling ring inside. The last remaining bit of sunshine brilliantly bounced off the faceted rock. She noticed the stone was twice the size of the one he gave her the first time he asked her to be his wife.

"Phil, it's beautiful."

"Well? It's yours if you just say the word." Faith kept her eyes on the ring as she slowly handed it back to Phil.

"I need some time to think about this."

"I understand. Keep it with you until you make up your mind." He closed the box and wrapped her fingers around it.

"Phil, I don't think I can make my—"

"Don't decide anything right now. I want you to be sure."

"I won't keep you waiting long for an answer. Okay?" she said, relieved to have a little bit of a reprieve. She tucked the ring in her small shoulder bag and picked up her shoes. If he had asked her that question on Friday, her answer would have been a resounding "yes". Somehow, after having dinner at "Novac's" restaurant and walking on "Novac's" beach, she just wasn't absolutely sure what she wanted.

"That's all I can ask for. I'll sit by the phone and wait for your answer . . . in the affirmative, of course. If the answer's 'no', I don't think I'll be able to come back and see you for a while."

"Phil . . . why are you saying that? I feel like you're trying to pressure me."

"Maybe I am." He took her by the hand and led her back up the beach toward the entrance to the restaurant's gardens. They wiped their feet, put their shoes back on, and ascended the wooden steps up to the courtyard.

Phil was quiet on the ride back to The Scrimshaw. When they were near the inn Faith broke the silence.

"I haven't said 'no', Phil. Please don't give me the silent treatment."

"I'm not. I'm just wondering what's going on in your head. And I'm thinking about having to go back home by myself. And wondering what I'm going to do if your answer is 'no'."

"Phil . . ."

"I'm not trying to be pitiful. I worry about losing you. I always worry about that. I lost you once and, believe it or not, it hurt me very badly."

"Phil, you don't know what hurting is. You didn't look very hurt in Seattle." Faith realized the conversation would turn nasty if she continued down that path. "I'm sorry. I shouldn't have said that."

"That's perfectly understandable. Let's not part on an unpleasant note. Okay?" Phil looked at his watch. "I'd better grab my bags at the inn and head on out. The ferry will be leaving in about twenty minutes."

Upon arrival at the inn, Phil noticed Alice reading in the living room, so he stuck his head in to speak.

"I'll be heading out now. Enjoy your evening."

She got up and walked to the door with them and bid him farewell. Phil held the front door open for Faith. Before exiting to drive Phil to the ferry dock, Faith turned and faced Alice.

"Thanks for the use of your car. I'll be back in just a few minutes." The look on Faith's face signaled to Alice that there was something up—something important.

Faith watched the ferry begin its trek across Nantucket Sound, waving until it was out of the harbor. As she looked out over the darkened water, she wondered if she had just bid farewell to her future husband or to a man she would never see again. Within a few days she would know the answer to that question. She had given Phil her word that she would not keep him guessing for long. Because of that promise, she knew it was time to come to terms with her real feelings.

CHAPTER EIGHT

When Faith walked through the inn's front door, Alice was waiting for her in the hallway. By this time in the evening, Alice had usually retired to her room, so this was out of character.

"Well?" she asked Faith.

"Well, what?" Faith replied, playfully giving her the silent treatment.

"Well, did he pop the question?"

"How did you know? Did he tell you!"

"He said nothing to me. You mean I'm right? Well, what did you tell him?"

"I didn't tell him anything . . . yet." Faith said, pulling the ring box out of her purse. She opened it up and turned it toward Alice, who stood with her hand over her gaping mouth.

"It's beautiful! Did you pick it out together?"

"No. He surprised me with it on the beach."

"How romantic! And you didn't give him an answer?"

"I told him I'd think about it and let him know," Faith answered.

"Good girl! Keep him guessing! Do you think you'll really marry him? Is that the way you're leaning?"

"At first, I felt good about it. But now I can't help but feel like something isn't right."

"Don't you trust him?" Alice asked.

"I don't think it has anything to do with that. We've

gotten over that hump. Phil's a changed man. It's more of a sad feeling. Sad over my life changing. It's hard to describe it. Is that crazy?"

"I don't think it's crazy a bit. You and Novac have been inseparable for the last few months, so your life will change in that regard. Obviously, you two can't be as close if you and Phil get married."

"Maybe that's it. I don't think I'm ready to give up my friendship with Novac. He's the best friend I've had in a long time. Maybe ever." Faith looked down at the ring and wiped away a tear from the corner of her eye. "Would I really have to give him up?" She chuckled a little as another tear rolled down her cheek. "Can't I keep them both?"

"Afraid not, honey. But I don't see why you can't still be friends. If Phil genuinely loves you, he won't deny you that friendship. But your life will change if you get married. You'll find yourself drifting away from Novac rather quickly, I presume." Alice put her arm around Faith and patted her on the back. "Life means changes, honey. But if you want to settle down and have a family, your priorities will be different. Novac would understand. I'm sure he'd miss you, too, but don't let that keep you from choosing marriage if that's what you want. You said, yourself, Novac's not the settling down type."

"You're right but change stinks sometimes!" Faith laughed again and stuck the ring back in her purse.

"When are you going to give him an answer?"

"I told him I wouldn't make him wait long. He wants to marry quickly if I agree. But, Alice, who'd help you around the inn?"

"Don't even let that enter into your decision. Your happiness is much more important. Besides, the end of the season is just around the corner. I'll be fine if you go off and get married. Really, I will." Alice gave Faith another hug.

"I guess I could come back over on the ferry and help out. Phil won't mind."

"Sounds good to me."

"Oh, by the way. Did Novac call while I was out?"

"No. Haven't heard from him."

"That's odd. He said he'd call and let me know how his doctor's appointment went."

"Why don't you give him a call?"

"I think I will. I'll let you know what I find out." They bid each other goodnight. Faith unlocked her bedroom door and flipped on the light. Kicking her shoes off, she sat down on the bed and dialed Novac's number. She listened as it rang eight, nine, ten times before she hung up the phone. A dark feeling came over her as she contemplated the possibilities. She brushed aside the bad thoughts and settled on the idea that he must've gone out to walk Doolittle. Or maybe he went to Fat Cat's to grab a bite to eat. However, he did mention that the doctors might want to keep him there overnight for more tests or observation. Now that Phil had left, she felt certain he'd get in touch with her soon.

The hot shower relaxed her and took her mind off Novac momentarily. Faith dressed in her pajamas and bathrobe and sat out on the patio with her magazines until worried feelings won over her attention. She went to the phone and dialed Novac's number again, but it rang and rang with no answer.

"Now I'm a little worried," she said to herself as she crawled between the cool bed sheets. "But I'm just going to wait for you to call me." She turned out the bedside lamp.

A crisp coolness was in the air when Faith awoke the next morning, making it difficult for her to drag herself out of the warm covers. But it was nearing Labor Day and every room at The Scrimshaw was booked for the weekend. A lot of work needed to be done so she couldn't linger in bed.

Several times during the day Faith slipped away to her room. She reached for the little velvet box on her bedside table where she had laid it the night before. Opening it slowly, she studied the ring, waiting for it to persuade her one way or the other regarding Phil's proposal. No answer came back from it. She slammed the box shut and placed it back on the table.

As the afternoon waned, Faith fretted over Novac's lack of communication with her. It seemed so strange not to be making plans for a bike ride or dinner outing.

By the time his call came that evening, her preoccupation over her impending decision had displaced her concern for Novac.

"Hello!" Faith said, nearly dropping the phone.

"Hi, baby," Novac's voice answered back. "Sorry I haven't called before now. I've been sort of detained."

"What are you talking about? I was starting to worry about you."

"I did receive a little bad news," Novac said with hesitation. Faith covered her mouth so he wouldn't hear her labored breathing.

"Um, yeah? Novac, what's the matter?" She really didn't want to hear.

"The bad news is the cancer has come back."

Faith closed her eyes and quietly whispered, "Oh, God. Oh, God. Please."

"The good news, well I guess you could call it good news, is they think it's contained to one spot and have scheduled an operation for early tomorrow morning. The doctors are going to remove a small section of my colon. Just like they did before."

"Oh, Novac! I'm so sorry! Where are you now?"

"I'm at the hospital in Boston. They did all that pre-op stuff. I'm staying at a hotel tonight and will return to the hospital early tomorrow morning."

"Do you need me at the hospital? I'll ask Alice if it's

okay. She'll insist that I go. I'm sure."

"No, no. I'll be just fine. Everything's all arranged and okay. I'll be in surgery and won't feel like having company. But thanks."

"Why didn't you call me on Friday to tell me?" Faith asked.

"I knew Phil was in town and I didn't want to spoil your weekend. How was it? Guess he's been tossing pennies from the ferry a lot. Seems he can't stay away! Did you have a good one?"

"Yeah, I suppose, but I'm still upset that you didn't let me know. Phil's understanding. He would've told me to go and be with you," Faith explained, not believing one word of what she said.

"You think so? Is he that sure of himself? He doesn't mind us spending so much time together?" Novac quizzed.

"Why should he? He knows we're just friends." Faith didn't want to tell him that she had kept the intensity of their friendship a secret from Phil. She was afraid he wouldn't understand and might try to prohibit her from seeing so much of him.

"Most men feel insecure about their woman hanging around with other men. They have a tough time with the concept of men and women being friends. It's not natural." Novac said.

"I don't see anything wrong with it."

"I didn't say there was anything wrong with it. It's just a challenge for us. Especially if the woman is pretty."

"Are you saying I'm pretty?"

"Not just pretty . . . beautiful. See, now I'm flirting with you. We have a hard time separating the two."

"You're a clown. Now go and get some rest. You have a hard morning ahead of you," Faith said.

"Yes, Mom."

"And Novac?"

"Yes?"

"Call me when you get released and I'll come visit you. Promise me. You really will call this time? Okay?"

"You'll be the first one I call," Novac replied.

"I'll be checking on you and praying for you."

"That's the best thing you could do. Don't worry. Everything will turn out fine. I've been through this before. Remember?"

"Bye, Bye. I'll be thinking about you tomorrow."

"Bye. Love you."

"Love you too."

"Hey Novac?" Faith said.

"Yeah?"

"Never mind." She almost told him about the ring, but decided the time wasn't right. "Talk to you later."

Faith wanted to fly to Boston to see Novac. She couldn't stand the thought of her best friend going through this ordeal alone. If she were the one in the hospital, he'd surely drop everything he was doing to be by her side. There was no doubt in her mind.

Later, she wandered to the kitchen and was surprised to see Alice sitting at the table, sipping a cup of tea. Feeling the need for some motherly advice, she tapped lightly on the open door before entering so she wouldn't startle her.

"Mind if I join you?" Faith asked.

"I'd love the company. I'm just having a cup of Earl Grey decaffeinated. Can I get you one?"

Faith shook her head then shared the news about Novac's surgery.

"I insist that you take some time off to fuss over him when he gets home. He'll need help with all kinds of things, I'm sure. I remember what my husband went through and how helpless he was during his illness."

"But you'll need me to help—"

Before Faith could finish her thought, Alice took her hand and squeezed it gently. "You will go take care of him. Period. End of discussion."

Faith knelt at the foot of her bed that night, just like she did as a child. "Lord, please heal Novac. Don't let him die. Give the doctors wisdom and steady hands, and to catch everything they need to find. Give him a fast recovery, please. Give me strength to take care of him. I'm so afraid, Lord. I ask for peace." Her words got softer and softer as she drifted off to sleep.

She dreamt she was walking on a beach by herself, looking at the sunset. It wasn't a pleasant walk, but one that left her feeling lonely and frightened. She stood on the beach staring up the hill at Novac's rose-covered cottage. Black clouds hung over the ocean behind her, moving toward her as the wind increased in strength. She knew she had to find shelter quickly, but only stood facing the cottage, waiting to be rescued by him.

She woke suddenly wondering what it all meant. With the details fresh in her mind, she replayed the dream a couple of times, trying to shake the feeling of dread which covered her like a blanket. Was she afraid of losing Novac? In the dream, had she turned down Phil's offer of marriage only to be a lonely old spinster? Was there any meaning to the dream or had it just been a release of anxiety she felt regarding Novac's cancer?

Faith rolled over and turned off the radio alarm clock; it was about fifteen minutes before the music normally would have come on. While brushing her teeth, the phone rang. She spat in the sink and ran over in time to answer on the fifth ring. "Hello," she said wiping her mouth with her washcloth.

"Did I catch you at a bad time?" Phil asked. "I wanted to call before you started your morning breakfast routine. I wish I could be there right now, waiting in the dining room for you."

"You just like to see me slave over a hot stove," Faith said lightly.

"Not at all. If you decide to accept my offer, you'll never have to work for the rest of your life. You'll be a lady of leisure to do as you please. How does that sound?"

"I don't know. I like my work." If he was prying for an answer, Faith didn't appreciate it. She was not going to commit herself one way or the other until she was sure.

"But wouldn't you much rather have free time to shop or play tennis with your friends, or whatever women do while their husbands are at work?"

"Not really," she answered. "Sounds like a dull life." Her voice drifted off as she envisioned those women she'd seen many times on Nantucket, shopping bags hanging from their arms. Could be fun for about a week or so, but not for an extended period. Since Phil was fishing to find out if she had made up her mind, she decided to do a little fishing on her own. "What if my friend were a man? Would you like that?"

"Is he gay?" Phil laughed. "He'd better be gay if you're going to be shopping with him."

"No, as a matter of fact, he's not." Faith was not laughing.

"Well, then I don't think I'd like that. I wouldn't be working my tail off to have you hang around with some man during the day. Who are you talking about anyway? Is this hypothetical?"

"It so happens Novac is a very good friend of mine. I'd hate to stop seeing him just because my husband felt insecure. It's an innocent friendship."

"Oh. You mean that guy with the kooky girlfriend, Saturn, or whatever her name is?" Faith detected a trace of jealousy in Phil's voice.

"Venus. Yeah, that one," Faith said tersely. "And she's not his girlfriend. They've been buddies for several years."

"If he's been telling you she's not his girlfriend, then he's kidding either you or himself." Phil's voice was becoming abrupt.

"What's that supposed to mean?"

"I mean, I saw them a day or two ago coming out of a hotel in Boston. I was across the street at a restaurant having lunch with a client. When I came out, I saw them."

"Did you say anything to them?" Faith couldn't believe her ears. Her hands trembled as she waited for his answer.

"I waved at them, but I don't think they saw me, or maybe they didn't recognize me."

"What were they doing? Just walking down the street or what?" She was sorry she had asked the question, but it was too late to take it back.

"Pretty much that. Walking together out the door and down the street. You sound jealous! Are you sure there's nothing between the two of you?" Faith couldn't tell if Phil was angry or just kidding her.

"There's nothing but friendship between us. That's all. I knew Novac was in Boston. His colon cancer has come back and he's having surgery today at the hospital. So, you're not telling me anything I didn't already know." She tried to sound calm and unfazed. However, the news about Venus being there with him stung her badly.

"Sorry to hear that. Seems like a nice enough guy. What are his chances? Is it bad?" Phil's tone didn't convince her that he was sorry.

"It can be if it's spread to other parts of his body. He went through this once before."

Phil abruptly cut her off. "Oh, wow! I just noticed what time it is. I've got a breakfast appointment to meet in twenty minutes. Gotta go! Love you. I expect to hear from you soon, my love."

"Okay. Go. Get to your meeting. I don't want to make you late. Love ya, too." Faith hung up feeling hurt by Phil's lack of concern about Novac. However, after hearing about Venus her own feelings of concern were a little confused. *How could he tell me I wasn't needed in Boston, but let Venus go along? He never mentioned one word about her being there when we spoke. He hadn't even called to let me know what was going on until yesterday. I'm supposed to be his best friend. His confidante.* She kicked the end of her bed. The more she thought about it the more betrayed she felt.

"I guess I should take the hint and wake up and smell the coffee," Faith said to herself as she changed into her work clothes. "He's never been mine. He'll never be mine, and he doesn't have to hit me over the head with a baseball bat to prove it." She threw a pair of black shoes on the floor, walked to the closet, and retrieved a brown pair, kicking the other pair as she passed them.

Just before exiting her room, she turned, walked to the small bedside table, and opened the ring box. She pulled out the ring and slipped it on her finger. A perfect fit, she thought. This was the first time she had removed the ring from the box. She liked the way it looked on her. A lot. *Is this meant to be?* She took off the ring and put it in its box before heading out the door to begin her day's work.

After her 10:00 break, Faith went to her room and took the brilliant ring back out of its tiny black box and slipped it on her finger. She debated about whether to wear it in public. It's beauty beckoned her to take it for a "test drive", but in her heart, she didn't feel it was right to wear it before giving Phil her official answer. Bad luck, or something to that effect, she thought. She sat on the side of her bed, staring at the tiffany-set diamond. *What would Novac think? He probably wouldn't mind at all*, she decided. *He has his own blossoming romantic thing happening.* With each thought Faith grew increasingly resentful.

"We had a pact, Novac," she said softly, still looking at the ring. "You weren't supposed to fall in love with anyone. And if you did, it was supposed to be me, not that aroma-therapy-sniffing hippie. You hurt me, Novac. Why haven't you been straight with me about Venus?" Faith walked over to her front window and looked at the street. "I should've known I couldn't compete with someone from your past, someone more exciting to you. But I thought you were starting to feel something for me and not just as a friend." Tears pooled in her eyes as she stared out the front window to where Alice's car was parked.

"Obviously, I was wrong. I do care deeply about you, Novac, and I always will. I wish I knew what I did to chase you into Venus' arms. I didn't mean it when I said I never wanted to get married. I was just venting. Letting off some steam. I do want a partner. Someone to grow old with. Someone to have kids with. Only, you made it very clear you didn't want that. Now look at me. I have a ring on my finger from another man and feel like a hypocrite for wearing it while I still have feelings for you. Rescue me, Novac! If there's any chance at all that I can make you happy, please, please tell me before it's too late. Just like they do in those movies we watch on TV all the time." She turned away from the window, held her hand out and pulled off the ring, placing it back into its box. She tossed it on the bed and reached for a tissue, feeling slightly sorry for Phil, who, with all his heart, desired to be a good husband to her. She blew her nose one last time and looked herself over in the mirror. "I do love you, Phil. Or maybe I hate you, Novac. I don't know what I feel right now. You and Venus are probably two of a kind. And now I've resorted to talking to myself like I've lost my mind! See what you've done to me!" she said, chuckling through the tears. Knowing she would only be changing sheets in empty rooms, she left her room and proceeded up the stairs to the guestrooms without repairing her makeup. No one would notice how red and swollen her eyes were.

After changing the last set of bed sheets, Faith looked at her watch and realized Novac should be out of surgery. She wanted to do something special for him to show her concern, so called the local florist and ordered some flowers to be delivered once he was able to return home. Her thoughts turned to Doolittle, who was being boarded and hating every moment of it, most likely. She requested that the florist tie a couple of dog bones into the flower arrangement for him and write on the card: "To appease Doo upon his master's return.". *Got that marked off my "to do" list, now onto the next.* But before she could think about the next chore to do, Alice gently tapped on Faith's door.

"Here. Read this." She handed the Nantucket newspaper to Faith. "There's an article right on the front page about Novac's cancer. I wonder how they found out about it." Faith took the paper and began reading.

"It says here that Novac said it's not life-threatening, and he will be getting out of the hospital soon. Okay. I know that. Let's see," Faith mumbled as her eyes skimmed down the page. "What! His companion, Venus Winter! Look right here!" she blurted at Alice. "It says his companion, Venus Winter, says he's feeling just fine and that they will be going home in a couple of days!" Faith's voice was beginning to sound shrill as she read the sentence over a couple more times. "They! Home! The article makes it sound like they live together or something! I wonder if Novac was around when she spoke to these people."

"Honey, that shouldn't matter to you now. You're about to become Mrs. . . . what's Phil's last name again?" Alice asked.

"St. John. That's his last name. St. John. But I haven't decided if I'm going to marry him or not. That's beside the point," Faith was perturbed that Alice didn't share her sense of disgust over the article.

"When are you supposed to give him an answer?"

"Soon. Real soon. I'll let you know when I decide."

Alice, not being one to try to exasperate, nor one to overstep her position tried to bring her back to reality by gently speaking up.

"You sound very conflicted, Faith. Please don't decide on the rebound. You may regret it if you do. I care for you and want the best for you," she said, touching Faith's arm lightly. "I suggest that you go back to your room and pray about it before giving him an answer. Then wait for confirmation from God."

Faith carried the newspaper into her room and reread the article. "Venus!" she said with hate in her voice. "Novac, you're a liar. You said there was nothing between the two of you." She threw the paper into the trashcan next to her bedside table and picked up the phone without heeding Alice's advice. *I need to look out for myself. Novac is wrong for stringing me along. Phil won't break my heart again.*

"Let's see," she said to herself as she flipped through the little green address book she kept in the drawer. "Phil will still be at work." She dialed the number and waited for the receptionist to answer. After punching in all the appropriate numbers to reach his extension, his voice answered, sounding slightly miffed by the disturbance.

"It's me," Faith said, hoping his tone would lighten up a bit at the sound of her voice.

"Honey, I'm meeting with a client at the moment. Is it urgent?"

"Let's do it, Phil." Her hand was shaking as the words came out of her mouth.

"Huh?"

"Let's get married." There was a noticeable pause as she waited for his response.

"You mean it?"

"I mean it."

"You can disturb my meetings anytime with news like that!" Phil was clearly excited. "Can you hold on a minute while I move to a . . . ah, guess I can't, this phone won't reach. I'll call you later. You'll be at home?"

"Should be."

"I'll catch you then," Phil said. "I love you, Faith."

"I love you too, Phil." Faith hung up the phone feeling like a hypocrite, an immature one at that. *Do I really love him, or am I just angry at Novac?* She wondered as she reached over and pulled the ring out of its soft box. She placed it on her finger and held her hand up in front of her face for one more inspection. "Guess you're officially mine now," she said to the ring as it sparkled back at her.

"Wonder how Novac will feel about this." She headed out her bedroom door to find Alice so she could share the news with her, feeling certain she was getting ready to get an earful of motherly advice. And, embarrassingly, feeling like she needed a good "talking to".

CHAPTER NINE

When Novac returned home that afternoon, Faith didn't have to wait long before the phone rang. Guessing it was Novac, she put on her sweetest voice as she answered. She wanted him to hurt with the news she was about to drop on his head. Hurt with as much pain as that article caused her.

"Hello? Faith?"

"Yes. It's me."

"Thank you for the flowers. And Doo thanks you, too."

"You're quite welcome. How are you feeling?" Faith asked, eager to drop the bombshell.

"Oh, much better. A little sore. Way groggy! Guess that's to be expected, huh?"

"Yep. I suppose so. Guess Doo was glad to see you?"

"Elated. He puddled right in the middle of the floor of the vet's office."

"How did you get home? I thought you needed me to pick you up," Faith asked. She decided to see how truthful he would be with her.

"A friend offered to give me a lift. I didn't want to bother you at work. Alice has been so nice about letting you off and allowing you to use her car. I didn't want to push it."

"Oh?"

"Besides," Novac started again, "I figured I'd need your help a lot now that I'm home."

"Oh."

"That's a hint."

"Oh." Faith didn't quite know how to respond to his request. "Where's Venus?"

"Home, I suppose. Why?" Novac asked.

"Just wondered. Thought she might be there helping you get settled in."

"Where'd you get that idea?"

"From the article in the paper. Alice showed it to me," Faith said.

"What article? What are you talking about?"

"There was an article in the Nantucket paper about you and your cancer surgery."

"What does that have to do with Venus?" Novac wondered.

"The reporters apparently asked her questions about you." Faith was agitated at Novac, believing he was skirting the issue. "Oh, come on now, Novac! I know she's been there with you!"

"She dropped me off at the hospital, yeah."

"And then she left?" Faith asked. "Or did she stay?" *Ugh! Why do I say things like that?*

"What's gotten into you, Faith? Why the interrogation? I don't know what she did. I was under the knife! Remember? I was a little out of it for a while, so lay off, okay?"

Faith realized she was sounding crazy, but she didn't like being deceived. Especially after what Phil did to her during their previous engagement. "Sorry. Can we change the subject?"

"Please. Let's talk about you. A safer subject. How have you and Phil been getting along lately? Still seeing him?"

"Yeah. I'd say so."

"That means things are good between you two, right?"

"Yeah. Things are fine," Faith said with a smile. She looked at the ring on her finger, convinced more than ever she was doing the right thing. Novac clearly wasn't jealous.

"Fine, fine? Or just fine?" he asked.

"Fine, fine, maybe?" she answered.

"Oh, really? Sounds like you two have gotten closer since we last talked. Things are progressing, are they?"

"You might say that. We're engaged." She took a deep breath, waiting for Novac's response. "We're getting married." The pounding of her own heart precluded her from hearing Novac's soft gasp. After a moment of silence, he spoke.

"That's wonderful, honey. That's what you've been wanting. I know you'll be happy. When's the big day?"

That was not the answer Faith wanted to hear. *You're supposed to pledge your love for me and beg me not to marry Phil. Does that only happen on soap operas? This is real life. Come on, Faith! Quit being childish and focus your thoughts on Phil—the man who wants to marry you. The man YOU want to marry!*

"I don't know. We haven't set a date yet."

"You'll be sure to let me know so I can be at the wedding, won't you?"

"Yeah, sure, Novac. Will do."

"You don't sound very happy for someone who's getting married," Novac said.

"Oh, I'm happy. I just have a lot on my mind. By the way, is there anything you need? Or need for me to do at your house?" *I hope the answer is "no".* She didn't care to Novac at the moment, even though he had just gone through cancer surgery. An odd sense of betrayal flowed through her body. Whether right or wrong, it was there.

"No, thanks. You'll have a million things to do from here on out. No more time for your dear ole friend, I suppose."

"Don't be silly," she replied. "I always have time to help out a friend."

"Actually, I could use someone to walk Doo from time to time. He'd love to see you. That is if Phil doesn't mind."

"Are you going to have to stay in bed for a while, or are

you able to move around?"

"I'll need to rest as much as possible for a little while."

"You know I'll help you any way I can," Faith said, although not feeling very sincere about her statement. "Well, I've got to go. I'll talk to you later. Bye."

"Congratulations, honey. I love ya."

Alice advised Faith to confront her feelings about Novac, then put it behind her forever. "You need to find out that man's feelings for you once and for all if it's standing in the way of your relationship with Phil. You must be certain that Phil's the one you want to spend your life with," she told Faith. "This may be your last chance to get to the clarity you need."

"Novac would've made his move by now if there's any interest," Faith said. "Besides, I've embarrassed myself enough by sounding jealous over Venus. I could never have the nerve to ask him if he has feelings for me. He made it clear to me from the start that he has no intentions of getting committed again."

"Then it sounds like you've clarified your own concerns. Time to put it to rest and concentrate on your future with Phil. It's not fair to Phil if you're hanging onto any feelings for another man. Let it go and take thoughts of Novac captive before allowing them to infiltrate your heart again."

"By the way, Phil is calling me tonight so if the phone rings, I'll catch it in my room."

It had been an especially difficult day for Faith, emotionally, so she decided to wash up, slip on her pajamas, retire to her room, and make it an early evening. She sat in bed trying to get her mind on the book she held, gave up, not realizing she'd dozed off. The phone ringing startled her.

She rolled over on her side, grabbed the phone's handset and immediately heard Phil's voice babble on and on excitedly about their upcoming wedding. He finally came to the purpose of his call—he wanted to settle on a date.

"Phil. It's been a rough day and I'm exhausted. I'm so sorry, but can we talk about this another time? I promise I'll call you tomorrow." The truth was she didn't know when she wanted to become his wife and had no good explanation to give him regarding her apathy.

She tried to put the wedding out of her mind and burrowed down into the bed like a rabbit, trying to stay warm against the slight chill in the air. Autumn was quickly nearing, and the summer tourists would be leaving the island soon, she realized, as she fell into a fitful sleep.

An approaching weather front caused the winds to pick up during the night. Branches from the bushes surrounding the patio tapped lightly on the patio door. She could see the shadows of the branches moving back and forth in the faint light from the streetlamp. Faith looked at her bedside clock and saw it was only 2:00 AM. With a moan, she rolled over, facing the door, determined to fall back asleep quickly. She gasped because she was certain she saw a person in the bushes staring at her, their face almost against the glass. *Am I dreaming?* When Faith pulled herself up in bed, the figure moved away abruptly. Realizing she was now fully awake, she remained still for a moment thinking about her next move. *This was no dream!* She tossed her covers off and slid her feet into slippers. *Lord, keep me safe*, she prayed as she drew in a long breath before dashing to the patio door.

She flipped on the outside light and cautiously looked through the glass door. Once she determined no one remained in the immediate area, she grabbed the fireplace poker and slowly unlatched the door, opening it just wide enough to ease her head and upper body out to look around. No cars were parked at the street, she noticed, and there was no sign of anyone wandering around the property. A faint floral scent was tossed around in the wind as the crisp air cut through her nightgown. Gardenias, she thought. Just like the fragrance she detected the night someone prowled in her room, waking her from sleep once before. "Lauralee? Is that you?" she loudly whispered, feeling a little silly after the words left her lips.

Maybe if she hurried, she would be able to spot the person from the widow's walk. Faith wrapped her chenille bathrobe around her nightgown and quietly started down the hallway toward the stairs leading to the widow's walk. Lauralee glared at Faith from the dark hallway portrait, causing a chill to come over her as she passed by. She climbed to the second floor and saw that the door to the stairs leading to the widow's walk was closed for the night as it always was. Faith slid the bolt over and carefully opened the door, hesitating a bit as the hinges creaked with age. Stepping as lightly as she could, she made her way to the top of the many stairs, pushing open the bolt on the second door which caused a gust of frigid air to blow against her face.

Familiar gray mist had settled over the island. The eerie glow of nearby streetlamps was all she could see through the foggy nighttime air. If anyone remained on the property, they would have no problem being concealed from her view. Faith wandered across the widow's walk to see if the view was any better from the other side. She could only hear the muffled sound of a car driving somewhere along a cobblestone road. Faint, scrambled noises also drifted up the hill from the direction of the harbor. Many nightclubs were closing for the evening. She tightly wrapped the bathrobe around her body. She turned suddenly to the sound of a nearby door being locked. Realizing someone had just thrown the bolt to the widow's walk, she rattled the doorknob and called out, "I'm up here! Please come unlock the door!" When no response came, she pounded on the door fervently.

"Don't lock the door!" she shouted, putting her ear to the

door to see if she could hear anyone walking down the stairs. Her efforts were pointless, she realized after a couple of minutes. Alice must've seen the door to the widow's walk wide open and thought a guest had left it that way. With Alice's room being on the first floor, she wouldn't be able to hear Faith's cries for help. Unfortunately for Faith, the evening was cool, and everyone would have windows closed for the night.

Accepting that she would be spending the night on the rooftop, Faith found the warmest spot next to one of the large, brick chimneys that flanked either side of the widow's walk. She needed to conserve every bit of heat she could, so she slid the chair up against the side of the chimney and curled up on the icy metal seat. She felt the cold sting through her bathrobe and gown. Faith pulled the bathrobe up over her head and tucked her feet, slippers and all, up under the robe, thankful that she had decided to wear a pair of socks to bed that night. Thick ones at that! This had been the first night it was cold enough to do so. When the wind blew, however, it cut through her like a knife. As she sat on the cold metal chair, she felt every bit of warmth leave her body. "Don't people die from exposure to the cold?" she asked herself, blowing into her stiffening hands to keep the circulation flowing. The misty air was causing her bathrobe to become damp and even colder.

Knowing there was nothing she could do to rescue herself from this situation, Faith relaxed the best she could in the chair, trying to think warm thoughts. She conjured up thoughts of drinking hot coffee, sitting by a fire, being curled up in her warm bed. Nothing worked. She couldn't keep her mind off how cold she was and the reality of the frigid air biting through her bathrobe. After she had been on the roof for what she estimated to be about an hour, Faith saw a dim light shining into the back courtyard. Hoping someone had awakened, she called out softly, not wanting to wake the neighbors. She didn't want to be rude, no matter how desperate she was. She walked to the small door and knocked again, calling out Alice's name. Still no answer. She went back, sat in the chair, and tried her hardest to go to sleep. Dawn was still a good four or five hours away.

Just as she began getting drowsy, the doorknob rattled, causing her to snap to consciousness. When the door opened, Alice appeared, looking extremely distraught.

"Faith!" she screamed out. "What are you doing up here? We've looked everywhere for you!"

"I think someone didn't realize I was here and locked the door." Faith still believed Alice must've done it and didn't want to distress her further. "I'm sure it was a mistake. I would've done the same thing if I'd seen the door open."

"Oh, you poor darling! When did this happen?"

"I figure about an hour or two ago."

"I can't imagine who'd have been up at that time to lock the door. The guests were all in for the evening long before that. Let's get in where it's warm." Alice shepherded a shivering Faith toward the door. She carefully locked the door behind them. "No one else is out there, right?" Alice asked before descending the staircase. Faith shook her head.

"Who all has been looking for me? You said 'we.'"

"One of the guests came and woke me up, saying he heard noises like walking on the roof. I noticed your lights on and both your hall door and your patio door wide open, so I was concerned. I called Novac to ask if he'd seen you this evening. He got worried and said he was coming right over. I was just about to call the police when I got the idea to check the porch upstairs."

"I'm glad you did!" Faith said. "Novac's here?"

"No. I only called him about fifteen minutes ago. When he said he didn't know where you were, the guest and I started searching the house and yard for you. Novac should be getting here soon, I suppose."

"I wish you hadn't called him," Faith said, remembering her thoughts from earlier in the evening. Alice led her into the kitchen and set a kettle of water on the stove to heat up. "He shouldn't be up and out like this. He needs to rest."

"Well, honey, I know how close the two of you are, and I panicked. I didn't know what to do. He was quite concerned when I told him I couldn't find you. I told him not to come out, but he insisted." Alice went to the cupboard and pulled out a box of tea. "I want you to drink some of this to warm up. It's decaffeinated. And don't worry about getting up early. I can handle things. I want you to rest. You've had a rough night."

Faith sat at the kitchen table, nervously stirring her tea.

"Honey, don't worry. Novac insisted on coming over. You know he really does care an awful lot about you."

"Oh, I'm not worried about him. What bothers me is if you didn't lock that door behind me, who did?"

"I don't know. I check that door every night before I go to bed, and it was closed up tight then. No one else would've been up lurking around at that time. But just in case, I'll quiz the guests in room number two when they come down."

"I'm not usually walking around at that time either, but I woke up and saw a face looking in through the glass door. It was dark, but I could see someone move away from the bushes when I stirred in bed and looked in their direction. I'm pretty sure I wasn't dreaming."

"Honey? Why didn't you wake me up?" Alice asked.

"I didn't see any real point in it. You said my doors were wide open?"

"Yes. Your patio door and the one to the hallway."

"I only left the hallway door open when I went to the roof. I know for certain I locked the patio door after I looked outside. I'm positive about it. Well, fairly positive. I'll be back in a minute," Faith got up from the table and slid her chair under. "I'm going to go check out my room. I don't like the sound of things."

Faith entered her room apprehensively, although she felt sure that if someone had been there, they were long gone.

While searching through her things, Nova walked through the hall doorway. She was startled by his pale, gaunt face.

"Faith! I'm glad to see you. I was worried!" He walked over to her and hesitated before bending down to give her a hug. "I guess I'm allowed to do that still, huh?"

"Sure. You can. You should've stayed home. You need to rest. How are you feeling?"

"I feel like I just had surgery, but I couldn't stay at home with you missing." He stood back and looked at her and squinted his eyes, tapping his finger on his cheek. "It appears to me that you're here. I think the case has been solved," he said in a deep dramatic voice.

"Yep. I'm here. Sorry you came all the way out for nothing." Faith was embarrassed that a fuss had been made.

"Where were you?" Novac asked.

"Up on the roof. I went up to look around. Someone had been prowling around outside on my patio. I got locked up on the roof."

"How did that happen?"

"We don't know yet. We're going to ask all the guests at breakfast if they saw anything. One of them helped Alice look for me. He woke her up because he heard me walking around on the roof."

"You said someone was outside prowling? Did you see his face?"

"I saw it, but I couldn't tell you if it was a man or woman or anything about the person. Novac, don't worry about it. You need to get back home and get some rest. How'd you get out here anyway?"

"Mrs. Graham's car. I have a key."

"Thank you for coming out to check on me, but really, go home. Right now. You don't look like you feel well."

"Okay, baby. I'm out of here. I'm glad you're back." Novac gave Faith a hug and a kiss on the cheek. "I love ya."

"Yeah. You take care. Thanks." Faith returned to the kitchen where Alice had just finished steeping another cup of tea for her.

"Here, honey. Drink up and get warm. I'm going to bed unless you need me," Alice said as she cleaned up the kitchen counter.

"Nope. I'll be fine. Thanks for letting me sleep in tomorrow. But Alice? You're up, too. You shouldn't have to do all the work yourself. That's not fair."

"It's quite alright. You just get some rest." Alice walked toward the door of the kitchen and turned around. "Make sure you turn out all the lights and lock the doors."

"Will do. Night, night."

Faith took her cup of tea and turned out the kitchen and hallway lights. She double-checked the locks on the doors and carried her tea to her room. She noticed the bureau drawer was half-open and several pieces of correspondence were lying on top.

"I didn't leave these here," she whispered and slid them back into the drawer. Her eyes skimmed over the room to see if anything else was out of place. Her closet door was open; however, nothing seemed amiss. The box that had contained her engagement ring was left open and sitting on the bed, but the ring was on her finger, so she was relieved it had not been taken. Her photograph album had been taken out of the drawer and was open to pictures of Novac and her at the beach. A slight whiff of floral fragrance teased her nose as she closed it. Faith lifted the album to her nose and sniffed. The person who had been in her room was wearing the same fragrance she detected in the air outside on her patio. It was not a manly smell, she thought as she replaced the album in the drawer, careful not to touch it too much in case a burglary had occurred. Faith felt completely violated as she looked around the room.

Walking over to the hook where she always hung her purse, she expected the worst. She looked to see if her wallet was missing or any other thing of value she may have stuffed in it, but was pleasantly surprised to find the purse undisturbed. Nothing taken or destroyed, she determined. No need to get too worried about the intrusion, she told herself. "Next time, be more careful about leaving your door open, you dimwit," she mumbled.

Faith decided against turning out the lights and trying to fall asleep; she was still too uneasy for that to happen. Instead, she pulled out her book and began to read. Her eyes kept wandering over to the patio door. The light breeze outside caused the bushes to sway slightly.

As the sun rose, she felt comfortable enough to drift into a welcome sleep. At noon, she woke up to the sound of guests talking in the yard outside her room. She walked to the front window, parted the long drapes, and watched as the couple from room #2 straddled the inn's bicycles. Alice was standing in the yard with them pointing out directions to some nearby site. Faith unlocked the window and opened it to call to Alice. "Did you ask them about last night?"

"They said they didn't hear a thing. They told me they went out to eat and came back and crashed about ten o'clock." Alice, carrying a red and white gingham checked dish towel, came closer to Faith's window. "I'll come in and talk to you," she said as she headed to the front steps. Faith was waiting in the doorway of her room as Alice walked up.

"I'll be dressed and out in just a little while," Faith said to Alice, who was now bending over to pick up an object from the hallway floor.

"Take your time. Did you sleep well?"

"I couldn't fall asleep until I saw daylight. I had a case of the creeps," Faith said.

"I don't blame you. I felt a little creepy myself." Alice handed Faith a small, dangling earring. "You must have dropped this, honey. It was in front of your door."

"Not mine." Faith replied, handing it back to Alice.

"Here. You keep it and ask our guest, Mrs. Comstock, when she gets back from her bicycle ride. You'll probably see her before I do. I'd better get back to work." Alice said, waving the red and white dishtowel around in the air.

"Leave the rooms for me to clean up," Faith called out to Alice.

"If you insist, honey. That's fine," Alice replied from the kitchen doorway.

As Faith changed into her work clothes, she kept thinking about the earring Alice picked up in the hall in front of her bedroom door. Did it really belong to Mrs. Comstock—or could the intruder have dropped it? Faith inspected the earring closely, studying the design, touching the iridescent beads, and noticing how long the earring was . . . a good one and one-half to two inches in length. *Surely dowdy Mrs. Comstock would never wear anything like this,* she thought, setting the earring back on her dresser. *Do we have anyone young and trendy staying at the inn right now?* Probably someone who came in inquiring about a room, she determined.

Faith cleaned the guests' rooms before heading out to 'Sconset to visit Novac and to fulfill her other promise of helping him with Doolittle.

Novac had left his front door unlocked and Doo nearly knocked her over with enthusiasm as she slowly entered. "Hey there, boy! You're glad to be home I bet!"

"You talkin' to me?" Novac called from the hallway.

"No! I was talking to your sidekick!" Doolittle was dancing all around Faith, hopping up against her legs, yipping in a shrill tone. "How are you feeling?"

"Oh, about as well as can be expected. I'm getting a little stir crazy just hanging around the house," he said, grinning. "I'm ready to get out and do something exciting. Like searching at midnight for a missing friend."

Faith's face exposed the embarrassment she felt, "I'm so sorry Alice called you. I never would've let her do that if I'd known. But there wasn't much I could do about it. Sorry."

"Don't be. I'm just teasing. To tell you the truth, it frightened me to hear Alice say you were missing. Nothing could've stopped me from going out there to look for you." Novac wrapped his arms around Faith and squeezed her. "Did anyone ever find out exactly what happened?"

"No one 'fessed up to locking the door," Faith replied. "The wind couldn't possibly have done it because the door has one of those sliding bolts."

"Seems we have a mystery here," Novac said, rubbing his chin. "Any clues, my dear Watson?"

"Nope. Well, except for the person I saw peeking in the window of my room. Guess that's a strong clue, wouldn't you say?" Novac nodded. "Then, I suppose that person is the same one who went through my room while I was on the roof."

"Was all your stuff still there?" Novac asked.

"Seems to be. Oddly, it looked like they flipped through my photo album. Moved a few things around. But nothing's missing."

"Well, that's good. You need to keep your doors locked."

"Excuse me, but I didn't think I would be spending my night locked on the roof. I just stepped out into the hallway to look for the intruder. Then I walked up to the roof because you can see all around the property. Besides, it seems like I strolled through your door just now without having to knock. Right? Take your own advice, Bud!" She laughed.

"Did you see anyone while you were up there?" Novac asked.

"No one."

"Did you call the police and report it?"

"No. I didn't think I really had anything to report. Nothing was missing."

"But you said you saw a person looking in your room.

Couldn't you give them a description or something?"

"Not really. It was so dark. I didn't get a look at the face. I'll tell you something if you won't laugh at me."

"What?"

Faith sat down and thought for a second before opening her mouth to speak. "At first, I thought it might be a ghost."

"What!" Novac broke into a large grin, then caught himself. "Sorry. I won't laugh."

"Yeah. People have told me there are ghosts at the inn. I saw a woman in the hallway one night, too. She reminded me of the woman in the portrait hanging near my room. You've seen it."

"You saw her face?"

"Mostly I noticed her clothes. She was dressed in something long and dark and just looked like a woman from that century. At least from what I could tell. She moved away very quickly."

"What makes you think it's the same person?"

"Just a feeling. Also, both times I caught a real faint aroma. Like perfume. Floral." Faith rubbed her arms to smooth the goosebumps that had formed.

"What kind of books do you read before going to bed? Maybe you need to lighten up your bedtime habits."

"I can see you're not taking this very seriously, so I'll shut up. Need me to walk your dog or something?" Faith asked curtly.

"Nah. Doo kind of walks himself most of the time. He does his business and then scratches on the door to come in."

"You definitely mentioned you needed someone to walk your dog for you, did you not?" Faith asked Novac, who was trying not to smile.

"I just wanted your sweet company. And I didn't have a chance to talk to you last night about your upcoming nuptials. Let me see the rock." He reached over before Faith could offer and pulled her left hand close to him. "Wow. Ole Phil's doing well for himself? Or did you pick it out?"

"He picked it out. It was a complete surprise," Faith said, yanking her hand back.

"It sure was. I can't believe while poor Novac was lying close to death in the hospital, his girl was snatched right out from beneath his nose." Faith tried to read Novac's face. *His girl? Is he teasing me?*

His face brightened. "I hope you'll be very happy. That's all I want for you. You deserve it, Sweetheart." He kissed her on the cheek. "You know I'm just kidding with you, don't you, about him stealing you away?" Faith rolled her eyes and nodded as he continued, "I confess the selfish part of me will miss you with all my heart. Our friendship won't ever be the same, but your happiness is much more important to me."

Faith wanted to ask him if "friendship" was all it was, but she'd made her mind up about marrying Phil and that decision was starting to give her the peace she'd been looking for. She and Phil had history, some good, some bad, but he was stable and not afraid to express his feelings for her. Forgiveness had settled in her heart, and she was ready to move forward and start a family with him. Novac, on the other hand, was only a friend. She had often heard people say that when a man gives you the "friend" label, you should believe that they are telling you the truth.

"Novac, if you don't need anything, I think I'll be getting back to the inn."

"When's the date?"

"What?"

"What do you mean, 'what'? When are you getting married?"

"I don't know exactly. Soon, I suppose. We haven't really settled on anything definite." Faith replied. She was uncomfortable discussing her wedding plans with Novac. She picked up her purse and headed for the door. "Call me if you really need something" she said, walking out the door just in time to run into Venus breezing up the front walkway.

"Well, hey there! Haven't seen you for a while!" Venus

said, looking Faith up and down. "Leaving?"

"Yep. Gotta get back to work. Thought I'd look in on the patient for a minute. Seems he's doing just fine." Faith walked past her without making eye contact. "See ya."

"Come back again when you can stay longer!" Venus called out to her. "And don't worry about Novac. I'm taking good care of him!"

"I bet you are," Faith whispered under her breath as she unlocked Alice's car. She glanced at her watch when she reached the stop sign at the end of Novac's street. *Four forty-eight. Phil ought to be leaving the office in just a few minutes.* "I'll call him about five-thirty," she said to herself as she drove along the narrow road leading back to the inn.

Alice was in the kitchen spreading mayonnaise on a slice of bread. Faith somberly walked in and closed the door behind her. "I need to discuss something with you if you have a minute or two. You must keep this completely to yourself."

"Honey, you know I will. Are you okay?" Alice replied, setting the sliced ham aside.

"I'm fine. I just have a lot on my mind. Let me tell you my plan and you can say 'yea' or 'nay.'" The two women sat huddled close together. Alice gathered Faith's hands in hers as Faith revealed what was on her mind. Faith glanced at her watch, got up and gave Alice one last hug before standing in the kitchen doorway, leaving Alice to ponder the words she just heard.

"Are you okay?" Faith noticed a glisten in Alice's eyes. She could tell Alice wasn't 100 percent okay but was putting on a brave smile.

"Do whatever will make you happy, dear. Don't worry one moment about the inn or me. We'll be fine. And I'm not just saying that."

Faith picked up the phone in her room and dialed Phil's number. It rang three times and when he answered he sounded out of breath.

"Phil. It's me. I need to ask you something very important."

CHAPTER TEN

Early the next morning, Faith's suitcases sat next to the inn's front door. When the doorbell chimed, she emerged from her bedroom dressed in a cream two-piece suit, piped in ecru. Her hair was neatly brushed back and tied with a matching fabric ribbon. This was bought to be her "going-away" outfit after her aborted wedding to Phil last year. She decided to ignore her superstitious feelings about the outfit being bad luck and wear it anyway. Faith had nothing else in her closet suitable for the occasion and time of year.

Phil handed her a bouquet of white roses as she opened the door. "You look beautiful!" He bent toward her and kissed her passionately just as Alice came walking down the hallway wrapping her bathrobe around her waist. She saw the embrace and started to turn around and head back in the other direction.

"Oh! Alice! Don't walk away!" Phil called. "We'll be going now and I just wanted to tell you how much I appreciate what you've done for Faith. You've been a good friend to her."

"Oh, my goodness. She's given me so much more than I've been able to give her. I've loved having her here. I feel like she's my own daughter. When she came to my room last night to tell me that you two would be eloping in the morning, I almost forgot I wasn't her mother!"

"I know she was pretty distraught when she arrived. I did

a rotten thing, and I just want you to know I'll treat her right," he said.

"I'm sure you'll be very happy. You're getting a wonderful lady," Alice said, smiling affectionately at Faith. "Faith, call me next week when you know your plans." Alice wrapped her arms around Faith and squeezed her gently.

When Phil wasn't watching, Faith felt around in her pocket for the penny she kept to toss over the side of the ferry. *Is it a bad sign that I have this penny? I'll toss it when Phil's not looking. Insurance that I'll see Alice again, should he ask.*

"Will do." Phil looked curiously at Faith, then shrugged and picked up her bags. Alice wiped away tears and bid farewell to them from the front stoop, watching their taxi drive away, slowly disappearing down the hill toward the harbor.

Later that morning, Novac phoned Alice and caught her as she was brewing the second pot of coffee for her guests.

"If this is a bad time, I can call you later," he said.

"I'm happy to hear a friendly voice, Novac. How are you feeling?"

"Doing okay, Alice. I can't complain. May I speak with Faith, please? If she's not too busy."

"Oh. Novac. I thought Faith told you."

"Told me what, Alice?"

"She and Phil left this morning to be married in Hyannis."

Novac took a deep breath. "Wow. Wow." He paused again. "If you hear from her, please give her my best."

"Sure, Novac. I'll do that. Take care of yourself."

It was a beautiful, clear morning in Hyannis as Faith and

Phil drove to the small chapel overlooking the shore. "I saw this place one day when I was driving around and decided right then and there this is where I wanted to marry you if you'd have me again." Faith smiled at him. "I can't believe we're really doing this." Phil stopped the car in front of the small stone church. "Faith, I just want you to know that when you called me last night, you made me the happiest man alive." He took her hand and kissed it. "I truly thought you were going to back out on me again. I thought you were calling to tell me you decided not to go through with it."

"No, Phil."

"You seem so deep in thought. Is something bothering you?" Phil asked.

"Not really. I guess I wish my mother and Alice could be here. It'd be nice to have some family and friends with us."

"Are you having second thoughts about eloping? We could wait and do it up with all the bells and whistles, if you want."

"No. I've made up my mind to go ahead and do it. We didn't have such good luck when we got wrapped up in elaborate plans the last time. In fact, I'm sure my mother wouldn't have come if I'd told her. She's still stinging about the twenty-grand she and my dad lost the last time we were supposed to be married."

"So, you didn't tell them about us."

"Nope." Faith looked out the window of the car.

"Are they going to be upset?"

"Yep. Well . . . maybe. I made the mistake of telling my mother we were dating again."

"What'd she say?"

"She said you'd burn me again if given half the chance— or something like that."

"You don't look like a happy bride."

"It makes me sad that my mom and I have this wedge between us now. We've always been so close. I thought she'd be happy because she sounded like she'd forgiven you and wanted me to do the same when I first spoke with her. Looking back now I think she meant I should forgive and forget. Her forgiving attitude had changed by the time I told her we were dating. I can't tell her the truth because I'm afraid she'll be ashamed of me."

"She hates me that much?"

"Hate might be too strong a word, but I wouldn't say that she loves you."

"Fair enough. Then how come she gave me the number where I could reach you on Nantucket?"

"She thought you were going to apologize and bring closure to everything. She wanted me to be able to get on with my life."

"Oh. But she sounded so happy to hear from me. At least I thought so."

"Well, if she was, she's singing a different song now. Believe me. I think she only liked the idea of the lifestyle you could offer me. Dad may have changed her mind."

"Are you sure we're going through with it this time?" Phil asked.

"Yep. We're going through with it. I was raised to make my own decisions and that's what I'm doing."

"Let me ask you one important thing. Do you love me and want to spend the rest of your life with me?"

"Yes, Phil," Faith answered, smiling slightly.

"Sure?"

"Sure," she answered.

"Then let's get in there! I see the minister's car over there next to the church," Phil exclaimed.

"How'd you get him to agree to marry us so quickly?" Faith asked.

"After I gave you the ring, I came to church here that Sunday and met him. He's quite a sailor. Took me out on his boat a couple of times during the week. Nice guy. I got him a good deal on some gear he wanted for his boat through some of my old connections. Said he'd return a favor for me.

He told me to call him up when we settled on a date. He was a little shocked to hear from me last night."

"I guess so!"

"I told him to give us time to get all the necessary paperwork done, and we'd meet him over at the church around 11:00."

Faith reapplied her lipstick and grabbed the bouquet. "It's eleven now. Shouldn't we go in and tell him we're here?"

"Then let's get in there and do it!" Phil replied, jumping out of the car and running around to open Faith's door before she had a chance. "Did I tell you how beautiful you look?"

"Yep. And thanks."

They walked through a side door and into a small office where a short, balding man in his mid-forties sat bent over a book. He took off his reading glasses when he heard them approaching his cubicle. "Hey! How's it going? Ready for the big day?" The man rose and shook Phil's hand enthusiastically.

"Elliot! Good to see you, man! I'd like you to meet my intended, Faith." Elliot extended his hand to Faith. "I like that name!"

"Thanks! Nice to meet you." Faith could tell by his face he was a kind man who seemed genuinely happy for them.

"Let's get started!" the preacher said.

"Sounds like a plan!" Phil answered, pulling Faith over to him in a sideways hug. "Ready to become Mrs. Phil St. John?"

"Ready!" she smiled back at him.

They exchanged vows in front of the small, nearly empty church with only the preacher's secretary in attendance, intently watching every moment of the service. When the short ceremony was over, the preacher introduced Faith and Phil as Mr. and Mrs. St. John, to the wild applause of the secretary.

"I hope you don't mind me crashing your wedding!" the cheerful woman said to the couple. "I've never actually seen anyone elope before! Curiosity got the best of me! Besides, you needed a witness."

"Glad you enjoyed it!" Phil chirped back.

"Preacher Elliot! You do an excellent job!" the secretary said.

"Why thank you, Miss Chastain. I'll be happy to do the same for you some day if Mitch is smart and fast enough to get you to the altar before someone else grabs you away from him!" The secretary laughed and every inch of her large body jiggled in delight over the comment.

"Mitch has had seven years to come around to my way of thinking. I keep telling him I'll get fatter and fatter the longer I wait! Eating is the way I cope with his uncertainty!" she laughed.

"He hasn't succumbed to your threats?" Phil broke in.

"Nope. I think he's one of those guys who likes his woman fat! The fatter the better! I'll have to try a different approach!" They all burst into laughter at her remark.

"We'd better get going, Elliot," Phil said. "I hate to rush off, but I have a honeymoon to get started!"

"Hey! I understand, my friend!" Elliot replied. "Don't blame you one bit for wanting a little time for yourselves. Give me a call sometime soon. I'd like for you to take me out on Bessie." Faith cut her eyes toward Phil looking curiously at him. Phil's face flushed slightly.

"Sure, Elliot. I'll call you in a week or two. Thanks for performing the wedding at such short notice!" They shook hands and Phil led Faith out of the sanctuary.

"Bessie? Did he know you when you owned Bessie?" Faith asked. "I thought you just met him."

"I'll explain in the car." Faith had a sick feeling in the pit of her stomach.

"Explain," she requested as they pulled out of the parking lot.

"Explain what?" Phil played ignorant.

"You know perfectly well what. Explain Bessie," Faith

said with her arms crossed tightly across her chest. "You didn't ever really sell the boat, did you?"

"Oh, yes. I did sell Bessie. Elliot was talking about Bessie II. I just bought her a few weeks ago. Actually, the person I purchased her from said I could try her out for a while before making my final payment."

"Why didn't you tell me? Is this the way major purchases are going to be handled in our lives? You kept it a secret because you knew I wouldn't be pleased, didn't you?" Faith asked. Her mind was clearly on his past deception regarding his original boat and how he seemed to love the boat more than he did her.

Phil was clearly shaken by Faith's displeasure. "I wanted it to be a secret. I know how much fun you always had on Bessie I, so I thought I'd surprise you."

Faith wanted to yell out "LIAR!" but held her tongue. After all, it was her wedding day, so she should try to behave in a civil manner toward the man she just pledged lifelong love and devotion to.

"Let's forget it. Okay? This is our honeymoon, darling. If Bessie II upsets you that much, I'll get rid of her. Promise. Now let's try to be happy," Phil suggested.

"Okay. If you say so."

"I love you, Mrs. St. John. I don't ever want to lose you again. Especially over a silly boat."

Faith smiled. It felt good to finally belong to someone who desired her in a permanent way even if it may not be the person she once hoped would want her. *Phil is a good guy. Stable. Devoted to me. He does love me with all his heart.*

"I hope you like where I'm taking you for our honeymoon. We're not going far. I rented a cottage on Cape Cod right on the beach. The crowds have gone away for the summer, so we should have a lot of privacy." He grinned at her in a devilish way.

"At first, I thought about going to a nice New England bed and breakfast inn, but then I remembered you live at one, so that wouldn't be much of a treat." Faith laughed at the remark. "By the way, why did Alice need to hear from you about your plans? What plans was she talking about?"

"I thought I'd go and help her on Saturdays until she closes the inn for the winter. It's the least I can do. She's been so good to me."

"Don't you think you should've consulted with me first? I don't want my wife working. I told you that. Besides, Saturdays and Sundays will be about the only time I'll get to see much of you," Phil said.

"I didn't realize you had the final word on everything I do. Besides, I thought you told me you didn't mind if I stayed at my job. It'll only be for another month or two. We'll have plenty of time together. You'll see."

"I don't remember saying that, but then you'll stop working. Right?"

"Right. If that's what makes you happy, I'll stop working. It might be nice to have a break from it," Faith conceded. "I'll need to rest up a little bit before we start a family."

"Hold on!" Phil's brow wrinkled a bit. "I think we should wait a while before we jump into that. We need some time to get to know each other. Do fun things! Just the two of us. Traveling. Sailing. You can't do those things lugging a kid along."

"Of course you can," Faith said. "Besides, you've been telling me for the last couple of months what a wonderful mother I'll make and how you can't wait to have a family with me. Why are you changing your story? I'm not getting any younger."

"I still feel that way. I just want to wait a while. Okay?" Phil pulled the car into a gas station parking lot. "Look here. This isn't any way to start a honeymoon. Can we lay off the controversial subjects for a while? I'd like to enjoy this trip. Geez! Now put a smile on your face and act like you're having an enjoyable time!"

Faith sat, trembling a bit, trying to hold back her tears.

"If I've said anything to upset you, I'm sorry. Forgive me?" Phil said, looking over at her. Faith nodded without making a sound. "We should be in Chatham before very long. I think you'll really like the town. Our cottage is right on the beach. Well, calling it a cottage is an understatement. This resort is quite magnificent. Golf course, tennis, pools, private beach . . . anything you might want to do is right there!"

"You sound like you know it well," Faith noted.

"I've seen it," Phil replied.

Faith figured she'd better not push the subject any further.

"I'm sure I'll like it. Sounds great! I guess if we want to play tennis, we can rent racquets, huh?"

"Oh, I'm sure we can. They have everything there. It's a classy place."

"Guess you plan to play golf?" Faith asked, hoping the answer would be "no." She'd never played a day in her life and had no desire to start.

"Brought the clubs. Might be an opportune time for you to take up the sport. They have top-notch pros there to get you started!"

"What if I don't want to play golf? Are you still gonna play?"

"I'd like to if it wouldn't upset you too much. There are loads of things you could be doing in the meantime. You like to sunbathe. And shop! I know you like to shop!"

"But I kind of thought we'd do things together," Faith said.

"We'll do lots together! I won't be on the golf course that much."

Faith sighed heavily. *Surely he won't prefer golfing over spending time together on our honeymoon? I'll cross that bridge when I come to it. I think he'll understand.*

The drive was pleasant along the coast of Cape Cod to Chatham. The historic towns were quaint, so they stopped in a few shops along the way and detoured off the main road to catch sight of the ocean. The windswept beaches sparkled under the blue September sky. Tall grasses rippled in waves of tan from the constant ocean breeze.

The Sandbar Resort was just as Phil had described. The property spread as far as the eye could see, clean and crisp. They pulled around to the front of a large building which housed the restaurant, gym, indoor pool, and the registration office.

After registering, Phil excitedly grabbed Faith by both arms and held her facing him. "I say we go to the cottage and unpack, then go for a walk around the property and let you see the place. The dining room here has a great dinner menu. I'll make reservations for, say, about five-thirty? Does that sound good?" Faith nodded. "We can go for a walk and retire early? What do you say?"

"Sounds like a plan!" Faith's spirits were beginning to lift.

The gray-shingled cottage was beautifully renovated and had a typical old Cape Cod feel. One wall in the small dining area was entirely glass, allowing a spectacular view of the ocean. Plush, cozy furniture filled the room, and a tiny stone fireplace occupied one wall of the living room.

English "flower garden" print upholstery covered the bedroom furniture, matching the thick comforter on the brass bed.

"It's beautiful!" Faith exclaimed as she peered into the bathroom, complete with a large jacuzzi.

"Let's go look around at the grounds," Phil said, pulling Faith by the hand back toward the living room.

The rest of the evening went just as Phil had carefully planned. After dinner, the honeymoon couple walked downtown to take in the last of the community's free band concerts in the park. The weather was clear and perfect.

"Let's take a walk along the beach. How does that sound?" Phil suggested. Faith eagerly agreed.

Once on the beach Phil gazed into Faith's attractive face, illuminated only by the light of the full moon, and kissed her tenderly. "The last time we were on a beach, I gave you this," he touched the ring on her finger, "And asked you to marry me. Although you didn't seem so sure." He chuckled. Faith bent her head over in embarrassment. "Right?"

"I guess you're right," she answered sheepishly. "But I'm sure now!" They embraced, but Faith's happy demeanor only masked things she still held in her heart. Being on the beach conjured up thoughts of Novac: the picnic in 'Sconset, the briar she stepped on, Doolittle, and countless hours spent divulging secrets only she and Novac shared. Guilt overtook the warm feelings. Then she turned her thoughts back to her new husband. A man opposite of the one formerly in her mind.

"It wasn't very long ago I stood on a beach, not too terribly far away from here, and asked you to become my wife. I can't believe I'm standing with you on my wedding day, Mrs. St. John." Phil bent down and gently took Faith's face in his hands and kissed her again. "Let's head back," he said as he slowly led her down the beach.

They climbed a flight of sandy wooden steps which marched across a windswept dune, ending directly in front of their cottage. A small lamp post lit the area outside their door, beckoning them to enter.

"Uh, oh! I forgot something earlier!" Faith stood at the front door, puzzled as Phil clumsily scooped her up into his arms and carried her through the doorway. "I was supposed to do that when we first went in."

"I completely forgot, too," Faith remarked as Phil carried her back to the bedroom and flopped her down on the floral comforter.

"Why don't you change into something more comfortable."

Faith smiled demurely. She got up and headed to her suitcases. Phil dug through his toiletry bag and carried his toothbrush into the bathroom.

"I'll see you in a few minutes, Mrs. St. John."

"I'll be waiting, Mr. St. John," Faith replied as Phil slowly closed the bathroom door.

After room service cleared away the breakfast dishes the next morning, Phil suggested they go into town. On the way to the concert the previous night, they saw a shop they thought looked intriguing, so they planned to visit it first thing in the morning.

"I never had a chance to get you a wedding gift. Let's go find something that suits your fancy! Does that sound like fun to you?" Phil asked.

"Sure does! But I haven't gotten anything for you, either."

"Don't worry about me. I have you. That's all I need!" Phil answered back.

"Good reply, but now I feel selfish for wanting a gift." Faith said. "I do want a gift!" she laughed.

"Then a gift you shall have!"

The store was stuffed full of every conceivable toiletry item, porcelain teacups, handmade dolls, lace tablecloths, and ancient trinkets. She had nearly given up hope of finding anything she wanted when she spotted an unusual necklace in a small glass display case. She asked the clerk to open the case so she could inspect the piece more closely, feeling sure it was much too extravagant an item to wish for. The clerk removed the necklace from its velvet box and placed the necklace in Faith's hand, explaining it was from the art nouveau period just around the turn of the century. The flowing, sinuous lines in the gold, along with the elongated freshwater pearls which dangled from the lavaliere, enchanted Faith. Phil noticed her intrigue and immediately told the salesclerk to ring it up. She was speechless as he tore the small price tag off the chain and hung it around her neck.

"But Phil, it's too—"

"Shhh. That's enough. You like it, right?" he asked. Faith

nodded as Phil pulled out his credit card and tossed it on the clerk's counter.

At lunch, her fingers lightly stroked the necklace around her neck. "Maybe a little too dressy to wear with my shorts, don't you think?"

"Looks perfect," Phil said to her, smiling proudly at how happy he had made her.

"I'm stunned. I don't think I thanked you properly for it!" Faith bent across to him and kissed him primly on the lips.

"That wasn't *properly*. You can thank me properly later." Faith shushed him, afraid the other guests might overhear their conversation.

"We're on our honeymoon! We're supposed to act this way!" Phil said in a slightly loud voice, embarrassing her further. The elderly man at the next table smiled and winked at them before turning his attention back to his newspaper.

"Looks like it's clouding up. What's there to do around here when it rains?" Faith asked, glancing toward the western sky.

"Faith, we're on our honeymoon . . ." His smile said everything. "I won't embarrass you by saying more."

At the resort office, the concierge passed Phil a note as they inquired about dinner reservations. Without reading it, he tucked it into the pocket of his slacks.

Outside, Phil looked up at the heavens and frowned. "It looks like a big one rolling in." Faith noted his pensive mood and wondered why the coming rain seemed to dampen his spirits when just an hour ago he behaved as if he looked forward to staying in, "honeymooning".

"Something on your mind?" she asked as they walked down the sidewalk toward their cottage.

"No. Not really. Just wondering if this weather's going to put a damper on our plans tomorrow."

Faith laughed. "Plans! I didn't think we had any plans except, well, you know, if the weather is bad." She squeezed his arm. "I thought you had lots of plans for stormy weather!"

"Yeah. That'll be fine. I just thought maybe you'd like to go to the beach and get some sun time."

"Ah, don't worry about me. That's sweet, but I don't have a big thing about going to the beach and getting burnt. I've seen a lot of the beach since I moved to Nantucket."

Phil unlocked the door to the cottage. "I'm going to take a shower and get cleaned up a little bit."

While Phil was in the shower, Faith couldn't contain her curiosity about the note he received from the concierge. She grabbed his pants off the bed and dug into the pockets: "Tee time 7:00 AM. Your partner will be Lewis Stewart. Enjoy!"

Faith waited, feeling miffed while her unsuspecting husband dried himself and shaved. A towel-clad Phil walked out to where Faith sat, noting the look on her face, and let out a long, sighing breath. "What's wrong now?" he asked. She sat silently. "I hopped into the shower in a perfectly good mood. Now you look like you wanna kill me or something, and I have a feeling my mood is getting ready to change."

"What am I supposed to do while you play golf first thing in the morning?" she asked.

"Play golf? What do you mean?" He played innocent.

"This!" Faith shoved the crumpled paper into his face. Phil opened it up cautiously.

"Oh, that. That's nothing! Don't worry about it." He tossed the paper into the trash can. "I made that tee time before we arrived. I thought you'd want to catch some sun on the beach."

"So, you cancelled it? It's supposed to be raining, so you won't be able to play anyway," she said, handing Phil the phone from the bedside table.

"I intend to play sometime on this trip, so you'd better get used to the idea."

"It's supposed to rain the rest of the week. Maybe you'd get used to that and come up with a plan B!" Faith retorted.

"So, I'll play in the rain. It's allowed. You can find some

way to occupy yourself for a couple of afternoons. I'll let you pick the days, and I'll work my tee times around them."

"I can't believe how selfish you're being. It's our honeymoon." She paused and took a deep breath, trying to hold back tears. "Listen to us bickering like a couple of bratty kids!"

Phil stood still, staring at her. "I want this to stop now! We're supposed to be enjoying ourselves. I don't know about you, but I'm not having fun right now." Phil walked closer to her; his towel dropped to the floor.

"Don't get any ideas, buster."

He laughed. "I was just going to kiss you. That's all." He wiped a tear off her cheek with the back of his hand and lifted her face up toward his. "Let's change the subject, how 'bout? Go get ready for dinner. I don't like to see you cry."

Faith gathered her toiletries together and closed the bathroom door, realizing Phil never gave in to her request and was going to play golf no matter what. Determined not to make the situation worse, she took a huge breath and opened the bathroom door. "Go ahead and keep your tee time if the rain doesn't bother you. I'll find something to do."

She closed the bathroom and stood in front of the mirror, staring at her reflection, trying to convince herself that by giving him permission to play she proved herself the more mature partner. Faith now understood what her coming role would always be in this marriage: peacemaker, mixed with a little "welcome mat," together with a large amount of long-suffering. *We are two independent, stubborn, somewhat immature people who will be spending the rest of our lives together learning how to compromise and put the other first,* she resolved. *I'd better get used to the fact that it might be a long, bumpy road to matrimonial bliss.*

CHAPTER ELEVEN

Alice grabbed the mail and thumbed through it, finding a postcard with a photo of a golf course. She flipped the card over to read the short, scrawled message: "Tell everyone I said 'hi.' Wish you were here! Love, Faith."

Funny message, Alice thought to herself. No mention of the wedding or honeymoon. "Wish you were here?" she whispered. "That's odd. I suppose their marriage took place this time." She stared at the card as if deciphering a cryptic message.

Alice had been lonely at the inn without Faith. The small, selfish part of her had secretly wished for Faith to back out of the wedding, run into Novac's arms and settle down on the island with him. She had grown fond of Faith's company and she knew, through conversations they had, Faith felt closer to her than to her own mother. Alice sensed an estrangement between Faith and her mother after her first wedding to Phil was cancelled only days before the date. When the wedding was called off, Faith's mother Rachel called to blow off steam to her good friend, Alice. At that time, Rachel insinuated a rift had taken place and she felt her daughter was impulsive and had poor judgment, even calling Faith a run-away bride. Alice didn't ask questions but reassured Rachel that Faith could take refuge at the inn. She would keep her busy and help her start her life over again.

Having lost her husband and knowing the pain of not

being able to plan a future with the one you love gave Alice nothing but compassion for Faith. It was her pleasure to offer respite for her dear friend's daughter until the hurt healed. Now, she had uneasy feelings about Faith's love life again.

She fingered the postcard and longed to hear from her "adopted daughter." *There must be more to this message. No new bride wishes to have an old woman along on her honeymoon. At least no happy bride would,* she thought.

Another note arrived from Faith a few days later. This one wasn't much more informative than the last. Inside the envelope on stationery bearing Phil's engraved name, Faith had written down her new address and phone number, along with the message: "The honeymoon is over and I'm trying to get settled into my new life in Hyannis. Please come visit me sometime. I miss you tremendously. Phil wants me to wait another few weeks before I continue my tasks at the inn. He thinks he's going to talk me out of it. He'd better think again. I'll let you know my plans soon. I love you. Faith."

Alice folded the note and slipped it back into the tan envelope. "Poor girl," she muttered softly. "I was afraid of this." She left her easy chair to change sheets in one of the upstairs guestrooms. She rubbed her tired shoulders and realized she would not be able to do this kind of work by herself forever. She would either need to hire another assistant or retire in another couple of years if Faith didn't come back to help. The steps were steep to walk up carrying supplies to the rooms, the weather was beginning to get colder, and the winter would be long and lonely.

Faith looked at a brown chair in her new living room and shook her head in disgust.

"That chair's gotta go," she said to herself as she wrote a message on a notepad. It still gave her an odd sensation to be in the house by herself while Phil was at work. Just the act of opening a cabinet or drawer caused her to feel like a nosy intruder. Her personal things, such as they were, had arrived one week ago via a Cape Cod courier service. Having familiar items at her new home provided more of a welcoming feeling, but the discomfort of living in "Phil's space" still overwhelmed her. He had given her permission to purchase anything for the house she deemed necessary to "feminize" it, with stipulations: no ruffles, no lace, no mauve, no flowered fabric, no chintz, nothing overstuffed or tufted. Those were his exact words to her. Anything else was fine if it was of excellent quality and sturdy . . . and, of course, not too feminine . . . and, preferably of a nautical theme. She looked around the room and realized he preferred things exactly the way they were.

She had been living out of several dresser drawers, half of two closets, and moving boxes that were stored in the spare room since her things were delivered, so the local furniture store down the street seemed the logical place to start her search for some items to help her survive in Phil's world. Phil left her a set of keys to his old spare car in case she had errands to run. She grabbed them off the hook by the door and took one last glance around the living room to make sure there was nothing else to measure before getting in the car.

After entering the store, she discovered it to be on the pricey side. Three salespeople stood, hungry for prey, as Faith self-consciously stepped deeper into the brightly lit showroom, feeling awkward and underdressed. A middle-aged man in a suit and tie approached, sneering condescendingly as he neared.

"We have no public restrooms," he grunted at her, "if that is what you were about to ask."

Faith felt her face flush as crimson as the bold shirt he wore. She debated whether to turn and leave in disgust, knowing that Phil would certainly have stomped out of there after delivering a few choice words. He had accused her of having her backbone surgically removed as a child and always chided her for not standing up for herself. She held her tongue and gave him the benefit of the doubt.

"I'd like to see a salesperson," Faith said to the man, who smirked at her and straightened his overpriced, stiff collar.

"I AM a sales associate, madam. Do you have a problem I can assist you with?"

"Yes. I have a problem with your attitude," Faith said, looking down slightly as to not make eye contact with him; she was not accustomed to standing up to bullies. She felt her face flush again and took a deep breath. "I would like someone else to assist me in selecting some items for my home. Someone other than yourself." She wished Phil had been there to see her put the salesman in his place.

"I meant no disrespect, ma'am, but if you feel that way, I'll get Bridgette to assist you." He walked away to the other salespeople who stood watching with interest. Studying his body language carefully, Faith tried to decipher what he was telling them. She was quite sure she read the "B" word on his lips as the other two glanced in her direction. A tall, pinched-faced woman walked over and extended a cold, boney hand to Faith.

"Hello. My name is Bridgette. May I be of some assistance to you?"

"Yes. I would like to look at a chest of drawers, a bed, and perhaps some living room furniture as well," she told Bridgette as they began to walk across the polished floor to the first bedroom display. Faith felt like purposely spending an obscene amount of money on furniture just to spite the salesman who was so rude to her. After a couple of hours and several thousand of Phil's dollars had been spent, she headed home. She was excited that the store would remove the old furniture and deliver the new furniture the following day. *When you spend enough money, people are willing to move mountains to get things done quickly,* she realized.

Once home, Faith began planning for the removal of the old furniture. *The disabled veterans would be happy to pick up Phil's old sofa and chairs,* she thought as she looked up the number. She explained to the man on the phone that she needed the furniture pick-up to happen as early as possible tomorrow because she was expecting the store delivery truck between noon and two o'clock. She had given this a lot of careful thought and knew the entire transaction must take place while Phil was away. If any remnant of his old furniture remained after the new things arrived, he would surely want to send back some of the things she picked out, she reasoned. *I'm taking him at his word that he wants me to feel at home. I can't wait to see the beautiful things I chose! I think it'll make him happy to see me so happy.*

The next day an unexpected blessing came in the form of a phone call from Phil, explaining that he had a meeting after work with his boss, so he'd be running late getting home, giving Faith four more hours to get the place ready for his homecoming. She opened the drapes at the south end of the living room, letting in copious amounts of sunlight. *Why would anyone cover these glass doors?* she wondered, checking to see how securely the drapes were hung. *I think I can remove these myself. Phil could be a bit of a stodgy "old man" in his ways and probably didn't want to fade the carpet,* she thought. "These have gotta go," she said as she yanked the end of the dark gold drapes. "Beautiful view concealed by horrifically ugly drapes!" she said to herself while admiring the colorful harbor in the distance.

Faith opened the doors and walked out onto the raised concrete porch to admire the new outdoor table and chairs she had purchased at the garden center. The sloping backyard still looked green although the surrounding trees had lost most of their leaves. She guessed Phil would tell her it was a waste of money to buy this furniture when winter was just a couple of months away. She shook off the thought and went back inside to begin straightening the house. The new dresser in the master bedroom needed to be moved over and sheets put on the bed, but first a pile of Phil's books and papers had to be relocated to another spot. He could be so funny and overly organized about most things, but why he piled one unsightly mountain of papers and books along the wall of the bedroom befuddled her.

Carefully removing one part of the stack at a time, she began setting the papers out of the way. The books started to lean, so Faith took the two top volumes off and placed them on the floor to brace the others. Something sticking out of a book on sailing caught her eye. Better judgment told her not to snoop, but she was now married to Phil, so there should be nothing off limits. The photo was of a boat remarkably familiar to Faith. "Good ole Bessie," she mumbled. "You caused a lot of hard feelings, old girl." *The true love of his life,* she believed.

In the photo, Phil stood at the bow of the boat. His image was very tiny. Someone was beside him—a woman with a red scarf tied around her hair. Faith took the photo over to the bright desk light for a closer look. No. She had never owned a red scarf and usually wore a cap when she sailed with Phil. This must be the woman Phil was seeing from Seattle. Just as she started to tear the photo up, Faith noticed a date printed on the bottom back corner and a short message.

"That was taken this past summer," she whispered, feeling slightly overcome with shock.

Let's do it again soon! What do you say? she read.

Faith scrambled through Phil's top desk drawer, found a small magnifying glass, and inspected the woman's face more closely. Without a doubt that was the face she saw looking back at her in Phil's apartment in Seattle. She would never be able to forget it. Phil looked happy, she observed. Further investigation of the photo under magnification revealed "Bessie II" on the side of the boat.

"Bessie II? He didn't even get Bessie II until this

summer!" she said aloud. She put the photo on Phil's desk, unsure about approaching him with this information. *Surely, he wouldn't have asked her to marry him unless he had put the other relationship behind him.*

Ignoring the photo proved unsuccessful as Faith finished rearranging things in the house. What should've been a happy time for her was anything but. The ominous feeling which had pervaded since she had said "I do" still haunted her, but she attributed it to marrying Phil in such haste—not to mention without her parents' approval, or even knowledge. She was raised not to make snap decisions about important things. "Regret will be the reward you reap when you make hasty choices," her mother always told her.

Faith's stomach began to churn nervously. She wondered if it was caused by the photograph or knowing Phil would be coming home soon, or both. She took a couple of antacids, propped her feet up, and waited for the sound of his footsteps on the front porch.

"Honey? Where are you? What the—?"

Faith roused, realizing she'd dozed off for a few minutes. She heard Phil grumbling about something as he walked around the room.

"Oh, there you are. What were you thinking? This is . . ." The disgruntled expression on Phil's face spoke loudly.

"So . . . there's no point in asking you how it looks?"

Phil was now quiet as he circled the living room examining her purchases. "Did you go to Cape House like I suggested?"

"Well, I don't remember you making any suggestion, but yes, that's where I went," Faith replied.

"I can't believe it!"

"Believe what?"

"I left explicit instructions with them about my likes and dislikes. I picked out a few things and told them you'd be in."

"Do you remember who you talked to?" Faith asked, trying her best to keep her temper under control.

"George. He always helps me there. Didn't you tell them who you were?" Phil snapped.

"Are you a local celebrity or something? How would I have known I was supposed to do that? Huh?" Phil sat down on the new couch and bounced a bit.

"I'm ignoring that comment." Phil ran his hand along the fabric. "Better be scotch guarded."

"George. Is he tall and stodgy looking. With a bow tie?"

"Suppose you could say about him."

"I told him off. He was rude and obnoxious."

"Right. Like I really believe you told him off. He's always been perfectly kind to me. You must've p.o.'d him somehow."

"Excuse me! He was rude to me from the moment I walked in the store! Why don't you ever believe me! You could try being on my side just once!" Faith said over her shoulder as she started to walk out of the room. Phil jumped off the couch and followed her.

"I'm sorry, honey," he said as he turned her around to face him. "I didn't mean to upset you. I was just surprised." Faith turned back around and kept walking. "You really did do a nice job. It's just not my style."

"How many people are living here, Phil?"

"Okay. You've made your point. Keep the living room furniture. My other furniture wasn't old so we can put it in the den. That den stuff is getting a little worn." Phil looked around the room once more. "By the way. Where is my other stuff?" Faith stood motionless. "Faith! Where is the furniture that was here?"

"I'm not sure."

"You're not sure! What did you do with it?"

"Gave it away," she said, barely audibly.

"What!?" Phil took a deep breath. "I hope you didn't say you gave it away. Do you know how much I paid for that stuff?"

"You should've told me not to."

"Anyone with half a brain would've asked!" Phil retorted.

"That's it! I tried to please you with this masculine junk! It wasn't even what I really wanted. I got it because I thought it would please you!"

"Don't think next time!"

"There won't be a next time! You are in charge of all the interior decorating from now on! Don't even think about pleasing me! I'll just live in Phil's world and not rock the boat. Okay? Speaking of boats . . . oh, never mind." Faith thought better of getting into a second argument.

"What does please you, Faith?" Phil yelled out to Faith as she walked down the hall and into the bedroom, slamming the door behind her. *Phil hasn't seen what I did to the bedroom furniture yet,* she thought. He banged his fist on the door and called out to her. In her anger she decided to throw open the door, exposing the newly redecorated bedroom to Phil for his criticism.

Phil walked up behind her, pulled back her hair and lovingly held it in a ponytail. Faith stood still, waiting for his blow-up.

"Honey. I think it looks great." She turned around to study his face. "Really. I do. It's pleasant, and homey, and a lot neater."

She desperately wanted to touch him and make everything okay between them but held herself back.

"I'm sorry. I didn't mean to hurt your feelings," he said. She leaned her head against his chest. "You worked very hard. I love you." Phil tipped her tear-streaked face upward and kissed her salty, wet lips. "Let's start over. Okay?"

"Okay," she whispered. Only she knew things weren't completely okay. There was still the issue of the photograph to address, but Faith needed to trust him right now. She made a commitment to him so she could feel secure for the rest of her life. She didn't take commitments lightly, and as long as she didn't bring up the subject, she could pretend everything was going to be all right.

There's a good explanation why that woman was on the boat with Phil, she reasoned. *There could've been other people along; someone had to be taking the picture. Maybe I'm wrong about the identity of the woman. Anyhow, now isn't the time to bring it up.*

She recognized the look in Phil's eyes as he stroked her face softly. At that moment she was glad she had purchased a new bed and mattress. The thought of being intimate with him on the same bed he and that woman had probably . . . .

"What do you say we christen the new bed?" he asked.

"But I haven't put sheets on it yet."

"I don't mind if you don't."

"It'll only take me a minute. I'll get 'em."

"I can wait that long." Phil lovingly watched Faith as she pulled the sheets out of thc lincn closet.

We've weathered our first big fight, Faith thought as she spread the bottom sheet out across the mattress. *Things will surely be easier from here on . . . I hope.*

CHAPTER TWELVE

Light from the rising sun sent streaks of orange through the bedroom curtains and onto the wall, rousing Faith from her sleep. She reached over to the other side of the bed, finding it was already empty. Curious to see if her husband was still home, she slid her feet into slippers, opened the curtains overlooking the terrace, and trudged down the hall toward the kitchen. The smell of fresh-brewed coffee was still in the air, but Phil was nowhere to be seen. A small note was taped to the cabinet door: "I didn't want to disturb you this morning. I'll be working late the next few evenings. I know it's Friday, but I have a big project to finish. See you tonight if you're still up. Love ya."

She barely saw Phil as it was. Now their time together was being cut shorter and shorter. After pouring a cup of coffee, Faith sat and ate a doughnut—a luxury she didn't have at this hour of the morning back at the Scrimshaw. Her mind wandered back to Nantucket. *It's breakfast time there. Alice is bustling around right now doing her morning chores,* she thought with a smile on her face. How she missed her friend. "I've got to call her," she whispered to herself. She wondered if Alice had heard from or seen Novac. If she had, she wondered how he had taken the news of her marriage. *I wonder if he's still spending a lot of time with Venus. Does he even care if I got married? Probably not,* she guessed. *But who cares? Not my concern anymore.*

The morning passed slowly as Faith made the bed and

washed laundry. A timer buzzed loudly in the kitchen. Ten o'clock. *Time to call Alice. She should be finished with her morning work now.*

"Hey!"

"Faith? Is that you?"

"One and only! I had to hear your voice."

"Where are you?" Alice asked.

"Home. Bored out of my gourd. And lonely."

"You know what? I've been lonely, too. I miss you horribly!"

"I miss you more!"

"You've got yourself a new husband! How's married life, by the way?"

Faith was afraid she'd ask her that. Brides she'd known in the past always beamed when asked that question, chirping back about how wonderful married life was. Not being able to lie, she needed to think up something quickly. "Oh, I'll adjust! Guess I'm just so set in my ways! Poor Phil! He'll just have to give me some time I suppose!"

"Not the answer I was hoping to get," Alice said with empathy in her voice. "Is everything okay, Sweetie?"

"Yeah! Fine."

"I'm not convinced. I know you better than that. That postcard. That's not the kind of message someone sends from their honeymoon." Faith sighed. Alice continued, "You can tell me, Sweetie." Faith sighed again. "I want to help any way I can."

"I'm so bored. I want to see you and to be back at the inn working, doing something I enjoy."

"You're not enjoying married life?"

"Does it get better?" Faith asked.

"I think it can. Or it can get worse. Depends on how badly you want it and how much work you're willing to put into it. No marriage is perfect. You know that, don't you?"

"Yours was."

"I beg your pardon, but it wasn't. We had our share of

hard times."

"From the beginning?"

"No. I wouldn't say from the very beginning, although we did squabble over money a lot when we were young and starting out. The hardest part was the middle. When our son was grown and had just moved away."

"How'd you get through it?"

"With God and love and patience."

"Um . . . "

"What has Phil said about your coming back to work?"

"He hasn't said much."

"You haven't discussed it?"

"We did briefly. He doesn't want me to. He said we won't have any time together. But we don't see much of each other now, so I don't know why it should matter to him."

"Would he mind if you worked while he's at work? I could use your help with the housecleaning."

"I don't care if he minds. I want to. Will you take me back?"

"Of course I will. But Sweetie, don't you think you'd better—"

"No! I'm just going to do it! Can I begin tomorrow? Maybe for only one day per week to start?"

"Sure. But be careful, Sweetheart. Don't make things worse, okay?"

"Okay. I'll fight the battle. How's Novac?" The words just popped out of Faith's mouth before she had time to think.

"Sad, I suppose."

"Why do you suppose that?"

"Because his best friend got married and left without a word."

"Why did I need to tell him? He's got Venus to console him. Right?"

"I guess. But don't you think he would've liked being told by you instead of me?"

"You mean you spoke to him?"

"Yep. He called here looking for you."

"What'd you tell him?"

"That you ran off and got married."

"What'd he say?"

"Not much. There was a lot of silence on the other end of the phone. He said, 'Whew!' or something like that. Then he said he wished you every happiness."

"Was that all?" Faith asked.

"Mostly small talk. But I did ask him about his health."

"Is he okay?"

"Far as I know."

"Is he still seeing Venus?"

"Since you brought it up . . . I didn't ask him, but I saw them together in town one day."

"Did they seem happy?"

"Faith! Why're you asking me these things, Sweetie?"

"Just curious. Did he seem happy?"

"Yes. He seemed happy. They were holding hands. She seemed happier than he did." Faith's silence told Alice more than her words could've. "Sweetheart. You're married now so it shouldn't matter anymore. Let it go. I know how you felt about Novac, but Phil's the one you love now. We should be talking about you and Phil, not your past."

"You're right," she said, not meaning a word of it. "I'll let him go. I'll see you in the morning?"

"If you feel that's the right thing to do. I'd love to have you here."

"I'm gonna take the 6 AM fast ferry, so I'll see you just before 7:00. Okay?"

"That's fine. Call me if you change your mind."

"I won't change my mind."

"Do you need someone to pick you up at the harbor?"

"Thanks, but I'll catch a taxi. You'll be busy. See ya."

"Okay, Sweetheart."

Faith didn't sleep well that night dreading Phil's reaction to her going back to work, but her desire to see Alice drove

her onward. Alice was her confidante in matters of love—
the only person in the world who knew the contents of her
heart. And the only person who knew how she once felt
about Novac and wouldn't judge her for the turmoil she was
now going through. But even if Alice voiced condemnation
concerning her actions—which she never would do—Faith
felt it would be justified. She realized she had acted in a
childish, impulsive way because she felt rejected by Novac,
so she impulsively ran into the arms of another man. A man
she thought had changed, a safe bet, underserving of being
hurt by her, forever her rock. But the memory of the photo
she found earlier still ate at her spirit, leaving her full of
doubt.

Phil was not thrilled, to say the least, when Faith rose
before sun-up, dressed, and headed out the door against his
wishes.

"I didn't marry you to have you run off and leave me here
by myself!" Phil yelled at her as she was leaving.

"Why did you marry me anyway? And by the way, I'm
driving the spare car to the harbor if you care to know!" she
shouted back, slamming the door and locking it behind her.
Inside the tough exterior she tried to portray to him earlier
was a trembling mass of mush. The question she shouted out
to Phil was one she herself needed to answer. Before their
marriage, Faith had been convinced of Phil's intentions: he
wanted to marry her because he loved her. His was a kind of
possessive love, but love, nonetheless. Could she say the
same about herself, she wondered? Did she marry out of
love? Or out of spite? Or perhaps, she married because she
had low self-esteem, and Phil desired her enough to pledge
his lifelong devotion to her? She pondered these questions

as she traveled down the twisting roads to the port. She was surprised at her overwhelming feeling of sorrow upon seeing the ferry dock again. *Am I doing the right thing?*

"Lord, forgive me. My behavior has been terrible, but I don't know what to do. I've married a man against Your will, and now I'm suffering the consequences. I want to make it work. Please forgive me for my impulsiveness and stubbornness."

She composed herself before boarding the ferry to Nantucket. How odd, Faith thought, to be feeling so nervous about returning to a place that had been home only a couple of months before. She didn't feel at home in Hyannis with Phil, and she was just far enough removed from Nantucket to feel she no longer belonged there.

The water was choppy, and salt spray coated the windows of the ferry. She determined her trip must be nearing its destination, so she moved to the outside deck. The island became closer and closer across the misty water and the familiar sights now warmed her soul—nothing had changed as far as she could tell. At least nothing on the island had changed. On the other hand, everything in her life was different. Faith left Nantucket a single woman, full of anticipation, hopeful that the security she had longed for would soon be hers. She was returning a married, anxious woman, wondering why she'd never felt so insecure in her whole life.

Unexpectedly, Alice had a taxi waiting for Faith at the dock. A young woman held a sign on which was written 'Welcome Back, Faith!'

"Your friend thought you might have a little trouble getting a taxi with it being so early in the morning."

"That was thoughtful of her," Faith replied.

"Yeah, after Labor Day lots of my friends went back to school. I got a place to stay here through the winter, so I can make some pretty good money carting around elderly rich people who brave the winter cold on the island."

"Sounds like a good idea to me," Faith said to the girl.

"Yeah. There's probably about three or four of us who'll stay on through the cold months." Faith climbed into the waiting car. "We keep busy in the Christmas season. You live here or just visiting?"

"Both, I guess you could say. I used to live here and now I'm visiting."

"Why'd you leave? I didn't think anyone left to go back to the mainland to live."

"Good question. Why did I leave?" Faith said softly.

"Sorry. Didn't mean to be nosy," the girl said as she swung the car around the final turn of the cobblestone road.

"I got married. That's why I left."

"Good reason, I suppose. I'd leave, too, if I found Mr. Right," she laughed. "Well, there's your friend!" Faith looked up on the front porch of The Scrimshaw where Alice stood waving like a crazy woman.

As the taxi drove off, Faith and Alice met halfway down the sidewalk and embraced each other like mother and daughter who had not seen each other for years. "Oh, honey, it's so good to see you. You don't know how much I've missed you!" Alice said, wiping tears away. Faith held onto her dear friend, not ready to speak. "Let me look at you!" Alice moved back away from Faith, holding her arms and looking deeply into her eyes. "You're not happy. I can tell from your eyes. They've lost some of their light."

"How did you ever guess?" Faith replied softly.

"Wasn't hard."

Faith snickered at Alice's remark.

"Come on inside and let's talk. I have everything ready for the guests' breakfast."

"Then you don't really need my help today?"

"You know what I need most of all?" Alice asked.

"Some coffee?" Faith half-joked.

"You silly goose! No! I need your company. I've been going crazy here with no one to talk to."

"You've had guests, haven't you?"

"That's not the same. I want someone to have a meaningful discussion with. Not just small talk. You're like a daughter to me. The women on the island are nice enough, I suppose, but they just want to talk about who's doing what and who's going where. They only want to gossip. They don't care about how you're feeling or about being a friend."

"I thought you had friends at church you hung around with."

"I do. But most of them have gone south for the winter. We're not spring chickens anymore. I've thought about doing the same myself."

"Going south?" Faith asked.

"Yeah. I knew when Jim died, my days here would be numbered. It gets too blasted lonely and cold. My blood's not thick enough for the winters on this island anymore."

"You never told me that before," Faith said as they walked down the hallway toward the kitchen where the aroma of coffee floated.

"I had you here."

"What do you mean?"

"I wasn't lonely anymore when you were here. I had a reason to stick around. Someone to care for and who cared for me, as well."

"Now you're making me feel guilty for leaving."

"Oh, not at all! I didn't mean to. I was thankful to have had your company even if it was for a brief time. You've truly been a godsend. I feel God sent you here to help me get over those hard months, and then it was time for you to move on."

"They were hard months for me, too. Remember?"

"I sure do," Alice answered. "So, I guess we needed each other. He has a perfect plan, you know."

"Don't you wish you knew what it was sometimes?" Faith asked.

Alice poured Faith a cup of coffee and sat. "Oh, I don't

know. Probably if we knew what His plan was for us, we'd be disobedient and decide we knew what was better, don't you suppose?"

Faith smiled, "You're probably right."

"His plan sometimes involves painful things."

"Are you trying to tell me something?"

"Honey, I'm just trying to say that marriage can be very difficult at times. Lord knows Jim and I had problems. But we always got through them, and we were stronger for those times."

"I don't think Phil and I will get through them."

"It only seems that way, but you will. Honey, you must be willing to work at it. You need to love him enough to give in sometimes, and he must do the same. I don't know what you're fighting about, but it's probably not anything Jim and I didn't go through. And I can tell you, there is light at the end of the tunnel."

"I don't love him." Faith said blankly, looking straight at Alice. "And I don't trust him."

"Oh." Alice was suddenly at a loss for words.

"Did you ever feel that way about Jim?"

"No, I didn't. There were times I didn't like him very much, but I never stopped loving him."

"I don't know what to do."

"I certainly can't tell you. I'm afraid to ask, but are you still in love with Novac?"

"I don't know what I think about Novac. I just know I made a big mistake. It has nothing to do with Novac."

"I wish there was something I could do to make it better. I hate to see you unhappy." Alice reached over and smoothed Faith's hair. Faith bent her head toward Alice's hand. "Have you spoken to your mother about it?"

"Ha! Not a chance! She acted cold when I told her I'd married Phil."

"I thought she'd be happy that you chose the man she said was stable. Does she resent him because the costly wedding was cancelled?" Alice asked.

"She'll always blame both of us. He broke her little girl's heart. And I impulsively cancelled the expensive wedding without giving him the benefit of the doubt. Mom and I have reconciled since that time, but it won't ever be the way it once was."

"I can understand her being upset at him for being unfaithful. But when he was here on the island, it seemed like he genuinely cared about you. At least whenever he was around me."

"I think he does. Sort of the way one would care about a boat or some other important possession."

"Um," Alice sighed. "Honey, do you think you're just being overly sensitive about something? Did anything happen between the two of you?"

"Nothing in particular." Faith took a sip of her coffee. "Did I tell you he bought another boat?"

"I'm surprised you allowed that after the first time." Alice held the coffee pot out to Faith.

"No more, thanks. Oh, I didn't know he bought the boat. In fact, I don't think he would have told me about it if it didn't slip out of the minister's mouth."

"Now you've lost me."

"Apparently, the minister who married us is a boating buddy of Phil's. He said something about going boating with him again sometime. Anyway, I asked Phil what he was talking about and he reluctantly told me about Bessie II. Can you believe it?"

"Bessie II?" Alice frowned.

"The gall of him! He even named it after the first Bessie! Oh! I found a picture of him with that harlot on Bessie II."

"You mean the one that he . . ."

"Yep."

"When was it taken?"

"It had to be after we got back together. But I don't know exactly when."

"Oh, dear." Alice gave Faith a sympathetic look. "Do you suspect he's still seeing her?"

"Maybe not since we've been married. He wouldn't have had a chance to. I'm always at home. Well, I was, anyhow."

"You need to talk to him about it. Sweetie, your imagination will drive you crazy if you don't," Alice continued. "It may have been something perfectly harmless."

Faith sighed and looked deeply into her coffee mug. "You're right."

"Is that why you've felt so downhearted since being here?"

"Not just that. I never realized what a control freak Phil is. He's gotta have everything his way."

"Faith, dear, those are things you have to work out. Everyone goes through stuff like that. Marriage means lots of adjustment. I'm sure he's had to adjust to you as well." Alice smiled at Faith. "Even though you are practically perfect." She winked.

"Yeah, I am, aren't I?" Faith laughed. "Okay. I'll try to put it all past me."

"Good girl!" Alice patted her hand.

"I'll get to work now. You can dock me for my break time."

"I will not. And I'm going to reimburse you for the ferry."

"No, you're not!"

"Oh yes I am. I selfishly wanted you back here. I'll get you back here for visits any way I can. I don't want it to be a financial hardship on you to come and see me. I know those ferries can be expensive."

"My husband's loaded." Faith teased.

"I'm a loaded old lady and it makes me happy to help you out. Even if you don't need it!" They laughed and Faith rose from the table and went about her old familiar chores of making beds and cleaning up the breakfast dishes.

At the end of her workday, it was with much hesitation that Faith left. She dreaded the inevitable clash that waited for her at home. Phil would demand that she never go back to the inn again. She would refuse to make the promise. They'd fight viciously over it and go to bed angry. Faith had the whole scene played out in her head.

"Same time, same place next Saturday," she and Alice had agreed as she walked out to the waiting taxicab. The ferry trip was not long enough to suit Faith. Phil would be waiting at home, impatiently drumming his fingers on a table, ready to attack the moment she stepped foot through the door.

When she arrived home, things did not work out the way she had expected. Faith entered an empty house and carefully made her way over to a light switch. A note hung on the kitchen cabinet. "Gone to dinner with a client. Won't be home until late. Don't wait up for me," it said. Relieved, she got herself showered and dressed in her bedclothes. A frozen dinner would suit her fine tonight. After watching an old movie on the television, Faith went to bed and quickly fell to sleep, not even aware of what time Phil came home.

Upon waking, Faith rolled over to face Phil's side of the bed. It was empty and looked as if it had not been slept on. He must've still been holding a grudge and decided to sleep on the couch, she figured. With a grunt, she rolled over and fell back to sleep, not wanting to face Phil's rage yet.

She looked at the alarm clock next to the bed. Eight o'clock. Phil would certainly be off to the golf course for his Sunday round. She shuffled down the hall to the kitchen and sensed something was odd. *No coffee? I see no sign of life at all in the house.* She walked from room to room. *No change of clothes lying around. No notes. Phil's side of the bathroom sink doesn't look like it's been used.* The phone rang. There was no voice on the other end of the line, only a brief pause and a hang up.

Phil's arrival home later in the afternoon was without fanfare. He walked through the door as if nothing had ever happened, put away his golf clubs and headed toward the bathroom to take a shower. "Hello," he said as he passed by Faith, who sat on the couch reading a book. She rose and followed him a few steps down the hallway.

"Good game?" she said, playing along with his charade.

"Okay, I suppose. How's Nantucket?"

"Okay, I suppose," she quipped.

"Surprised to see you back," he said as he closed the bathroom door and turned on the shower.

What did he mean by that? She thought. Did he think she'd abandoned him? Or maybe he thought she would stay there the entire weekend.

The ringing phone caught Faith by surprise as she sat down on the couch. Something told her not to pick it up this time. After a few minutes, she checked the message recorder to see if a message had been left. A youthful female voice played back to her. "Phil? If you're there, pick up the phone! Oh, Phil? I hope you get this message before Faith comes home. Let's not let so much time pass before we get together again, okay? Hope you had a good round of golf. I straightened up Bessie a little before I left. The key's in the usual place. I'll be seeing you again soon, I hope!"

The message ended and Faith was barely able to catch her breath. The water was still running in the shower, so Phil had not heard the phone ring. Faith saved the message for later reference, if needed. Memories flooded back to a note she found in Phil's jacket pocket once before. The message on this note was almost identical. It alluded to a weekend on the boat, making it sound like it was a regular event. The only difference being the first time she found out in time to call off the wedding. This time she was too late.

I won't be naïve and believe he was meeting up with a male golf buddy. He'll want me to think that, but this time I have evidence. Although this wasn't a face-to-face meeting with his other woman, as before, she felt just as humiliated to hear her voice over the phone.

Stunned disbelief swept over her as she nervously

pondered the prospect of facing Phil with her knowledge. *Should I approach him outright or pry the truth out of him little by little? Will he deny it or try to justify his actions? Phil is an expert at that when he feels he's been treated unfairly,* she thought. Maybe it was something he did out of rage and would never do it again. He'd beg her forgiveness, telling her how much he loved her and didn't want to lose her again. The whole ugly scene played out in her mind.

When he came out of the shower, Faith looked for any sign of guilt in his mannerisms. Finding none, she decided to play it cool for a while, seeing if any confessions would come her way. None did that day. Nor did any come in the following days.

Toward the end of the week, there was still no sign of guilt in Phil. He'd come home from work each evening full of the usual small talk. Nothing more was mentioned about her job at The Scrimshaw until Thursday.

"What are your weekend plans?" Phil asked.

"I intend to continue my Saturday job as long as Alice needs me."

He threw his hands up in the air, "Fine!" he said. "Don't expect to see much of me on the weekends either! I've tried to be as flexible as I can with you and your whims, but this time you're the one driving the nail into the coffin!"

"What's that supposed to mean?" Faith asked, half expecting a confession from him.

"I mean I've been bending over backwards trying to make this marriage work. It's been obvious to me since day one that you have an ax to grind with me. You sulk around acting childish and miserable! You've made it clear you're unhappy!" Anger shown in Phil's eyes as he spoke. For a moment, Faith wondered if she *was* the cause of all of it.

"I've been feeling like you were the one unhappy with me," Faith said. "You haven't liked my choices in furniture. You've made fun of me often. Not to mention, I've felt like an outsider a lot of the time. I feel like you're keeping things from me. Like for instance, I didn't even know you'd bought another boat until the minister mentioned it."

"That was a mistake. I should've told you." Faith nodded as he continued. "I was afraid. I didn't want to lose you. I bought Bessie II only because I didn't think you'd ever have me back." Phil wrapped his arms around Faith and held her tightly against him. "Now you are back, and I'm so lucky."

"Why didn't you come home the other night, Phil?" she asked.

Phil shook his head and chuckled softly. "I guess that was pretty silly of me. I'm sorry for doing that."

"What do you mean?"

"I was trying to make a point. I wanted to make you afraid of losing me." He chuckled uncomfortably. "I acted like a two-year-old." He held her more tightly and kissed her on the top of her head. "It was wrong. I drove around town with my clients until late, then we went and sat on Bessie until the sun came up. I took my golf clothes with me so I wouldn't have to come back to the house and run into you. These guys are big golfers. I'm sorry I worried you."

Faith told herself she must've been mistaken about the phone message. He had been entertaining clients. That's all. She went to bed that night feeling a little calmer about the situation, yet cautious until she knew the whole story. Still, the memory of the female voice played over and over in her mind.

When Phil was at the office the next morning, Faith continued her usual routine of straightening up the house for the weekend. She gathered up a bundle of dirty laundry and carried it to the washer. On her trip back to the bathroom to pick up a dirty sock she'd dropped, she noticed a small, while folded-up piece of paper on the floor. It must've fallen out of Phil's golf shorts, she surmised. After unfolding it, she immediately recognized the handwriting as matching that on the photo of Bessie II. "Call me anytime, day or night. I love to hear your voice. Let me know if the coast is clear to visit you again next weekend." A scribbled heart along with a phone number ended the message. The area code was the same one Phil had when he lived in Seattle. The truth was now plain. She felt she'd given Phil every benefit of the doubt and had been a fool to believe him. She knew she only had about two or three hours before he'd arrive home. Faith picked up the phone and dialed quickly.

"Alice?"

"Faith? Is that you?"

"Yes. Alice." Faith was still shaking from her recent revelation. "I'm coming home. If you'll have me back."

Alice detected the tremble in Faith's voice as she spoke and knew not to ask too many questions. "Honey. You know you're always welcome. When are you coming?"

"Tonight. If that's okay."

"I'll be waiting for you. Does Phil . . ."

"The answer is 'no'."

"You can tell me when you feel like it, honey. I'll have your room ready for you tonight."

"Thanks."

"You're very welcome. You know that I love you and will do anything I can to help."

"I love you, too. See you about eight."

Faith gathered her necessities together, packing them in the very collection of bags she first took to Nantucket. Thinking she may need evidence, she removed the tiny cassette tape from the phone's answering machine and safely tucked it in her purse. When Phil walked through the door at 5:15 PM, she was sitting on the couch with suitcases stacked around her.

"I'm going away, Phil. When you feel you can tell me the whole truth about your affairs, you can come and find me. If I haven't heard from you within a week, I'll send for the rest of my things. You can pick up your car at the ferry dock. I'll leave the keys under the mat." Feeling a little like a pack mule, she took the first load of things and set them outside the door while she went back in for the remaining items. Phil stood silently, not making a move to help her. From the quick glimpse she caught of his face, Faith could see he was not going to stop her from leaving. He simply watched as she shut the door behind her. Driving off she wondered if that would be the last time she'd see Phil, the house, and those ugly gold bedroom drapes.

CHAPTER THIRTEEN

The moist evening air blew through Faith's wavy hair as the ferry danced over choppy waves. A pit formed in her stomach as the events of the past day began sinking in. Looking around at the other passengers, she wondered if they could tell that she had just left her husband. *Does a person who committed a shameful thing have a guilty look about them?* Phil didn't. Phil's poker face never gave him away. No one would ever suspect Phil of cheating just by looking at him. Unlucky for Phil, he was sloppy with the physical evidence.

The boat's undulation caused Faith to feel queasy, so she took a seat close to the restroom for the remainder of the trip. While sitting there, she wondered how long it would take for Phil to be in contact with her—if ever. *If he hasn't done anything wrong, surely he'll call me this evening.* "Don't hold your breath," she whispered as she leaned back on the bench.

Realizing she had dozed off for a minute, she woke to an announcement of their momentary arrival at Nantucket Island, gathered her bags, and moved to the end where she would be disembarking. The larger baggage, which was piled together on the deck of the ferry, was hastily unloaded by a couple of young men and left on the dock. Knowing her things would be too heavy to carry down the sidewalk by herself, Faith left her suitcases and took her valuables with her to hail a cab. As she walked past the darkened sidewalk benches, a man caught her eye, stood, and approached her. She felt a touch on her shoulder and let out a startled gasp.

"Novac!" she exclaimed, once she realized who it was.

"You remember me!"

"What're you doing here?" she asked.

"I visited Alice this afternoon and asked her how you were doing. She said to go to the ferry dock at eight o'clock and see for myself. So here I am!" Speechless, Faith stood and stared up at Novac's wide smile. He seemed much older than she remembered. From what she could see in the darkness, his hair was growing back much grayer than it was previously. "Are we just going to stand here or do you have some more bags to get?" he laughed.

"I have more bags."

"I knew you would. You never travel lightly. You always visited me at my house with a tote bag the size of Rhode Island." Faith realized he was trying to make her smile. How much information had Alice given him, she wondered. They walked back down toward the ferry to retrieve Faith's bags.

Without words, they carried the bags to where Novac had parked Mrs. Graham's familiar old blue Nova. He opened the trunk and stuffed as much as he could in there before piling the rest on the back seat. "I really have missed you," he said, turning around to face Faith. She didn't know how to respond to his statement but was glad he could not see her flushed face. They drove toward The Scrimshaw as they had many times together in the past.

"I meant what I said," Novac said tenderly. She smiled at him and bent her head down, pretending to inspect her fingernails. Instinctively, she covered up her left hand, annoyed that she was still wearing her wedding ring. She wanted no reminder of Phil or her recent abandonment; however, she wasn't ready for the finality symbolized by removing the ring.

"Did Alice tell you anything?" she asked him.

"About what?"

"About me."

"Nothing except that you were coming for a visit."

"Um."

"Faith, you know Alice would never betray a confidence. I suspect there's more to it than just a visit, but I didn't pry. That's your business." Faith remained silent. "Words can't describe what I'd want to do to that man if he's hurt you in any way."

"I appreciate that, but I can handle him."

Alice was waiting at the door to greet them, looking first at Faith and then at Novac. "Oh, Sweetheart, it's good to have you here." Alice embraced Faith in an especially motherly way and whispered in her ear, "I haven't said anything to him." Faith smiled and looked straight into Alice's eyes. "Let's go put your things in the room. Novac? Can you stay a while?"

He looked at the two women and realized they must have things to talk about. "I'd better be getting back to Doolittle. He's probably wondering what's happened to me."

"Thanks for picking up Faith!" Alice said as he headed for the door.

"I'll be talking to you later," Novac replied.

"Thanks," Faith said, shutting the door behind him.

"I owe it to you to tell you the whole story," Faith said to Alice.

"You don't have to tell me anything."

"You're nice enough to let me stay here. Besides, I want to tell you."

"Then let's go get comfortable. Want some ice cream?"

Faith awoke the next morning, mindful that Phil never called the previous evening. She suspected what his silence meant but cared very little. All that mattered was that she was back in her old room, sleeping in her comfortable bed, and near people who genuinely wanted the best for her. The old routine would be cathartic.

A chill was in the air, signifying crowds would be dwindling to almost nothing on the island until the Christmas surge began. The inn would be closing soon to the public—a time Alice had been dreading since the death of her husband. The loneliness was crushing to her spirit. With Faith's future being uncertain, Alice could only hope she would be able to stay on at The Scrimshaw for a long time to keep her company and offer a helping hand.

Sunday came and went with no word from Phil. While getting ready for bed, Faith sighed, pulled off her wedding band and unceremoniously slipped it into a travel tote, where it would remain if things did not get settled between them to her satisfaction. Sitting in bed, she wrote a letter to Phil stating all her suspicions and giving him one week to respond. She rose early on Monday to make sure the letter went out in the morning mail pick up.

Tuesday evening, Novac called to check on Faith. Alice kindly explained to him that she didn't want visitors for a while so she could do some soul-searching regarding important decisions in her life.

The next morning, Alice handed Faith a cup of coffee, as well as a long, slender box tied with a fat red ribbon. A card imprinted with the address of the island florist was pinned to the ribbon.

"Phil?" she asked Alice who shrugged and encouraged her to rip it open quickly. "If you need a shoulder to cry on, I'm here waiting. - Novac". She read the message aloud to Alice. "Oh, well. Not what I was hoping for."

"I know." Alice said wistfully. "But your friend is reaching out to you."

"I promise I'll talk to him. Just not now. I'm not ready."

"Understood."

"I need to see where I stand with Phil first."

"Honey, I do understand," Alice replied.

The Friday afternoon mail finally brought a letter from Phil:

"*Faith,*" he wrote, "*I'm disappointed in the way you have handled this. You should have faced me with your concerns. You asked me to respond within a week to your allegations. Here's your response. I've tried to be a good husband to you and give you everything you've wanted. Do what you must do with your life, just as I have done. I won't stand in your way. - Phil*".

Faith read the letter to Alice. "What do you think?"

"I think the same thing you're probably thinking."

"He didn't deny anything."

"No. He certainly didn't," Alice added. "I think you got your answer."

"Wow." Faith could hardly hold back the tears, surprised by the sudden sorrow that came over her.

"Get it out of your system, Honey. I don't blame you one bit." Alice held Faith as one would hold their very own child. "This soon shall pass. Life will be beautiful for you again, I promise. I know it doesn't feel that way right now."

"What would you do, Alice?"

"I can't answer that for you. You've got to do what you feel is best. But start off by praying about it. And often."

"Right. But it seems the only thing I can do is leave him for good. He's obviously not going to change," Faith said through sobs. She looked at Alice for her reaction. Alice shrugged.

"That's something you have to decide after you've calmed down and given it serious thought. Now is not the time to make that decision. You need some proof that he has a girlfriend . . . don't you think?"

"I don't know how to do that. I'm not going to just pop in some weekend and catch him. I think I'd kill him!" Faith reached into her purse and pulled out a tiny tape cassette from the answering machine at the house. "I do have this tape still. I kept it as proof, should I need it."

"Then I'm guessing that Phil doesn't know you have this?"

"Yep. He has no clue. That should be proof enough if he ever tries to deny a relationship with her."

"You still need to call him and face him, I think."

"I don't think I could bear that," Faith said, shaking her head.

"Honey, if you're going to leave the marriage, you need to be free of any doubt in your mind. Then you've got to figure out whether or not to forgive him and try to make a go of it."

"I'm not a brave person. I've got a great big yellow streak down my back."

"I understand completely, so I'm going to give you a push."

"Like how?" Faith asked. Alice picked up the phone and handed it to Faith.

"Dial his number."

"Right now?"

"Now. Get an answer from him."

"I don't think it's a good . . ."

"Now, honey," Alice said firmly. "Put him on the spot and get it off your chest. I don't like to butt into things I'm not involved in, but this time I need to push a little for your peace of mind."

Faith's hands trembled as she slowly punched in the telephone number. "He's probably still at work, so I don't think I . . ." Alice gave Faith a stern look and she resumed punching in the numbers.

"Phil St. John speaking."

"It's me," Faith said to Phil in a breathy voice, her heart pounding.

"Yeah. Did you receive my reply?" Phil's voice was very businesslike which made Faith feel uncomfortable.

"Yes. I did."

"Was it to your satisfaction?" he asked.

"I'm not sure what you mean by that remark."

"I mean did it answer your questions sufficiently?"

"It skirted around the issues. So, I think you need to do a better job of clearing things up."

"Like how?"

"Phil. Be straight with me," Faith said, gathering her strength from Alice's presence. "Are you seeing someone?" The other end of the phone was silent long enough that Faith knew the inevitable answer. "Well?"

"Faith, darling. I've made mistakes, let's just say. You've been so cold and even confrontational with me lately. I felt like I'd lost you."

"So, this is the way you try to mend things? By seeing another woman behind my back? Great plan there, Phil!"

"Look, Faith. I'm willing to try to patch things up between us if you want that. We could start over again. Be the way we used to be."

"How long have you been seeing her?"

"Just one time recently. After you made it clear it was over."

"And how did I do that?"

"By going back to Nantucket. I knew why you were really going back."

"And would you care to share the reason with me?" Faith demanded.

"Because you were still in love with Novac. It was written all over your face when you were around him."

"That's not true! And it's also not true that you just started seeing that woman again. Phil, admit it! You've been seeing her all along! She's been flying in from Seattle the whole time we've been back together. I saw the photo in the book. I heard her voice on our answering machine the morning you stayed out all night. You've never changed, and you never will. You never stopped seeing her."

"Why should I try to deny it? You've already made up your mind. So, why did you call?"

"To hear it from your mouth. Don't worry, Phil. I don't want anything from you except the truth. I never want a penny from you, and I won't interfere in your life. Just tell me the truth. Tell me if it's true or deny it outright."

The silence that followed told Faith two things about Phil. First, he had been seeing the other woman all along. Second, he was not worthy of her trust.

"I have my answer. And I can't think of anything else I care to say." Faith slammed down the phone, completely crushed. She went to her room and gently closed the door behind her. Alice fought the urge to knock on her door, knowing she needed to be by herself to think things over. Periodically, until the lights went out around ten o'clock that evening, she would pause and listen at Faith's door to make sure she was okay.

The next morning, Alice was surprised to see Faith up so early, getting breakfast ready for the couple of guests staying at the inn that weekend. Bagels and fruit had been laid out, along with muffins Alice had made the night before.

"Sleep well, honey?" Alice asked Faith, who was sipping a cup of coffee.

"Actually, I did, surprisingly enough. Sorry I wasn't good company."

"I figured you wanted to be left alone."

"You were right."

"I see you found the antacids. I have a new bottle of them in the medicine cabinet if you need them. Upset stomach?"

"Yeah. Probably because I skipped dinner last night. Well, that and the fact I cried until about nine. That always makes me nauseated."

"Honey, if you don't want to talk about it, fine. But did you get things straightened out with him to your satisfaction?"

"It may not have gone the way I hoped, but it got settled.

For me, anyway."

"That's good." Alice popped two English muffin halves into the toaster.

"My hunch was right. He's had a girlfriend all along."

"I'm so sorry."

"Don't be. I did a stupid thing by running off with him after he'd been unfaithful to me the first time. I shouldn't have trusted him. I'm to blame."

"Don't be silly! You're just a trusting person. But that's a good thing." Alice pulled the hot muffin halves out of the toaster and tossed them on a plate. "Here. For you. I remember how much you like these with honey on them."

"Oh, no thanks. Not this morning. My stomach's still churning. I'll eat a little later. Guess I'm still wound up from yesterday."

"Are you going to divorce him?" Alice asked, wondering if she was overstepping her boundaries by asking.

"I'm not going to do anything except stay here. If he wants a divorce, he'll ask for one. Call me crazy, but I would feel guilty making the first move. I always believed that marriage is forever. Divorce was never in my vocabulary."

"Honey, you shouldn't feel that way in this case. Phil made the first move by having a mistress. I understand how you feel, but even the Bible says infidelity is a valid reason to leave a spouse. I'm not trying to push it, but you have given him two chances."

"Well, if he wants a divorce, he'll get it. I don't want a penny from him. I told him that, so he doesn't have to worry about his precious money. I'll get a full-time job to support myself if I need to."

"You'll do no such thing! You have a job here and a free place to stay as long as you want."

"You don't need me here during the slow season."

"I was serious when I said that I may take some time and head to where it's warm during the winter. Of course, I won't leave this year, but it's inevitable."

The sound of footsteps down the stairs caused the two to jump to their feet and walk to the dining room. "Good morning!" Alice sang out to the young man who entered the room. He was soon followed by an older woman who, judging by their similar facial features, was his mother. "Come in and get something to eat! Did you find your rooms to be comfortable?" Alice asked, then turned to Faith and whispered, "Go call Novac. He'll be good medicine for you."

"He doesn't need to be bothered with my problems."

"He called here asking about you last night. I told him it wasn't a suitable time," she whispered. "Now, go call him, okay? He's dying to talk to you." Alice shooed her out of the dining room.

She thought about Alice's decree, then headed up the stairs to straighten the guestrooms. The last thing she wanted was to take advantage of her generosity by not putting in a good day's work. As long as Alice was giving her a place to stay, Faith felt it was the least she could do to help out in any way possible.

"Did you call him?" Alice inquired at lunchtime.

"Not yet. I had work to do first." Faith tried to avoid the subject. She felt uneasy about the idea of calling Novac.

"You're free now," Alice commented, making it clear she wasn't going to leave until Faith promised to contact Novac.

"Why is this so important to you?" Faith asked.

"Because I think right now you need to feel special. Novac always did that for you."

"But I'm afraid."

"What do you have to be afraid of? He was your best friend in the world only several months ago. He's the same person. He hasn't changed."

"I have."

"Not that I've noticed."

"I'm bitter. Frightened. Insecure . . . and married."

"If I remember correctly, and tell me if I'm wrong," Alice began, "when you first arrived here on my doorstep, you were in that very same condition. Except you hadn't quite made it to the altar. Novac certainly noticed your good qualities the moment he met you. And you were an emotional mess. Remember?"

"I remember."

"Well, I remember seeing you walking around with a smile on your face just after you two ran into each other on the beach. Remember?"

"I remember."

"Well then?" Alice smiled at Faith and led her over to the phone in her room. "I want you to be happy."

"But Venus?"

"What about her?" Alice asked.

"They . . . you know . . . they might be . . ."

"They what? Might be friends? An item? Honey, they knew each other before you came around, and he still chose to spend time with you. I think Venus will be ancient history once you get reacquainted with him. Please know that I'm not encouraging you to romance Novac. You're still a married woman. I want you to have a friend who can give you a male point of view and who will support you. I feel as though you and I are close friends, but I'm old enough to be your mother. You don't need motherly advice. You need the closure only he can provide so you can figure things out using your head and not just your heart."

Faith sat quietly, pondering all that Alice was saying.

"You two got along like two peas in a pod. You were inseparable."

"Okay, okay!" Faith dialed his number while Alice looked on with a smile.

"Novac?"

"Yep. This is Novac. Faith?"

"Speaking."

"I'm glad you called. I've been worried about you."

"Why?"

"Because you seemed so despondent when I saw you

last."

"Yeah, I was."

"Care to talk about it? I mean, you don't have to if you don't want to," Novac said. "I'd love to see you."

Alice patted Faith on the shoulder and walked out of the room.

Faith sighed, "I've missed you so much." She couldn't believe the words came out of her mouth and was slightly humiliated by her admission.

"Three months, two days, and I'm not sure how many hours. You didn't exactly tell me you were leaving, you know."

"Sorry."

"I'll be right over. I bought Mrs. Graham's old car. She didn't need it anymore."

Faith laughed. "Novac! You really can afford a car that isn't always breaking down!"

"But it makes me seem more eccentric to drive a clunker, don't you think? Okay, so I'm a little cheap, too." Faith chuckled at his comment.

"See you in twenty minutes," he said.

"See you." Faith hung up the phone and ran into the bathroom to wash her face. While reapplying her makeup, someone knocked on her door.

"See. It worked!"

"What?" Faith noticed that Alice was referring to the smile on her face. "Oh!"

"Are you going to see him?"

"In twenty minutes," she said, looking at her watch.

"Well then, I'd better let you get ready." Alice winked and walked out of the room.

True to his word, Novac arrived at the door twenty minutes later, carrying a red rose.

"Welcome back," he said, handing it to Faith.

Novac reached out and gave her a tight hug. "I'm allowed to do that, aren't I?"

"I suppose no one's going to stop you."

"You're right. No one could stop me! And better not try!" he added. "Let's go sit somewhere and talk. We've got three months, two days and some odd hours to make up for." He took Faith by the hand and led her to where he'd parked the Nova. "My chariot awaits you!" Faith laughed at the sight of the car which had mud splattered all along the bottom of the doors.

"I'm glad you cleaned it up for me. I'd be embarrassed to be seen in it otherwise!" She'd forgotten how easy it was to be around Novac. No words needed to be spoken for them to understand one another's feelings. *What a contrast,* she thought, *between this and my life over the past three months.*

Every day had been a struggle between Phil and her. Every day brought with it misunderstandings and arguments. *Phil and I were unevenly yoked, for sure. If Novac wondered about that, why didn't I see it? He hadn't changed and never would've.*

Life was going to be different now. She could feel it with each breath she drew in. At last, she was home.

CHAPTER FOURTEEN

Faith concluded that Alice was right about connecting again with Novac. Novac understood. He always understood what she was going through. Their times together proved to be the balm needed to soothe the sore spots left on Faith's heart. They quickly fell back into the routine they once shared as if there was never a three-month gap in their friendship. A deal was struck between them that Phil's name would not be brought up unless it was absolutely necessary. And so far, Faith had not asked Novac about his relationship with Venus either, although she was still around, there was no mistake about that. She had her way of popping up unexpectedly when Faith and Novac were together, but there seemed to be no serious relationship between the two of them, that she could tell.

On Saturday morning, Faith awoke with an ominous feeling about the day, unsure of why this mood had come over her. Perhaps a dream she couldn't quite remember had triggered some buried emotion. Or maybe she was suffering from one of those strange seasonal change disorders she read about in the magazines. A cup of coffee would snap her out of it for sure. She headed to the kitchen and started a pot of coffee as she had done many times in the past. The aroma filled the chilly kitchen air as she began gathering the silverware and dishes to put out in the dining room.

When Faith poured the dark coffee into her waiting cup, a wave of nausea came over her. The flu had been going around Nantucket for the last week. One of the inn's guests spent the better part of last weekend in bed until she felt strong enough to withstand the ferry trip back to the mainland. Faith laid her head down on the kitchen table trying to shake the feeling.

"Didn't sleep well last night?" Alice's tender voice asked.

"I'm not sure. I feel kinda sick. I woke up feeling a little off and now it's getting worse." Alice put the back of her hand on Faith's forehead.

"You feel a tad warm to me. Go lie down and get some rest. I don't want you to end up like Mrs. Cantrell last weekend. Remember how sick she was? Poor old thing. You just run on now and do as I say."

"I'm okay, I think. It was just a 24-hour bug or something."

"What did you have to eat last night, honey?"

"A bunch of greasy stuff. I don't really want to think about it."

"You'll learn. The older you get, you know to stay away from that kind of food. It makes me queasy every time."

"I'll be okay."

Faith continued feeling shaky as the day progressed. Not wanting to worry Alice, she kept it to herself and went about her chores the best she could, taking frequent breaks to sit down and steady herself.

Faith nervously ripped open the package she purchased on one of her trips into town earlier in the week. She read the directions on the back of the box and proceeded to the bathroom. Minutes later, she walked past the staring portrait of Lauralee as she trudged down the hallway to Alice's room.

"Just a minute!" Alice called out from behind the closed door. When she saw Faith's ashen face, she tilted her head sympathetically at her. "Still not feeling well are you, honey?"

"Alice? I need help." Faith's pleading face frightened Alice. She took her by the arm and led her to an easy chair.

"I'll call the doctor."

"No, Alice. You don't understand." Faith held out the white stick to show Alice, who looked confused. "I'm pregnant."

Faith was still groggy from her midday nap when Alice came to the door.

"Honey? The phone's for you," Alice spoke through the crack in the door.

Faith's fingers fumbled for the phone next to her bed. "Hello?" She wasn't awake enough to be nervous about who might be on the other end of the phone line.

"It's me! I told Alice to wake you up," Novac said.

"Thanks."

"No problem. You shouldn't be sleeping at 3:00 anyway."

"Go away, Novac."

"Ooh. Someone woke up on the wrong side of the bed."

"I'm not feeling well."

"I'm sorry. I wanted you to go riding with me. I found a new place over near the bogs that has an easy path. There was one spot that was a little bit marshy, but we could ride around it. My bike almost got stuck when I went there to check it out. I thought we could pack a picnic. You know, those chicken salad sandwiches you made that time we went to the lighthouse. If you could do that, then I could bring some of those—"

"Novac?" Faith interrupted. "Obviously you didn't hear me. I don't feel well."

"You were okay last night at the crab house. You ate like there was no tomorrow. Let me tell you something. When a man takes a woman out to dinner, he likes to see her eat.

Take Venus, for example, she'll only eat fruits and vegetables. I don't know how anyone can exist on carrot sticks and yogurt and hummus. You want me to get takeout from the Crab House? You really enjoyed that."

"Novac!" Faith screamed. "Shut up! I don't feel well, and I certainly don't want to hear about food right now."

"Do you need me to bring you anything?"

"No. I'm fine. I just want to rest."

"I'll leave you alone and let you go back to sleep. I'll call you later to see how you're feeling. Okay?"

"Okay. Thanks." Just as Faith hung up the phone, Alice tapped on the door and poked her head in.

"The mail just came and here's a certified package for you." She walked over to the bed carrying a large manila envelope. Alice's strange expression and the careful way in which she carried the package told Faith this was not an ordinary piece of correspondence. Reluctantly, she took the envelope from Alice and read the return address.

"Boland, Bradford & Lowry, Attorneys at Law, Hyannis, Massachusetts."

"Phil?" Alice asked with a worried look.

"Guess we'll find out."

"Want me to leave you alone?"

"No!" Faith pleaded, grabbing Alice's hand. "I have a feeling I'll need you here." Faith tore open the end and slid out a small stack of papers. Letting out a sigh, she flipped through the pages, reading only a word here and there. "Well. He's done it."

"Phil?"

"Yep. He's filed for a divorce," Faith said. Alice bent over Faith's shoulder as they read the first page. She pointed at a section halfway down the document.

"Of all the nerve!" Alice cried out. "Abandonment! You didn't abandon him! You need to fight him on this! He can't do this to you!" Faith sat in stunned disbelief as they read on. "That's lousy. He doesn't want to pay you any alimony!

That's why he did this! He knew that if you filed and told them you wanted a divorce because of his dalliances, he'd owe you something. Honey! You need to set the record straight! You've got that tape. There are probably several people you could find who would vouch for you. Other people are bound to know he was fooling around!"

"Alice?"

"Honey, you don't deserve this! Not at all!"

"Alice?"

"What, Honey?"

"I'm not going to fight him," Faith said calmly.

"What?"

"I'm not going to fight him. I just want to get it over with. He can have his divorce."

"Aren't you going to tell him about the baby? You deserve to get child support or something!"

"No. I'm not going to tell him. I don't want to have anything more to do with him. I don't want my child to have anything to do with him, either."

"Honey, it's his child, too. Don't you think he should—"

"No! What he doesn't know won't hurt him. Besides, think of it as a favor I'm doing for him. He won't have to pay child support. I don't want his lousy money, and he won't have to feel any guilt over deserting his son or daughter while he fools around with his trash."

"Are you sure? Wouldn't you want to know if you were in his shoes?" Alice asked.

"Of course I would. And so would you. But you and I have scruples. Phil's cut out from a different piece of cloth."

"Faith. Give it a little thought. However, your secret's safe with me if you decide not to tell him."

"Thanks," Faith said, sliding the papers back into the envelope. "Been a little too much excitement for one day."

"One beginning, and one ending. And big ones at that," Alice said. Faith nodded as she looked toward the window.

"What am I going to do, Alice? How am I going to take

care of a child when I can hardly take care of myself? Don't get me wrong but I may have to find a second job. I'll have an extra mouth to feed. Babies aren't cheap. And please don't say 'child support'."

"I'm going to help you. You know you'll always have a place to stay here, and I'll pay you enough to cover your expenses. I'll even put a little aside in a college fund. My kids are grown and don't need my money. It'll be nice to have a little one around!"

"I can't allow you to do that because I won't be much help around here."

"Hush! You're like family to me and family takes care of family. It'll be a pleasure. Your mother is my best friend, and she'll be happy to know you're well taken care of on the island. What I pay you will be our little secret. I'm not trying to replace her, but I'll feel like a new grandmother again!"

Giving her abdomen a gentle pat, Faith looked at Alice with reddened eyes. "I love you, Alice. If you're sure about that. I certainly don't want to take advantage of you."

"I won't take 'no' for an answer," Alice said.

"I really appreciate . . . *we* really appreciate your kind offer."

"No problem. No problem at all," Alice grinned at Faith. "I'm so excited! Aren't you? How are you feeling about the whole thing?"

"I'm not feeling anything except nauseated at the moment," Faith answered.

"Make yourself a doctor's appointment as soon as you can. Don't worry about the cost. I want to help." Alice noticed the shock on Faith's face. "Remember, I won't take 'no' for an answer," she said before Faith could protest.

That evening, Novac popped in unexpectedly to see how she was feeling. "Stunned" is the only way to describe his reaction when Faith told him the news. Faith noticed a change in his demeanor throughout the remainder of his visit, which confused her, but his parting words shed light on the thoughts behind his actions.

"I suppose Phil will be overjoyed enough to change his wandering ways, huh?"

She wasn't in the mood to get into a big discussion with Novac, so she left the remark unanswered. Besides, Novac still held secrets about his love life close to the vest. Specifically, his relationship with Venus. He had admitted, though not in full detail, that things had progressed between them during Faith's absence. Whenever Faith stopped at Novac's house, Venus would surface. If she went into town with Novac, like the ever-present shadow, Venus would be lingering somewhere nearby. Novac seemed completely oblivious to the fact he was being stalked by this woman with whom he had once been intimate. It had become increasingly evident that Venus had no intention of letting go of territory she had once claimed. Although it stung, she reminded herself it wasn't her place to stand in their way. Her life was now taking a new path; she must allow him to live his life as he pleased.

Within two weeks the worst of Faith's nausea had passed, leaving her with waves of energy followed by uncontrollable sleepiness. The doctor gave her a clean bill of health, assuring her that everything was progressing right on schedule for a woman who was almost three months pregnant.

The resumption of her bicycle outings with Novac proved to be a pleasant diversion after her morning routine at the inn. Bundling up against the chilly ocean breezes, they would set off for some new destination, exploring the natural beauty of the island. Novac remained more "buddy-buddy" toward Faith the past couple months; his flirtations had stopped. She understood and appreciated the space he was giving her to come to terms with her feelings as a new life grew inside her—one that was half Phil's.

"Over one-third of Nantucket is protected conservation land," Novac explained as they sat down and took a break overlooking the windswept shoreline of Surfside. "Are you sure you're okay?" Novac asked Faith as she sipped water from her bottle.

"Oh. Fine. Just a little winded, but I'll be alright." She was warmed by his ever-increasing concern. "The doctor said I should be getting exercise." She took another swig of water and set the bottle back in its holder on the side of her bicycle. "I don't know how much longer I'll be able to keep this up, though."

"Don't push yourself."

"I won't. Don't worry," she responded. Novac put his helmet on and offered her a hand as she rose from the rock she'd been sitting on.

"You've been putting on a few pounds lately, I've noticed," Novac innocently commented as Faith bent and pulled down the legs of her sweatpants over her socks.

"Oh, shut up!" she barked back to a shocked Novac.

"Didn't mean any harm by that. You're supposed to be gaining weight. Right?"

"You didn't have to mention it," she said as she snapped the latch on her helmet. Novac covered his mouth with his hand and backed away from her cautiously.

"Can I mention that you've gotten a little . . . well shall we say . . . touchy lately, as well?"

"No!"

"Then I won't mention it."

They rode back in the direction of the inn, taking a couple of breaks along the way. Alice was in the yard cutting chrysanthemums. The bright yellow, bronze, and lavender brought life to the otherwise fading yard. Trees had lost their leaves, and the grass was now a drab brown in contrast to the crisp, deep blue autumn sky.

"I want to take you two girls somewhere tomorrow if you like," Novac said as he and Faith walked alongside Alice. Alice shaded her eyes against the bright sinking sun and looked at Faith. Faith nodded and smiled.

"I'm afraid my bicycle days have long passed," Alice said to him.

"I'll drive you in style. Besides, I'm not too crazy about this one here pushing herself as hard as she's been doing. I think maybe it's time for her to start putting her feet up a little and slowing down." Novac wrapped his arm around Faith as she rolled her eyes.

"Exercise is good for me," she said.

"I'll have to agree with Novac, Honey. It's been making me a little nervous to see you ride off on that thing lately. What if something happened to you and you were out in the boonies somewhere?" Faith rolled her eyes again and grunted.

"I can see I'm not going to win this one. Two against one."

"Tomorrow then? I'll pick you up around nine in the morning or whenever you're free?"

"Sounds good," Alice answered. "Where are you taking us anyway?"

"To the cranberry bogs. We're going to watch them gather cranberries."

"Oh," Faith said sarcastically. "Sounds exciting."

"It's an island tradition. You'll see. Lots of folks will be there." Novac could tell he wasn't convincing Faith. "Trust me."

"Sounds like fun to me," Alice chimed in. "We'll be ready around nine o'clock." Novac kissed both ladies on the cheek and mounted his bicycle. As he rode away, Alice turned to Faith, handing her the bouquet of mums from the garden.

"You really shouldn't be so hard on him. He's crazy about you, you know."

She patted Faith on the shoulder. "Go put those in a vase of water please, if you don't mind." Faith wondered how Alice could be so sure of Novac's feelings for her.

The next morning, the crisp fall air felt good to Faith as

they looked out over the oceans of brilliant scarlet. Just as Novac had said, many islanders and tourists turned out to see this spectacle.

"This bog used to be the largest in the world," Novac said, pointing out over the expanse. "They had to divide it up to conserve water. Isn't it beautiful?"

"Gorgeous," Alice commented. "Where are the bushes?"

"They submerge them under water and kind of beat them with a machine to make the cranberries float to the surface. See? They've flooded the area with about a foot or so of water."

"Ingenious," Alice added. "In all the years I've been here, I never knew this was going on."

"You were busy at the inn." Faith said.

"I really need to get out more often."

"I'll try to make sure you do," Novac said, smiling at Alice. A young woman in sunglasses sidled up close to Novac, causing Faith to take notice. Feeling intimidated by this bold move, Faith possessively moved in closer on the other side until she felt Novac's arm brush up against hers. "Getting cold?" he asked, looking down at her.

"Not really," she replied. A faint smile crossed Novac's face.

"Pretty amazing, huh?" the other young woman murmured to Novac. He nodded and draped his arm over Faith's shoulder. The woman slid the sunglasses down her nose and peeked over the top of the rims at Novac. Faith recognized the lavender eye shadow and crystal blue eyes instantly. Novac was so enraptured watching the harvesters he had not yet caught on. The bandana-style scarf she wore wrapped around her hair, combined with the dark sunglasses, had completely concealed her identity until now. Faith let out a faint gasp that caught Novac's attention.

"I was wondering what happened to you," Venus whispered to Novac. He took his arm from Faith's shoulder and fidgeted from one foot to the other.

"I see now," she hissed.

"I don't want to talk about that here. Okay?" he said.

"Then when do you suggest we discuss it?" Venus asked, staring straight ahead at the bog.

"We had a long talk, and I think everything was settled then," he replied.

"To your liking, maybe." Venus added. Alice and Faith moved away and slowly walked out of earshot. Novac's eyes followed them. He clearly wanted to run away from Venus, but she seemed determined not to release him before finishing her thoughts. From Venus' body language, Faith could tell she was a woman desperately in love with Novac. Her facial expressions were that of a woman frantic over losing her man, and Faith feared she would be willing to make every effort to win him back. She looked down at her own sensible clothing and felt dowdy compared to the young woman arguing with Novac. Venus' slim, lithe body moved like that of a dancer's as she bent and swerved with each dramatic statement.

Novac walked away from Venus, leaving her there to brood. Several onlookers watched as he grabbed Faith by the arm and led her and Alice to his parked car.

"I'm sorry, ladies," he said as he started the Nova's engine. Only silence greeted him back as he pulled onto the road. "That insufferable woman! She's crazy, I tell you! Crazy! I am convinced she has a screw loose in that blonde head of hers. I swear I can hear it rattling when she moves."

"May I remind you that you are the one who—" Faith bravely began before being cut off.

"Don't go there, Faith!" Novac barked back. No one said another word. The entire, winding trip back to The Scrimshaw was silent. Novac walked the two ladies up the front sidewalk to the porch, holding the door open for Alice who was eager to get inside. "I'm sorry about the excitement," he told her.

"Don't worry about it," Alice said. "Maybe I don't need

to get out more often," she chuckled at Faith as she walked past her. Novac and Faith were alone on the porch, avoiding each other's eyes.

"We need to talk, Novac."

"You're right," he replied. "Wait until I've cooled down some. Okay?"

"Your call."

"Why don't I pick you up and we'll get take-out and eat it at my place tonight?"

"Are you sure we'll be safe there? We won't have any unexpected guests, will we?"

"I certainly don't think so. Besides, if they're unexpected I couldn't possibly predict that, now, could I?"

Faith grinned. "Guess not."

"See ya later."

"Yep. Later." Novac walked away without bestowing the usual kiss on her cheek.

Faith nervously awaited dinnertime, mentally compiling a list of questions she wanted to ask him concerning his relationship with Venus. For several weeks, she avoided the subject, not caring to hear details of what may have transpired between them while she lived in Hyannis, married to Phil. She reasoned that Novac is a grown man and Venus is a grown woman; they have a history that occurred before she met him. She was about to talk herself out of the meeting with Novac just as he knocked on her bedroom door.

"Ready to go?" he inquired.

Faith smoothed her slacks down and replied, "Ready as I'll ever be." She grabbed her purse and jacket.

"Faith?"

"Yeah? What?"

"Oh, never mind," Novac said, deep in thought. "I just wish you weren't so nervous about talking to me."

"Shouldn't I be?" she asked.

"I don't think so." He led her out the door of her room, past Lauralee's solemn gaze.

"I won't be out too late," Faith called to Alice, who was reading in the living room.

On the way to 'Sconset, Novac stopped at the Crab Hut and ordered two crab sandwiches and fries to go. Faith held the bag in her lap as they drove down the slightly rolling Old South Road to the small road leading to Novac's cottage. Her stomach growled as she breathed in the delicious aroma which rose from the containers she held. When they arrived, Doolittle was elated to see them and danced around the cottage, letting out tiny yips.

"You can't have any of this, old buddy," Novac said to him as he carried the bag to the kitchen table. "Unless your Aunt Faith has any leftovers when she's finished. I, however, intend to eat every bit of mine!"

"Aunt Faith," Faith began sarcastically, "is ravenously hungry so don't bet on it, little nephew!" She cast a sideways glare at Novac, wondering if she was only the dog's "aunt" in his mind.

"Sorry, Doo. Guess you're out of luck," Novac said, opening the first Styrofoam container and handing it to Faith. "Dig in. Don't wait for me. What can I get you to drink? A beer?" Faith patted her abdomen. "Oops! Milk for you!"

After dinner they moved to the living room couch. Doolittle jumped up beside Faith and propped his head on her lap. She stroked him tenderly while collecting her thoughts about the morning's events.

"Well? What do we need to talk about?" Novac asked, knowing good and well the subject at hand.

"How about let's start with this morning, hmm?"

"Okay. Um. Where to begin . . ." Novac tapped his cheek with his fingers. "Well, Venus was pretty upset," he began.

"Yes. That's a given."

"She felt like I'd been avoiding her."

"Okay. Keep going. Have you been?"

"I suppose there has been a certain degree of avoidance on my part."

"I thought you told me the two of you had ended your relationship. You made it sound like she was okay with it."

"I may have stretched the truth a little. She was actually very upset with me when I told her it was over."

"And?"

"And she kept calling me for a couple weeks afterward, trying to get me to change my mind."

"Has she quit calling?" Faith asked.

"For the most part. She just physically shows up now."

"I've noticed."

"You must've let things progress between you two while I was in Hyannis, huh? Please understand, what you do with your life is your business, but this morning I felt caught in the middle of something that made me feel extremely uncomfortable."

"I get it, and I apologize for that. But hear me out," he said, turning to face Faith. "When you left, I was . . . well, for lack of a better word, devastated. I knew you were engaged to Phil and intended to marry him. I just didn't think you'd actually go through with it."

Faith looked puzzled at him as he continued.

"I suppose I was just interjecting my own feelings into the situation. I didn't want you to go through with it. You were my best friend. It was always easy being around you. I couldn't imagine you'd find someone else you'd rather be with than me. Pretty selfish, right?"

"No. Not at all," Faith said, shaking her head.

"Venus was there, waiting in the wings. Well, backing the story up, she took care of me and watched my house while I was in the hospital. She hardly left my side. I felt like you had deserted me."

"I'm sorry," Faith whispered.

"I don't blame you. You and Phil had big plans to make. That was exactly what you should've been doing." Novac took a deep breath. "Well, to make a long story short, Venus and I started seeing a lot of each other while you were gone.

You would think I'd learned something from past mistakes, but the lessons apparently didn't sink in too well. She started getting overly possessive and jealous of any woman who spoke to me. I wasn't seriously interested in her and thought I made that clear. She was just someone to hang around with. But she began pulling the same stunts she did previously like talking about moving in together and I had to put an end to it before she got her hopes up too high."

"You broke her heart."

"I guess you could say that, but she was getting crazy! Believe me. Some of the things she was doing were absolutely insane. I won't get into all the details because she's not here to defend herself, but I was actually afraid of her."

"Are you still?"

"Yeah. A little. Especially after this morning. So, there you have it. If you want to steer clear of me, I wouldn't blame you one bit."

"Novac. You're my friend. I couldn't possibly go away because of a dumb mistake you made."

"It was dumb, wasn't it?"

"Yep. Real dumb. But I'm guilty of the same. Only I married my dumb mistake! So . . . I guess that makes me dumber, huh?"

"Not at all. Just more trusting and loving. I, on the other hand, don't trust many people and love very few. And I certainly have never loved Venus!" Novac took Faith's hands in his. "I do trust you and I do love you. So there. I have no intention of messing things up between us by . . . oh, never mind. Enough said. You look tired."

Faith yawned, then smiled at Novac. "I do need to be getting back. I'm fading."

"You need your rest. Let's go," he said, helping her to her feet.

Later, while lying in bed, Faith pondered the meaning of Novac's words "I have no intentions of messing things up." Her eyes grew heavy with sleep before her mind had a chance to draw conclusions regarding the remarks.

Around six o'clock the following morning, Faith awoke to a strange sensation within her body. Once fully awake it occurred to her—she had just felt her baby kick for the first time. She ran her hand over her abdomen, amazed at the movement deep inside that signaled that her baby was alive and well. Until now it seemed unreal to her that an actual person could be growing inside her womb. Aside from the nausea she had experienced, the gradual swelling of her chest, and occasional flutter she felt deep inside her fuller abdomen, her body had seemed remarkably unpregnant to her. Completely without her permission, it was now changing and producing a child to care for. Someone for her to love. Someone who, God willing, will love her in return.

CHAPTER FIFTEEN

Nantucket was alive with lights and songs of Christmas! And tourists, once again, arrived to witness the beauty of the gaily decorated downtown area. Alice opted not to take reservations at The Scrimshaw during the famous Nantucket Noel celebration. This would allow her to spend quality time with Faith and give her a chance to attend the festivities around the island without working. Novac was pleased to be her escort. Venus had not made any more surprise appearances since the encounter at the cranberry bogs, which made them both feel less vulnerable being out together.

On Christmas Eve, Faith talked Novac into staying in a guestroom at the inn so they might all be close together. Doolittle had a comfortable little bed set up in the kitchen. The floors could easily be cleaned in case of an accident, Alice had noted. Before bedtime, the three of them cozied up together around the fireplace as Alice read from the book of Luke in the Bible, the story of Christ's birth, followed by a reading aloud of Dickens' Christmas Carol. Faith imagined the ghost of Marley in the dimmed light of the living room. Shadows danced around the antique-filled room as they listened spellbound to Alice's expressive voice making the classic tale come alive. Upon finishing, she slowly closed the worn copy of the book, holding it close to her chest.

"Jim and I used to do this every Christmas Eve. Thanks for letting me bore you to death with my traditions," she said quietly to not break the spell.

"It's a beautiful tradition, Alice. Thank you," Faith murmured. Novac smiled and helped Faith to her feet from the low couch from where they all sat. "I'm gonna turn in now. Don't mean to be a party pooper."

"By all means, Honey, get to bed. It's been a long day."

"Goodnight. See you two in the morning. Goodnight, Doo." Faith bent to rub the dog, who was curled up on the rug in front of the fire, licking his feet.

"Sweet dreams," Alice and Novac said in unison.

Faith slid into bed and wrapped the warm covers tightly around her shoulders, eagerly anticipating the next morning's surprises. First, they would go to church for the Christmas service, then packages would be opened around the grand tree in the living room.

Is Phil alone tonight, she wondered? *Who will he spend Christmas with? Has he thought about me once?* As she drifted off to sleep, she didn't notice the shadowy face peering through the frosted window of her room.

"Faith! Faith! Get up!" A voice startled her from a sound sleep. As she groggily sat up in bed, she noticed the smoky haze that filled her room. Flames crept up her bedroom curtains. Her body felt heavy and tired as she unsuccessfully tried to drag herself out of bed. Coughing, she flopped back down and covered her face with the covers. "Faith!" Novac's voice called out once more. "Open the door!" Her throat was parched as she tried to muster up the energy to speak. The door flew open with a mighty thud. Novac ran to Faith, scooped her up, wrapped her in a blanket, and carried her out of the smoky room as firemen pulled up in front of the inn.

"We need help over here! She's pregnant!" he shouted to the firefighters as they ran past him to the front door of the inn.

Several neighbors stood in their yards, shaking their heads at the scene they were witnessing. Alice was talking to the couple who lived next door, asking them if they had seen anything suspicious, while firefighters sprayed water on the front corner of the inn where the fire was contained. The outside wall of Faith's room was charred and smoke billowed from the broken windows.

The captain walked over to Alice who was talking to a Nantucket police officer. "You were very lucky to have caught it early. These old houses burn up in a flash. Seems like that front quadrant is the only part that's sustained damage. We've got it under control. The inspector will come out and look around to see if he can rule out arson. Did you make any fires in the fireplaces?" he asked Alice.

"We had a fire in the living room fireplace before we went to bed. But it was out by the time I turned in."

"Where's the living room located? Over that way?" He directed his flashlight beam at the left front corner of the inn.

"Yes. It's over there," Alice said.

"I was inside lookin' around. It seemed to check out okay."

"Did the young lady have a fire in her bedroom fireplace that you know of?"

"No. I know she didn't for sure."

"Any guests have fires?"

"No. No guests here tonight, except Novac, and I know he didn't use his fireplace. Right?"

"Right. I went straight to bed."

"Yeah. Okay. The inspector will take a little look around. Check the wiring and all. Sometimes the wiring in these old places is pretty worn. We've seen a number of fires start that way."

"All the wiring's been recently updated," Alice informed him.

"Well, he'll check it out just to make sure," the fire chief said. The paramedics bent over Faith, covering her face with a mask.

"We're gonna take her and get her checked out at the hospital. She sucked in a lot of smoke. She's reviving okay, but we need to make sure she has what she needs. Since you said she's pregnant, we don't want anything happening to the baby, either."

"I'm going with her if you don't mind, Alice?"

"I'd feel better if you did, Novac," she replied. "I'll be okay here. Sadie next door said I could sleep over there tonight."

At the small hospital Faith, now fully alert, took deep breaths into the oxygen mask. A nurse intently watched the screen displaying her blood pressure and oxygen saturation. She removed the mask and said, "Take a few deeps breaths and let me see what your numbers look like while breathing without it. Okay. Good. I think we're safe leaving the mask off."

A sonogram was ordered. "I've been feeling the baby move around," Faith told the doctor.

"That's a good sign. Just lie back slowly," Dr. Hoffman said as he punched a few buttons on the machine. He squeezed some warm gel on her swollen belly and moved the wand around to spread it. "There we go. A great view of the baby's head."

Anxiously, Novac watched as the fuzzy image appeared on the screen above them. A small foot moved past and was quickly out of sight. Another light image moved from one side to the other on the screen.

"Heart's beating okay and the baby is very active. Two arms and two legs. That's good! Do know the sex of the baby? Because I know it!"

"No! I want to be surprised," Faith responded.

"Then mum's the word," the doctor said as he wiped Faith's abdomen and braced her back so she could sit up slowly.

Novac groaned. "Are you sure you don't want to know? Won't the suspense kill you?"

"Speak for yourself. I like surprises."

"I still think we're looking at a delivery during the first

week of May," Dr. Hoffman said as they walked toward the door of the examining room. "I want to keep you here overnight as a precaution. A nurse will get you in a room, and I'll check on you first thing in the morning."

"Thanks, doctor."

After Faith got settled in her room and the nurse took her vitals and left, she turned to look at Novac, who had the TV remote in his hands, flipping through the channels.

"Anything you want to see?" Faith shook her head, so he turned the television off and walked to her side.

"Do you wish Phil could be here to share this with you?" Novac asked.

"Not a chance!" Faith snapped back.

"Don't you think he has a right to know?"

"Nope. He signed his rights away with those divorce papers. I told him I didn't want a thing from him, and I meant it. I don't want his support or visits or anything!"

"Nothing?"

"Well, maybe only one thing." She looked down at her protruding stomach and caressed it lovingly. "I'll keep this part of Phil."

Novac remained quiet for a while, staring ahead at the monitors on the hospital room wall. He finally broke his silence.

"May I be with you when the baby is born? That is, unless there's someone special in your life by that time."

She paused before answering. "There already is someone special. Very special. And I would be honored."

Relief passed over his face and he took her hand in his.

"Now go get some sleep. Santa's on his way!"

"I'll be here bright and early to check on you."

"Go stay with Alice. She's pretty shaken over everything. Let her know I'm alright," Faith requested.

"Will do, baby." Novac bent over Faith and kissed her tenderly on the cheek and gave her sock-covered foot a squeeze as he walked away. "I'm so happy you're okay. You had me very worried. Goodnight," he said over his shoulder.

Meanwhile, back at The Scrimshaw, the fire investigator, accompanied by a Nantucket policeman, thoroughly checked the grounds around the inn.

"Seems the fire started here," the inspector said, waving the flashlight's beam over the outside corner of Faith's room. Looks like someone tried to catch several other places on fire, but it burned out before spreading. See. Look." He pointed the flashlight at several smaller areas where the surface of the wood siding was charred.

"Someone?" the officer asked. "So, you think—"

"Deliberately set. Yes. It sure seems that way." He continued explaining how the fire must've made its way into Faith's bedroom through a broken window, catching the drapes on fire, and causing the room to fill with smoke.

"Well, I'll be! What do we have here?" The inspector reached into the shrubs surrounding the front corner of the inn and pulled out a gasoline can. "This is certainly proof of the fire being intentional, I'd say. Probably wasn't much gas in the can to begin with or this old structure would've been an inferno. No one in their right mind would try to set a fire using a lighter and gasoline. Good way to set *yourself* on fire."

Novac pulled up and parked at the curb behind the fire truck and walked up to the two men.

"Good evening, gentlemen."

"Are you the other person who was staying here when the fire started?" the police officer asked Novac.

"Yes, sir. I was in an upstairs room. My dog's barking woke me. We left him in the kitchen, and he was going crazy because he heard something. I walked downstairs and smelled smoke, so I banged on Faith's door to try to rouse her. Alice was in the hallway, but Faith wouldn't answer me, so I kicked in the door.

"Your dog must've frightened off the arsonist. We found a tiny bit of char outside the kitchen window, too. And a lighter. The prowler was obviously on this side of the structure, too. Thankfully, his attempts were unsuccessful. Not a *particularly good* arsonist. Thank God."

None of the neighbors who had assembled in the darkness recalled anything of significance to tell the officer. Sadie next door, however, was the only one awake when the fire began and was the one who called 911. She relayed what she saw to the inspector.

"I just finished walking my dog Midge around eleven. We were inside and she started barking at something moving outside the window. I thought it must be the cat from two doors down rummaging through my bushes looking for mice. She does that some nights. Midge just wouldn't stop barking so I opened my door to scare off the cat. Midge ran out the door and I heard a dog barking inside of The Scrimshaw, so I figured *that* was upsetting Midge. After I brought her in, I peeked through my door's window and saw someone looking into the car parked at the curb. Alice told me she had a guest staying over, so I didn't think anything of it. It was dark and my window was a little frosted, so I don't know if it was a man or woman, but the person didn't seem to be causing any trouble . . . just looked through the car window and walked back toward the inn. I peeked out one last time before turning in for the night and saw smoke pouring out of the side corner of Alice's house."

The officer took notes and asked Alice to look around the property as best she could and see if anything looked amiss to her. He escorted her as she carefully perused the front and back yards. "What do you keep in there?" He pointed the flashlight's beam at the small shed at the rear of the property. The door was slightly ajar.

"Yard things. My gardening equipment. A lawn mower, fertilizer, shovels. That kind of stuff."

"Do you keep gasoline in there?" he asked.

"I have a gas can with a small amount of gas in it. I always try to use it up toward the end of my mowing season.

Seems dangerous to keep it around. I'm afraid of explosions. There's probably enough for one mowing at the most." Alice pulled the shed door wide open while the cop shined his flashlight into the cramped space.

"Where do you usually keep the can?"

"It's supposed to be right here next to the mower, but it's gone."

"Good thing you didn't keep it full. Your house might've been a total loss."

"You mean that was my can . . ." Alice was horrified.

"Sure looks that way. Someone emptied it and tossed it in those bushes. They didn't have enough fuel to finish the job."

Because The Scrimshaw was designated as a potential crime scene Alice was told she could not enter yet, so Sadie kindly offered her a guestroom to stay in for the night. Novac went back to his own house with Doolittle. The events of the evening had worn him down, so he bid Alice goodbye and told her he'd come back for his things when he was allowed to go inside.

The front corner of The Scrimshaw Inn looked blackened and cold in the early Christmas morning light. Novac shook his head sadly at the sight and walked to Sadie's doorstep to check on Alice. They welcomed him heartily and continued their discussion of the previous evening's events over a second pot of coffee.

"The hospital called me to say that they are releasing Faith as soon as someone can get there to pick her up. She must stay calm and in bed for a couple of days to regain her strength. Sadie, I hate to ask, but do you have an extra bed for her?"

"Of course, Novac! It'll be my pleasure to have her here. Now go on and pick her up!"

Novac was all too glad to wait on Faith's every beck and call after they returned to Sadie's house. She lay on the couch, covered in soft blankets. Alice watched as Novac tenderly sat next to her, his hand placed protectively around her shoulder as Sadie droned on and on about her dog. It was obvious his mind was somewhere other than on the terrier, who was now "opening" his stocking full of treats. Novac's face couldn't hide the feelings he had for the woman beside him—a woman who wanted more than anything to hear him proclaim those feelings for her but would have to be content just sharing Christmas morning with him by her side. Faith leaned her head against Novac's warm arm as the baby gently wiggled inside her. As if it were second nature, she placed his hand on her belly. For a few moments, they slipped into their own little world completely oblivious to the fact they were being watched by someone through the tiny ornate window on the side of the house—someone not happy about the scene they were witnessing.

CHAPTER SIXTEEN

After opening their presents and finishing breakfast, Novac led Faith into a private room, drew in a deep breath, paused a moment, and looked straight into her eyes. "Faith. I have something to tell you. I didn't think it was important at the time but now I have a weird feeling." Faith widened her eyes as she braced herself for whatever revelation Novac was about to dump on her. "I didn't mean to scare you! It's nothing too terribly bad, I guess. It's just that, well, remember when you showed me the earring Alice found outside your door at the inn?"

"Yeah. What about it?"

"I didn't say anything at the time, but I bought a pair of earrings just like those for Venus once. It was for her birthday. They're handmade by a lady who lives on Nantucket."

"Yeah? And?"

"The next time I saw Venus, she asked me if I'd found the earring at my house. She was afraid it had fallen out while she was there."

"Why didn't you say anything to me?" Faith asked.

"I didn't want to get things stirred up."

"What do you mean 'get things stirred up'?"

"I was too embarrassed to tell you I had bought earrings for her. Besides, she had caused no harm, so there seemed to be no point in bringing it up. I know how you feel about her."

"Yeah, and with good reason, I think you'll admit," Faith

said.

"Maybe so, but now I have a strange feeling about how the earring got in the house. Venus may be a little eccentric, but I never in a million years would've suspected she'd do anything violent or aggressive."

"And now? Do you think she's capable of it?"

"Definitely." Novac's serious face told her there was more story to come. "When I went home last night to walk Doolittle there was a message on my answering machine. It was from Venus. She was crying and yelling and not making a whole lot of sense. She said something about seeing me and my pregnant girlfriend at the Baby Stuff store in town during the Christmas festival. Then she said some gibberish about how she knew I was spending Christmas Eve with you without even once thinking about her and how she might be lonely. She said some indecipherable stuff, then rattled on and on about our last Christmas together. I think she's really gone off the deep end this time."

"So . . . what are you getting at? You mean she thinks the baby is—"

"Let me finish. She also said she wasn't going to put up with it any longer and that I had betrayed her for the last time." Novac took a deep breath before continuing. "I think she's been watching us, and I also think she's behind the fire at the inn." Faith gasped as Novac continued, "I took the tape from the machine to the police station early this morning and told them what I've told you. They had no other suspects, so they were happy to get the information."

"But Novac, you don't have any real proof of anything except that maybe she's a little crazy."

"I realize that. It's just a strong hunch. They're going to check into it."

"And Alice? Does she know?"

"I pulled her aside just before I went to pick you up at the hospital. I didn't want Sadie to hear and blab to her friends." Novac put his hands on Faith's shoulders and looked straight into her eyes. "I'm going to stay at my house as much as possible until they find out who caused the fire, or at least until they clear Venus. You'll be safer here if I leave. And I don't feel good about leaving Doo by himself for very long. If Venus is behind all of this, she's likely to harm my home in some way. The same way I believe she tried to destroy the inn."

"It sounds like I'm the one she wants to harm. The fire was at my corner of the house," Faith said.

"She probably thought I was there with you," Novac responded.

"I never thought about that. If she thinks the baby's yours, then all of this makes sense. Novac, are you sure you'll be okay staying there?"

"Doo will let me know if he hears anything. He has an uncanny way of knowing when there's trouble. Just like Lassie!" he laughed. "Besides, he can smell Venus a mile away. Don't worry. I'll be fine. They'll be watching her carefully, and there's still a possibility she's not involved."

"I can't imagine anyone stooping low enough to do a thing like that. Even as angry as I got at Phil, never in a million years would I have caused physical harm. But believe me . . . I might have fantasized about it."

"I don't blame you, but you're not Venus."

"I'll agree with you there," she said.

"She's a very passionate, emotional person. Her life is guided by her emotions. She loves strongly and she hates strongly. There's very little in between."

Very little in between her ears, Faith wanted to say but refrained. Faith, strangely, felt a little envious about the way Novac described Venus. No one ever described her as loving passionately or reacting very passionately about anything. She secretly yearned to possess this zeal and wondered if her lack of it might have contributed to Phil's desire to see another woman. *Am I boring? I've always had a tough time openly expressing my feelings. I want a little bit of that* *passion and boldness. Maybe Phil would've been more interested in me and stayed faithful. I wish I had the boldness to just come out and tell Novac my feelings, but I'm afraid it would run him off, just like it did when Venus wanted to move forward in their relationship. But if I stay this way, will Novac grow bored of me? Maybe if I—*Novac's voice snapped Faith back to reality.

"I'm going to look for Alice and give her the lowdown on what we just discussed." He patted Faith on the back. "I'll be back in a few minutes to tell you goodbye."

Novac left the room and found Alice sitting in Sadie's library, glancing through a gardening book while Sadie lay fast asleep in her plush recliner. Keeping his voice low, he explained why he planned to stay at a distance for a while—for everyone's sake; Alice listened with concern and touched his arm softly, nodding in agreement.

"Please be safe," she murmured, closing her eyes while whispering, "Watch over them dear Lord. They're both so special to me."

As she waited in the adjoining room, Faith found it difficult to get the conversation she had with Novac out of her mind. *Is Venus really so upset that she would harm me? And Usher was attracted to her spontaneity and passion? The only spontaneous thing I've done in the name of love was to give Phil a second chance and marry him and look where that got me! I guess I'm doomed to remain sensible, unemotional, and guarded.*

Novac walked back to where Faith waited. "Bye. I'll call Sadie and check on you. And call me whenever you need anything, and Doo and I will be here in two shakes of a lamb's tail." He kissed her lightly on the cheek. "Take care of baby what's-his-name."

Novac stopped at the store to buy groceries for his days of seclusion, then he picked up two burgers for dinner. He arrived at his home in 'Sconset just after dark and plucked a small pink note from his front door which read: "I need to see you. If you get home soon, come down to the beach. I want to show you how sorry I am." Novac recognized Venus's handwriting immediately. It was now completely dark outside, and he was hungry, so he decided not to venture out to the cold, deserted shore.

He kept a light on all night as he drifted in and out of sleep. With each creak or rustle he heard, he peered out the windows of his small cottage, only settling back into a fitful sleep after convincing himself Venus was not around.

CHAPTER SEVENTEEN

epairs were well under way on the burned portion of The Scrimshaw. The damage was superficial except for one badly charred wall where flames created a hole around the front window in Faith's room. The wood floors in her room were ruined from water and smoke, as were many of her personal items. Burnt drapes were taken down and the blackened windows cleaned.

Faith moved her unharmed belongings up to a guestroom on the second floor. Since much of her clothing and paper items had been ruined by smoke and water, Alice kindly gave her a shopping spree as a belated Christmas present and had contacted her mother to fill her in on what had happened. Faith occasionally phoned her mother now and was relieved to find her more sympathetic than anticipated concerning the breakup with Phil. The prospect of a grandchild obviously had a softening effect on her mother's disappointment, Faith figured.

A check arrived in the mail inside a card.

"You must be needing maternity clothes by now, and, of course, a few baby things! I'm sorry we couldn't make it there for Christmas. We do want to see you soon if that's all right with you. We miss you and love you. Mom and Dad."

Faith put the card aside and wondered how they would accept her friendship with Novac. The last thing she wanted was for her mother to be suspicious regarding the baby's paternity or to draw any false conclusions regarding Novac and her marriage ending. Her relationship with Novac was totally innocent, but if Venus believed he was the baby's father, so could her mother.

Her mother's philosophy had always been that if your husband is taking care of you financially and isn't abusing you, then don't rock the boat. A slight indiscretion here and there on your husband's part was no reason for alarm, she felt. Faith didn't agree with her mother's way of thinking and was afraid her mother would believe she left Phil frivolously to run off and have an affair with Novac.

"I want to see you; please don't think otherwise, but I don't need anymore 'Venus' stress in my life. I think you understand," she told him during their next phone call.

"You're right about that."

Faith read her mother's card to Novac. "I didn't want you to take it the wrong way if I suddenly asked you to get lost," she said with a giggle. "My mother is the type to get a bee in her bonnet and pop in unexpectedly."

"I completely understand. But you can't stop me from dropping by when I happen to be in the area," he said. "I need visual evidence that you're taking care of yourself."

"Fair enough. I appreciate your concern."

Novac and Faith made no plans to see each other in person for a while to quell any suspicion concerning their relationship—not only because of the danger she was in, but because her mother was genuine in her desire to visit soon.

No one had heard from Venus for a couple of weeks. Her friends at the community theater didn't know her whereabouts, and Novac had not been harassed by any more phone calls or visits. She remained the only lead the police had concerning the fire at The Scrimshaw, but still no solid evidence had surfaced connecting her with the crime. As far as anyone knew, Venus dropped off the face of the earth without so much as a peep.

One evening while Novac slept, Doolittle began barking. Novac slipped on his shoes, draped a bathrobe around himself, and walked through the darkened living room to the back door where the dog stood guard. By this time, Doolittle danced around frantically.

"What's the matter, boy? It'd better be for a good reason for waking me up at this hour of the night." He flipped on the kitchen light and looked at the clock. "I took you out before I went to bed." Novac rubbed the sleep from his eyes. "If you've gotta go, you've gotta go, I guess. Come on!" He opened the back door and stepped out into the cold air. "Make it fast, Doo!" Doolittle ran to the back of the yard and barked.

Novac saw in the distance the faint outline of people standing on the beach under the moonlight. Several had encircled something which lay on the ground in front of them. Flashlights glowed eerily as the group hovered around. He could make out none of the words as he watched with interest. Only muffled sounds drifted on the breeze. A vehicle pulled up alongside the scene, headlights shining brightly.

Curiosity got the best of him. Novac went back inside and grabbed the clothes he had thrown on the floor next to his bed. As he bundled himself up, Doolittle remained outside the back door, barking. Novac grabbed his flashlight and headed out the front door, down the small road to the beach entrance. Low tide left the beach wide and wet. Doolittle ran ahead and stood at the group of people waiting for his master. "What's happened?" Novac asked.

"Looks like someone got in some trouble," one man answered. "Probably fell off a boat or something, don't you think? No one would be out swimming this time of year. Not good to swim out there any time of year, really." Several men nodded in agreement.

"Yeah. The surf here can pull you under real quickly if you're not careful. I almost got myself in some trouble out there once," another man added.

"Anyone call for help yet?" Novac asked.

"Yeah. Cops are on the way."

"Man or woman?" Novac asked. An uneasy feeling passed over him as he gazed at the blanket-covered mound on the sand.

"Woman. Looks fairly young from what I can tell."

Novac resisted the urge to look under the blanket. If his suspicions were correct, he'd know soon enough. An ambulance drove onto the beach, followed closely by a police car. Two men got out of the ambulance and walked to the motionless bundle on the sand. An EMT uncovered the body briefly enough to confirm that the victim was well beyond any lifesaving attempts and quickly covered it back. Novac caught a brief glimpse of the bloated body, but it looked unrecognizable to him—although the long hair lying across her face was familiar. While the techs loaded the woman's lifeless body into the back of the ambulance, Novac and Doolittle made their way back to the cottage. He had always claimed to have a low tolerance for anything morbid, so he knew the sight of what he just witnessed would live on in his mind for an exceedingly long time.

Sleep eluded him. Novac turned on his bedside light and held the pink note in his hands, wondering if the message was the cry of a desperately distraught woman. He read the words over and over, analyzing each one for meaning. "Come down to the beach. I want to show you how sorry I am," he murmured, eyes fixed on the piece of paper. "Sorry for what, Venus? Sorry that you said some of the things you said? Or sorry for the fire? Was that you, Venus? Did you set that fire? What were you going to show me that night?" Novac murmured.

He rose and went to a table and pulled out his lap desk, opened the lid and began to write. Doolittle curled up on the floor next to his feet and went to sleep. After an hour of meditative pauses followed by his pen flowing freely, Novac removed his reading glasses, rubbed his eyes, and shut the lid to the desk. The sky was beginning to brighten as he got up to start a pot of coffee. The sight of the vast black-blue ocean took on a new identity to him now. No longer was it just a calming sight out his back window—it was a reminder that it claimed the life of the young woman found on the beach only hours ago.

Novac sat on the couch with his cup of coffee and leaned his head back, drifting off to sleep only to be awakened by hot coffee spilling in his lap. "Dog blast it!" he yelled, jumping to his feet, dabbing at his pants with the blanket from the back of the couch. He unzipped and pulled the pants off and tossed them to the floor. Doolittle stood and slid his paw down Novac's leg.

"Can't you see I've got a little problem here? You're gonna have to wait a minute. Go cut your claws or something! You scratched the heck out of my legs when you did that."

He walked down the short hall to his room in search of a clean pair of pants. As he stood in front of the open curtains, he admired the sky—deep electric blue with the faint, peach outline of clouds hanging over the horizon. He pressed his face against the window and stared down at the hazy beach. The only evidence of the previous evening's tragedy was tire tracks barely visible near the top of the beach, the rest now covered with the rising tide.

Novac trudged his way back to the kitchen, donning his dry pants.

"Blast it! You, you, you, DDDDOG!" He kicked, missing Doolittle by a good five feet. "Couldn't wait just a couple of minutes, could you?" he said as he grabbed a wad of paper towels off the counter and soaked up the puddle on the floor.

When the phone rang early at The Scrimshaw, Alice called out to Faith; a million thoughts ran through Faith's mind as she picked up the phone next to her bed.

"What's up, Novac?"

"They found Venus," he replied.

"Oh, yeah! Where was she hiding out? Has she been arrested?"

"No. Nothing like that." Novac let out a long sigh and continued, "She's dead."

"Oh my gosh. How? Why?"

"A girl washed up on the beach late last night near where I live, so I called the police to find out what they knew about it. They didn't want to tell me anything, but when I told them I believed it was a friend of mine, they confirmed it was Venus. Someone went to the morgue and identified her."

"How did it happen?"

"They didn't see any sign of foul play and said she probably had been drinking. They'll do an autopsy. A few days ago, someone along the beach found a little rubber raft that looked like it had been slashed with a knife. I told the police about the note I found on my door. They suspect it was suicide."

"I'm sorry," Faith said weakly. "I know she was crazy and all, but I can't help feeling sorry for someone who's sad enough to do that."

The coroner's report confirmed Novac's suspicions— Venus's blood alcohol level was so high she couldn't have saved herself in the rough surf even if she had wanted to. Sand was found in her lungs, leading the coroner to declare her cause of death to be drowning. He stated that her body remained submerged in the frigid water for as many as two or three weeks. Novac's pink note may have been the last correspondence anyone had with Venus.

On the day of her funeral, many of her friends at the community theater attended as well as several other artists she had gotten to know during her five years on the island. Then everyone adjourned to the west end of Nantucket and scattered her ashes just as they felt she would want. Since Novac wasn't feeling well that day, Faith stayed close by his side at the cottage.

"Even if I had felt okay," he told Faith, "I don't think it

would've really been a good idea to go."

"Why?" Faith asked.

"I'm sure all of her friends knew about her feelings for me. No telling what she said to them about you and the baby. It could've created a scene."

A couple of days later, Novac walked along Main Street past some of Venus's favorite craft stores when a young man came running out of one door.

"Novac!" Novac turned toward the voice. A slender young man approached him, his hair tipped in pink, an earring in his nose. Novac recognized him as being one of Venus's close friends from the theater group. "I was hoping I'd run into you someday!" Out of breath, he continued. "I'm Adam. Venus and I were pretty close. I don't know if you remember me or not." Novac nodded. "Can we go sit somewhere and talk for a minute?"

"Yeah. Sure," Novac replied. They found a bench on the sidewalk outside a candle shop and sat down.

"I don't think Venus would mind me telling you this, so here goes. She had a lot on her chest the night she died." Adam bent his head over and shook his long, pink-tipped hair. "Man, I hope it's okay to tell you this."

"Go ahead. Venus is gone. What is it?"

"She was really mad at you."

"I already suspected that," Novac said. "Although she had no reason to be."

"Yeah, well, in her mind she was really crazy about you, and it just got the best of her," Adam said.

"I don't think you brought me over here to tell me that."

"No. Well . . . the truth is . . . she was really flipped out on Christmas Eve and took off from the party saying she was going to put an end to you and your new girlfriend. She'd had too much to drink. She drank like a fish sometimes, you know."

"Yeah, I know," Novac replied.

"Well, I caught up to her and asked her what she was

going to do. I said I hoped she wasn't gonna do anything stupid. She just smiled and said she thought she might try to smoke you out. I didn't exactly know what she meant, and I'd been drinking a little bit myself, so I don't remember much about the rest. But the next morning she called to tell me 'Merry Christmas.' She said she'd screwed up the job and was going to be leaving."

"Did you see her after that?" Novac asked.

"Just for a minute. She stopped by my apartment to pick up a few things. She kissed me goodbye and told me she tried to burn down that inn with you and your girlfriend inside."

"So, you never heard from her again?" Novac asked.

"Yeah. She called me later from somewhere and said she was going to go to your house to confess everything and beg your forgiveness. I told her she would end up in jail. She said that wouldn't be possible because afterwards no one would be able to find her. I didn't know what she meant exactly, but then I found a note on my door telling me goodbye and how much she appreciated my friendship and so on. It was obvious she was going to kill herself. I just didn't know where to look for her."

"Wow."

"I don't think she'd mind me telling you. She was going to tell you herself. I just don't want her to have died with that on her conscience. She wanted your forgiveness," Adam said.

"She's got it."

"Phew! I feel better. She was really a special girl, you know."

"Yeah. I know. She was special to a lot of folks," Novac assured.

"No hard feelings?"

"No hard feelings," Novac replied. "And I don't want any of her friends to have hard feelings toward me, either."

"Hey. You gotta right to love anybody you want. She wasn't wanting to share. You know? She really flipped when she found out your girlfriend was having a baby. She saw you two coming out of a baby toy store and you were rubbing your girlfriend's belly. Ooh! She talked about that for days!"

"It really isn't anyone's business, but I meant it when I said I didn't want any hard feelings from you guys, either. To set the record straight, Faith is just a really, really good friend. The baby's not mine. Her ex-husband is the father. I didn't throw Venus over for Faith. Venus and I were over with long before that. She pursued me. I didn't pursue her. Okay? No hard feelings, right?"

"Right. You mean she was all worked up over nothing," Adam stated. They looked at each other in silence, understanding the irony of the situation. "Wow," Adam said as they both sat still for another minute not speaking a word. They realized that Venus let her own imagination get the best of her and it had cost her dearly. The men stood, shook hands, and parted company, each leaving with a heavier heart.

CHAPTER EIGHTEEN

As May arrived, preparations began being made at the inn for the arrival of the baby. Faith's downstairs room now had a nursery area, separated from the rest of the room by a brightly colored floral screen. Every Saturday during the off season, Alice visited the local secondhand stores and church thrift sales looking for toys and accessories that might be needed. It had become Novac's job to drag furniture around the room as Faith tried to decide the best arrangement for easy diaper changing and feedings. He took it upon himself to "childproof" the inn, covering all the outlets and moving all small objects away from low shelves, making sure furniture was secure against the walls and could not be tipped easily. Faith repeatedly reminded him it would be a year before the baby would be walking around, to which he'd reply, "You never know. He might be a fast learner! Better safe than sorry."

"He?" Faith asked. "Are you sure about that?"

"Yep. That's what I said. He."

"What makes you so sure?"

"I just have a sixth sense about those things," Novac replied.

"You have so much experience with babies. Right?"

"I don't need to have experience to know what I feel. I think it's a boy."

The final childbirth class had come and gone, leaving Faith feeling a little anxious about Novac's role in the birthing process. He had been pushing himself hard so that everything would be perfect for the big day. Alice insisted on helping every way she could, but Novac would not hear of it. He ran errands for Faith, commuting back and forth between his house and the inn, sometimes several times a day. Whenever he had a spare hour or two, he continued to work on his book. It obviously was taking its toll on him. He was beginning to look tired and thinner than usual. This did not comfort Faith. Novac was going to be her childbirth coach and needed strength to make it through her labor. He had already expressed concern over seeing all the "blood and guts," as he put it.

Over the last several weeks, Faith's sleep was uncomfortable and scarce. She found herself spending most of her day in a recliner that had molded itself to her new, enlarged shape. Alice stayed busy getting supplies ready for the inn's tourist season and hired a lady to give the place a deep cleaning. Faith was allowed to help with a few chores—taking reservations and anything that didn't require her to be on her feet too long. The physical work around The Scrimshaw was proving to be difficult for Alice to accomplish by herself, so she decided to rent one room only under the condition they didn't mind the presence of a new, fussy, baby in the house.

While folding laundry, Faith answered the phone.

"Hey, Faith. I know it's only two weeks away from your due date, but I have business in Boston that will keep me there for a while. Don't be worried. I'll check on you every day—at least once. You aren't allowed to go into labor without me."

"Is this a joke?"

"Afraid not. I wish I could do something about it, but it's important for me to be in Boston." Novac realized how that sounded after the words came out of his mouth, but not before Faith replied.

"This is important, too, Novac! How long is 'a while'

anyway?"

"I don't know yet. But I assure you . . . I WILL be there for the baby's birth! Promise. I'm leaving in the morning and will check up on you when I get there. Love ya."

While he was away, he called Faith a couple of times a day to check on her, as promised, but on the morning of Faith's weekly prenatal checkup, she began bleeding lightly. The doctor told her to get there immediately. When Novac called, Alice told him Faith had not returned from her appointment yet.

"Faith said that the doctor has some concerns about the baby, so he scheduled her a sonogram," she told him.

"Let me give you the number where I'm staying," Novac said. "Call it as soon as you know anything, but please, do not let Faith call. I want to hear the news from you. She'll sugar coat it so I don't worry. After you give me the news, I'll call her once she's home."

"If that's what you want. I'll call you and tell you what I find out. Are there certain hours call you between? Will you be in meetings?" Alice asked.

"No. Call me any time. I'll explain later.

An hour later, Dr. Hoffman called Alice with an update on Faith.

"Faith gave us written permission to give you medical information on her condition," Dr. Hoffman explained. *Condition?* Alice wondered.

He continued, "Faith has a condition called placenta previa. She's bleeding because the placenta is trying to become partially attached from the uterine wall. This can be serious, so she's being flown to Boston Medical to be watched and treated. They are much more capable of handling emergency situations such as this. The sooner we get her there, the better. We don't want to wait until the bleeding gets heavier," the doctor advised. "We'll make the arrangements. There's an air service we use for transporting patients. She should be leaving in about 30-45 minutes. If you can get a few things packed for her, we can send a courier to pick it up at your inn. Wait. She's telling me that she already has a bag packed for the hospital. Let me give you a heads-up about one other thing. Should the bleeding get heavier, she may need an emergency C-section and possibly a transfusion. Otherwise, they'll watch the bleeding and hope for a natural birth. But I'll stay in touch with the physicians at Boston Medical. She'll be in great hands there. Here, I'll let you speak with her."

"Thanks for taking care of her, doctor."

"Alice? Please don't worry. I'm fine. It's just a precaution," Faith said. "By the way, my bag is sitting inside my closet."

"I'm glad to hear you're okay. I was worried about you. I'm going to fly to Boston to see you as soon as my guest leaves."

"Please don't go to any trouble. I'll be okay. But I need you to call Novac and let him know what's going on. He'll be so disappointed to find out he won't be coaching me during labor."

"I'll call him right now. He checked up on you earlier and left me a number to reach him at. He was genuinely concerned."

"Tell him not to worry. It's so strange to think that the next time I see both of you, I'll be a mother!"

"How exciting! I can't wait, Honey. Take care of yourself and I'll be praying for you. Keep me posted about everything . . . if you are able to call. I love you!" Alice said.

"I promise. I will. I love you, too."

Immediately upon hanging up, Alice dialed the number Novac gave her.

"Boston Medical," the female voice answered. Alice was dumbfounded. Why had Novac given her the number of a hospital? She repeated the number to the woman to make sure she dialed correctly. "Yes, ma'am. That's the number you dialed. How can I help you?"

"Room 267, please," Alice said. When Novac told her he was in room 267, she had assumed it to be a hotel.

"I'll put you right through."

"Hello?" Novac said.

"Novac? Alice."

"Oh, Alice. What did you find out!"

"Why are you at the hospital? I thought you went to Boston on business," she said.

"I'll explain later. How is Faith doing, and the baby?"

"They're on their way up to where you are," she replied.

"Boston?"

"She's having problems, and the doctor feels she needs to be at a larger facility than Nantucket's hospital. Just in case."

"Just in case of what? Is she okay? Is the baby okay?" Novac asked.

"In case she needs a transfusion or something. Don't worry. They'll be okay. She'll explain everything to you when you call. She is probably going to have a C-section and was disappointed that you wouldn't be able to coach. I'm not entirely sure I understand it all myself. Now, why are you in the hospital?"

"Having tests."

"I don't mean to pry, but is something wrong?"

"Yeah. I think so. Don't tell Faith. Promise me. That's why I didn't want her calling me here."

"Cancer?" Alice asked, holding down the fear in her voice the best she could.

"There's a strong possibility it's spread. I don't know for absolutely certain yet, but they think when they removed that small section of colon during the last bout, it already may have spread. Some lymph nodes were affected and removed at that time. I wasn't good about going in for follow-up liver scans. When I finally did have a scan, there were a couple of very tiny spots on my liver. They wanted to check it out further, but I stupidly refused, or I should say, denied it. I elected not to go through chemotherapy or radiation. I got deathly ill from it the last time and couldn't bear the thought of going through it again. My doctors fought me about it, but I didn't figure it would make much difference if it had already spread to my liver. I was feeling okay at that time, but not now. If I had it to do over I would've tried the treatments. It could've bought me more time. That was stupid of me."

"I wasn't aware you were feeling poorly."

"Yeah. I could tell something wasn't right, but the timing was bad. I couldn't let on to Faith. I haven't been feeling well for quite a while."

"She noticed you'd been losing weight," Alice said. "We both noticed. We just thought you were working too hard and not taking care of yourself."

"That was partly true, but not the whole story."

"Novac . . . I'm devastated. I don't know what to say."

"Just don't say anything to Faith."

"She needs to know," Alice said.

"She'll know when the time is right, but this isn't the right time. She's got herself to care for now. And soon she'll have a baby to care for, too."

"Sounds like you should've done the same for yourself."

"Hindsight is twenty-twenty, as they say. I was an idiot not to get myself checked out when I first began feeling bad. Back when Faith and I first met. I knew some of the symptoms were there, but it was easy to ignore them on the days when I felt fine. I just wanted everything to be perfect. I waited a little too long."

"There's a chance it's not cancer, right?"

"There's a chance. A small chance. The scan I just had should give us more information."

"Are you going to be able to see Faith when she gets there?" Alice asked, changing the subject.

"Oh, yeah, sure. I wouldn't miss seeing that baby being born for anything. She can't do it without me! Uncle Novac is the first face he'll see in this world!"

"Are you delivering the baby?" Alice teased.

"Maybe I'll be the second one he'll see," Novac chuckled. "Is Faith really coming to Boston Medical?"

"She should be on her way to Boston now."

"Don't tell her I'm here. I want to surprise her. And please say nothing about my health to her," Novac said.

"I would never want to do anything to upset her," Alice assured. "You *will* keep me posted about the baby. Right? I can't go anywhere because I have a guest staying at the inn for a few days."

"I'll call you every time anything happens."

"You take care, okay? I will keep you in my prayers every day."

"Thanks, and I promise to keep you informed," Novac said.

Novac changed from his hospital gown into some street clothes and periodically checked with the information desk while awaiting Faith's arrival at the hospital. When she was finally admitted, he pushed his hospital bracelet up under his long sleeve and met her clutching a vase of flowers he had purchased at the hospital flower shop.

"Novac!" Faith shouted. "What are you doing here!"

"I wouldn't miss this for the world," he said, bending over her, smoothing back her hair, and kissing her on the cheek. "I hear you've been having some problems."

"Some. I might be a mom a little sooner than we expected."

"You'll be a great one, too," he said.

"How did you get here so quickly?"

"I was already in Boston. Remember? Alice told me where I could find you."

"I can't tell you how happy I am to have you here," Faith said.

"Not half as happy as I am to be here."

"Are those for me?" Faith said.

"And who else would they be for?" Novac said, handing the flowers to Faith. She sniffed at several and read the card.

"They're beautiful! Thanks."

As the nurse wheeled Faith to her room, Novac walked alongside her carrying the suitcase. "I've been rehearsing everything we've learned in childbirth class. I think I'll remember it if I don't pass out. Let's see, it's breathe, push, push, push, scream, or something like that."

"Novac?"

"Yeah, baby?"

"I don't think you'll need to rehearse anymore."

"Why's that? You're firing me?"

"Novac, they're going to be taking the baby."

"What do you mean?"

"I mean I'll be having a C-section. I'm sorry, Novac. I know that's not what we counted on happening. I put you through all those classes for nothing."

"Baby, I did all of that because I wanted to. It was a privilege being there with you. Seeing the look on your face as they explained the birthing process and everything. I'm just so honored you wanted me to be your coach. Alice told me they might have to do a C-section. I was teasing you about the breathing and all. Am I still going to be able to be in the delivery room when he's born?"

"There you go again," Faith said.

"What?"

"He. You said 'he.'"

"I don't like calling the baby 'it'. Babies shouldn't be 'its'."

"Agreed. But what about 'she'?"

"But that would be wrong."

"What makes you so sure? You've just been pulling my leg, haven't you?"

"Trust old Novac." He winked at Faith. "As I was saying, may I be in the delivery room with you? Is that allowed?"

"I can't tell you the answer. But I suppose I'm allowed to

have any coach I want: mother, husband, friend . . . whatever. Right? I guess we'll know as soon as the doctor sees you standing by my side in the delivery room. If there is a delivery and not a C-section. By the way, how's your conference going? Or is it some other kind of business trip?"

"It's going well. After the baby is born, I should be finished with everything I need to do. At least for a while."

"You never told me what kind of business you had in Boston? I just assumed it was a conference. When are you finished?"

"It's over. I'm just here on other business. Meeting with my agent and the publishers. The usual. They want to see how far I've come on my next book. We need to plan the marketing strategy. Book signings. Talk shows. Celebrity stuff. You do know I'm a celebrity, right?" He winked at her.

"Oh, right."

"What's wrong?" Novac asked.

"I had hoped you'd be around some to see the baby. It sounds like you'll be back on the road soon."

"I can assure you. I'll spend as much time as I can with you and the baby. I promise."

"I'm glad you're here now. Did I already say that?"

"You did. But it's nice to hear again."

"Mrs. St. John?" the doctor asked as he walked into the hospital room.

"Yes?"

"I'm Dr. Neal," he said, shaking her hand. "I want to have another sonogram done to make sure there have been no changes since the doctor on Nantucket saw you. Air travel isn't the best thing in your condition, but unfortunately, it couldn't be avoided in this case. I'll feel better if we see that no harm was done."

As Faith tried to stand, she felt a warm sensation between her legs. "I think my water just broke!"

"Don't try to stand," the doctor ordered. "Let's get you down to the delivery room now. We don't have any time to waste." He had the appropriate staff paged immediately.

Faith looked down toward her lap and gasped. She understood the doctor's panicked look. Novac saw her bloodstained pants and turned an ashen color.

"You'll be okay, baby. You're in good hands, I'm sure." He dashed along beside them as the doctor wheeled her chair quickly down the hall, not even waiting for a nurse.

"Doctor?" Faith asked. "What's happening? Will the baby be okay?"

"We're going to do all we can to make sure you and the baby are okay. You're beginning to hemorrhage. We're going to do an emergency C-section. I'm sure your physician filled you in on all the details. Correct?"

"Yes."

"He informed you about blood transfusions I assume?"

"Yes."

"I'm not going to order that unless I'm absolutely sure you need it. Rest assured. But it is a lifesaver. Nothing really to worry about," the doctor explained as he began the prepping process on Faith. "The anesthetist will be here momentarily to administer the epidural."

"Am I allowed to stay in here while the baby's being delivered?" Novac asked.

"In situations like this, we really prefer no one else in the delivery room. We'll make an exception sometimes for husbands if the wife is adamant about it." The doctor looked at Faith. "Well?"

"I'm adamant about it. I must have him in here with me," she said as the nurses helped her remove her clothes and put on the appropriate gown. They got her onto the table and hooked up monitors.

"I guess you're in," the doctor said to Novac. "Please understand that if the situation becomes more serious, you'll be asked to leave."

"Understood." Novac walked over to Faith's side and held her hand as the anesthetist came in. Faith was rolled over on her side while he painstakingly injected the liquid between her vertebrae. Monitors beeped and catheters were hooked up. Novac turned his back on most of the process, not wanting to watch.

"Are you ready to become a mom?" the doctor smiled. "And a dad?" he asked as he turned toward Novac.

"I think I'm going to be one whether I'm ready or not, Lord willing," Faith replied.

Novac bent down and whispered in Faith's ear, "I must be getting old. I don't remember the wedding or the conception." Faith smiled at him.

"Right now," she said, "I can't say that I remember either one myself. Oh, Lord, please be by my side and keep the baby safe," Faith prayed as they started the procedure.

Novac held her hand tightly as a red, wrinkly baby was lifted out of Faith's abdomen.

"Would you like to cut the cord, Mr. St. John?" the doctor asked.

"Nope. Pass on that one. I'll leave it to the expert." Novac waved his hand toward the doctor as if to shoo him away.

"Congratulations!" the doctor said as he clipped the cord. "Looks like you have a healthy baby boy!"

Still grasping Faith's hand, Novac bent down and placed a kiss on her tear-moistened cheek. "Great job. You're wonderful and your son's terrific. I love you."

"I love you, too," she whispered back. "Tell me now, how did you know it was a boy?"

"Brilliance, I think. That and when we went for that sonogram together, the one about mid-way through your pregnancy . . ."

"Yeah?"

"You were pretty choked up and started blowing your nose. I was watching him when he turned toward the screen and flashed me. There was no mistaking it."

"So, all along you really did know but you were pretending not to know. Or actually you were trying to fool me into thinking you didn't know what you were talking about."

"Whatever."

The doctor continued working on Faith as the nurses cleaned the baby up. "You're a mighty lucky woman, Mrs. St. John."

"Yeah, I am."

"Your blood loss was minimal compared to what it could have been. The fact you were already here at the hospital when the hemorrhaging began saved the baby's life and perhaps your life as well. I'm keeping you at the hospital for a few more days," he said as he continued suturing. "You'll need to gain back some strength. You lost more blood than the average mom does during delivery, but like I said, you were mighty lucky."

A nurse walked over to Faith and set the baby down on her chest. His tiny, wrinkled hands flailed around as he tried to squeak out a cry. "Oh, Novac, look!"

"He's beautiful. Just like his mother." Novac turned his face away from where the doctor stood working on the sutures.

"You made it through!" Faith said. "Blood and guts and everything! I'm proud of you! You said you'd never be able to do it."

"Funny how you don't think about things like that when you're faced with a serious situation," Novac said. "All I was thinking about was you and the baby." Faith smiled. "By the way? Does he have a name?"

"I've been working on it, but this all took me by surprise. What about Calvin Russell St. John?"

"Really?"

"You don't like it?" Faith asked.

"I love it. But are you sure?"

"I'm sure. You're the best friend I've ever had. It seems only right to name him after you."

"I'm honored," Novac said as he caressed her shoulder gently with his fingers. The doctor looked curiously at them as they settled on the name, seemingly confused by the conversation, but walked away to scrub up in the labor room sink.

"Do you want to hold him?" Faith asked.

"Are you sure? I might drop him."

"I'm sure." Novac lifted the baby ever so gently from Faith and nestled him in his long arms.

"Little baby Calvin," he said, entranced with the baby's tiny face.

"Cal."

"Cow?" Novac asked.

"Cal, you silly. I'm going to call him 'Cal.'" At that moment, the baby squeaked out another cry.

"I don't think he approves," Novac said, stroking the baby's soft, fuzzy head.

"Just the first of many decisions I'll make he won't approve of, I'm sure."

"If he's a normal son, I think you're probably right about that." Novac bent his head over and kissed the baby softly on the cheek. "I love you, Cal. You are such a lucky, lucky little boy to have this lady here for a mother."

"I'm the lucky one," Faith said, as she reached over and patted Novac on the side of his leg. "I'm the lucky one for sure."

Alice couldn't wait until Faith arrived home with baby Cal. One brief visit to the hospital was not enough to pacify her for long. Her arms were aching to hold the newborn baby. She loved everything about babies—their fragrance, the softness of their skin, even the way they cried. Any apprehension Faith had regarding Alice's offer to live at the inn with Cal, was erased on her first evening back.

By the end of that week, Alice had practically taken over caring for Cal to the point where Faith felt she needed to ask permission to spend time with her own baby. She was thrilled that Alice was so in love with her new son but found it necessary to have a little talk with her. She chose her words carefully.

"The doctor said I am healed enough to take over full responsibility. Thank you so much for your help while I was recuperating. I couldn't have done it without you," she said over dinner. Oh, how she hoped Alice would not take offensive at what she said.

Alice seemed to understand, however, and she apologized profusely for being so selfish with the baby. "If I ever step on your toes, please don't think you'll hurt my feelings by saying so. I'm tough. I can take it. When my son was born, my mother-in-law insisted on staying with me to show me the ropes. I didn't ask her to; she just took over, much to my dismay. It's not that I minded her help. I needed it because I knew very little about raising children. My own mother had just had back surgery and was unable to help, so she only thought she was doing me a favor."

"But I do need your help. I don't know what I'm doing," Faith said.

"Maybe so, but not to the extent my mother-in-law helped me. I guess I was acting exactly the same way. I apologize."

"No harm done and no apology needed."

Novac couldn't stay away either. He was drawn to Cal as a moth is to a flame. Every day he would stop by and check on the baby's progress, staying long enough to give him a bottle, diaper, and put Cal down for his nap. Faith gave up and decided to just consider herself lucky to have two friends who were so interested in her son's well-being.

One day when Novac arrived at the inn to take Cal for a stroll, Alice noticed he was not his usual "chipper" self. Sensing something wrong, she pulled him aside.

"Have you heard anything about your tests?" she said to him as they stood on the front sidewalk. "It's been a while and I've been concerned. You look like you've lost more weight."

"I've heard," Novac replied, looking off past her gaze.

"And?"

"And the news isn't good." Alice held her hand over her mouth and bent her head down.

"Have you told Faith?"

"No."

"Don't you think it's about time?"

"Maybe. I don't know what to say to her. She's been through so much."

"She's stronger than you think. You can't hide it from her much longer. She knows you so well. She's bound to figure there's something not right." Alice said.

"They removed more lymph nodes while I was there. They came back positive. They ran further tests to see if the cancer has spread. My liver scan wasn't good. I'm still waiting for the results of the other tests," he sighed. "Alice, I need to be truthful with you. I don't feel like it's going to turn out okay this time. My body is letting me know in a lot of ways. I shouldn't have ignored it, but Faith's health was more important to me."

"That doesn't make any sense, Novac. She needs you to be as strong as possible. Selfishly speaking, you're not much good to her if you let yourself get worse. When you love people, you take care of yourself for their sake. Don't you want to have a long life together and be able to see that little boy grow up?" Alice realized immediately after the words left her lips she may have gone too far. She looked at Novac's face and tried to read the look on his wrinkled brow.

"You're absolutely right, Alice. I screwed up. As I told you on the phone, at that moment it seemed like the right thing to do. I'll tell her, but not until I know the results of the last tests."

Alice bowed her head slightly and whispered the words, "I'm sorry. God's got this." Novac's long arms reached around her and held her tightly.

"I'm sorry, too. I really am."

The results were not what Novac hoped for but were exactly what he suspected. Faith had to be told their remaining time together would be brief. Alice gave Faith the day off from the inn and encouraged her to accept Novac's invitation to drive out to the lighthouse for a picnic, without the baby. Alice even insisted on preparing her almost-famous meatloaf sandwiches and cheese bread; Novac only had to supply the basket and blanket.

He picked up Faith at the inn promptly at noon. For the first time, Faith noticed a change in Novac's physique as he walked ahead of her to the car.

As they drove to the lighthouse, Novac seemed uncharacteristically quiet, so Faith broke the silence.

"It feels wrong to be leaving Cal behind. Do you think I'm overly protective?"

"That's normal. I think you're a perfect mother," he replied.

They found a good, grassy spot for the blanket, and unpacked the basket. Faith talked about Cal's funny faces, Cal's amusing noises, Cal's reactions to everything. Novac enjoyed listening to her gush over being a mother but inwardly struggled knowing he was about to spoil the moment with news of his health.

"Faith," he said softly, "I've delayed telling you some things—things I should've told you about a long time ago.

Please accept my apology." His gaze was on the blanket before turning his eyes toward hers.

She gasped, dropping her sandwich onto her plate. "No." Her hands were shaking. "I knew things were going too well in my life."

"My trip to Boston wasn't for business. I lied to you. I was there to have medical tests run. That's why I got to you so quickly; I was already at the hospital."

"And . . ." she whispered.

"It isn't good." Novac told Faith of how the cancer had returned and spread. By the time they left, he had spared her no detail about his worsening condition.

She didn't take the news well. All Novac could do was stand back and give her breathing space as she dealt with the deluge of feelings racing through her heart and mind.

Over the next few days, Faith kept a low profile, staying absorbed in Cal's daily routine. Novac tried in vain to get her to open up, but she kept her distance emotionally. She felt as if his inevitable passing would not hurt as much if she shut down just a little of the feelings she had allowed herself to have for him.

Months passed and the treatments Novac was receiving seemed to be of little use. He went through them because he felt he had to give his life every chance he could.

It took every bit of courage Faith could muster to spend time with him at his cottage, taking care of many of his daily needs. It crushed her to see him in an almost helpless position, struggling to get up and perform even the most menial tasks. A nurse was assigned to help most afternoons when Faith couldn't be there.

On the day that Cal took his first step, Novac took a turn for the worse. The nurse took him to the doctor who suggested that he be admitted to Boston Medical for an experimental therapy they'd had some satisfactory results from in later stage colon cancer cases. Novac protested loudly at first but remembered his wish to do anything possible to further his days with Faith, so he agreed to go.

At Alice's insistence, Faith took time off from work to be with Novac in Boston. Never had she felt such dread as she did upon entering the hospital doors. But this was time to be strong for Novac's sake.

At first, the treatments he received seem to bring him some relief. His nausea was less, and the CT scans showed that the spots of cancer had slowed in spreading. But the doctors warned Novac and Faith that his condition was still very grave. Not wanting his illness to drag on and knowing his outcome did not look promising, no matter how many drugs were pumped into his body, Novac spoke frankly to Faith when no one else was in the room.

"Sweetheart . . . you and I both know these treatments will be useless in the long run," Novac whispered as Faith bowed her head. "My choices seem to be to drag out this misery and *maybe* get a few more days, or to not fight what my body wants to do naturally. I'm not afraid of dying and you need to get on with your life. I know where I'll be after I leave this world. You taught me that. What do you think?"

"Novac . . . I can't make that decision for you. I don't like either choice," she spoke into his ear. Novac touched the corner of her eye and wiped a tear away.

He made the decision to discontinue his experimental treatments and to call in hospice and palliative care.

Her next few afternoons in Boston were spent by Novac's bedside, reading to him and filling him in on all of the details surrounding Cal's development into an energetic ten-month-old. Alice kept Cal during her absence and told her stories of his antics. Faith had her Bible with her and read Novac verses he heard her recite on their daily bike rides together. Verses that comforted and intrigued him, enough that he would often sit at his cottage in the evenings and pull out his own copy and meditate on the meanings. Sometimes, the next day, he would ask her if he comprehended the passages correctly. It thrilled her to think that he now cared about his eternity and that he didn't want to ever find himself in a "unevenly-yoked" situation, should he find his one, true, forever love.

When she ran out of new stories to tell about Cal, her work, or gossip from town, she recalled memories of the good times the two of them shared. "Do you remember the night we met?" she asked.

"How could I forget that? You hated me," Novac replied weakly, a smile crossed his face.

"I didn't hate you." Faith leaned in close to him so she could hear his words.

"Well, then you were repulsed by the sight of me."

"Maybe a little."

"But you made sure you ran into me again."

"I think the medicine's making you hallucinate," Faith teased.

"You may not realize what you were doing at the time but admit it, you wanted to see me again." He smiled and Faith swabbed his dry lips with ointment from a nearby tube. She offered him an ice chip, but he shook his head.

"I wanted to see you again." She brushed his cheek lightly with the back of her hand.

"You're a sweet liar," Novac said. Faith bowed her head and smiled. Novac closed his eyes and dozed for a minute as Faith studied his drawn face. She felt a mild twitch from the long, thin hand she clasped between her own. "Faith?" Novac spoke softly.

"Yes, baby?"

"I'm sorry," he spoke, and smiled, looking her straight in the eyes.

"Sorry about what? About getting sick?"

"Yes and no. Sorry I messed up our lives like this," his words were barely audible. She squeezed his cool hand and patted it softly.

"You haven't messed up anything, Novac. You gave my life back to me. You know that don't you?" He smiled at her.

"I just want you to have . . . the security and love . . . you deserve," he whispered.

"I know, baby, I'll be fine," Faith reassured, giving his hand another squeeze.

"You sure will." Novac winked and smiled. "I'm tired. I need to go to sleep now, sweetie. I love you."

"I love you, too." Faith took a deep breath. She knew the meaning of Novac's last statement to her and held onto his hand tightly, as if her touch could sustain his life just a little longer. She remained in the room for a few more hours watching every rise and fall of Novac's chest until his breathing became shallow and his face paled. Occasionally, the nurse looked in to see if anything was needed.

As Novac's life quietly and unceremoniously departed, Faith could not help but be aware of the irony in the situation. Ten months prior, in this very hospital, Novac stood next to her, holding her hand as a precious life came into the world. With her head bowed, Faith mouthed a silent prayer as the attending nurse approached the bed.

Faith covered her red, swollen eyes with dark glasses, and descended the flight of stairs leading to the parking garage. The bright sunshine stung her eyes and seemed to be mocking the solemnity of the afternoon. "How dare you!" Faith shouted in her mind as a young man drove by smiling, chatting to a girl in the seat next to him. *Can't the world pause for one minute? Doesn't anyone realize what just happened inside the hospital? Wasn't Novac's death worth a reverent tip of the hat, or a brief respectful bow of the head?* She yearned for some acknowledgment from the afternoon lunch crowd that flew past her in eager pursuit of a quick burger. No one obliged her. No one shared her monumental grief. Faith never felt so alone in her entire life. Totally alone.

After the funeral in Vermont, Faith returned to Nantucket to be greeted at The Scrimshaw by Alice, Cal, and a middle-aged man holding a large envelope.

"Faith," Alice said, hugging her. "Mr. Griffin is here to see you. He's Novac's attorney. I'll leave you alone."

"Nice to meet you, Mrs. St. John," the gentleman said as he shook Faith's hand. "May we have a seat over here?" He led her to the sofa and began pulling papers out of the envelope. Mr. Griffin was a comical-looking man, with small glasses riding the tip of his nose, upturned eyebrows, and a ring of hair encircling a shiny, bald dome. He was as unlikely an attorney by his appearance as Novac was a best-selling author. "Novac was very special to me, too. He was a great guy." Faith nodded, still confused by Mr. Griffin's visit.

"I have here his will. You probably already know that he left just about everything to you."

"No. I had no idea," Faith responded. "I never gave it any thought."

"Well, he did. He wanted me to meet with you as soon as possible and give you this." Mr. Griffin handed Faith the envelope. "You don't have to open it now. Why don't you wait until you can be by yourself. If you have any questions, I'll be staying here at the inn this evening. Mrs. Woodson has been kind enough to offer me a room."

Mr. Griffin rose from the sofa and shook Faith's hand again. "Novac mentioned to me that your little boy is a very special little guy. He told me all about him. Cal, I believe he said his name is?" Faith nodded. "He was very fond of you, both. Go and get settled in. I know it's been rough for you. Oh, he requested that you pick Doolittle up from the kennel sometime this week."

"Thank you," Faith whispered through her tears. Mr. Griffin patted her gently on the back. Faith held the large envelope close to her body as she walked to her room.

Alice entertained Cal in the backyard while Faith sat on her bed, preparing herself mentally for what waited in the envelope. She drew in a deep breath. As she cautiously loosened the glue, three keys fell from the opening she made.

She fingered them gently and slid the papers out, placing them carefully on her lap. The top paper was a hand-written letter. Clearing her eyes, Faith moved closer to the light and read:

"My Dearest Faith,

"If you are reading this letter, my soul has left this earth and my physical pain is finally gone. I am so sorry that I can't stay with you, baby. 'Goodbye' is a word I never wanted to use in the same breath with your name.

"As you will see from this letter, I am leaving you the four possessions that have meant the most to me in my life. In this envelope there are keys to open three of them.

"The silver steel key is to my Nova. Do with it as you wish. I think it's a fine car—contrary to your feelings!

"The large key belongs to the door of 'House of Alvin'. I certainly have no further use for it. I'm trusting that I'll have a new, improved home where I am now. And cleaner, too, I assume! It makes me incredibly happy to leave my earthly home to you so that you will always have a place to call your own and somewhere to raise our precious Cal.

"The tiny worn key fits my lap desk. I want you to cherish it as I always have. It belonged to my father and his father before. My intention was to give it to Cal someday. You'll have to do that for me now. Inside the desk you will find all the secrets I held so close to the vest. I hope by reading these things you will understand my ways a little better. God knows, you knew me better than anyone else on earth, but I'm afraid I wasn't always completely upfront with you about my feelings. There's no need for me to go into all of that in this letter. Read my romance, my love story, if you prefer. I want you to promise me that you will continue the story I began to write and give it to Cal when he's older. You'll find it all in the lap desk. You have my permission to look in it. It's all yours now. My secretive lap desk where I kept my heart locked up with a small key. Forgive me, baby, for handling things the best way I knew how.

"Forgive me, also, for the horrible mess I left for you at the cottage. Don't eat anything in the refrigerator for your own health's sake. Now is your chance to clean the house up like you've been itching to do since the day you first saw it. Enjoy!

"The fourth precious thing is my old friend, Doolittle. No key required for him. Please take care of the little fellow. I've had a long talk with him and explained that I would not be coming home. He's a good listener and will remain faithful to you until his days are over (he assured me).

"Lastly, I want you to know that Cal's financial requirements will be taken care of, as well as your own. I have set up an account in your name that should cover all your worldly needs. Bob Griffin will fill you in on the details. I want you to be able to relax and enjoy Cal as he grows without worrying about money. There should also be enough for you to go buy a new hat if you desire. I know how fond you are of hats!

"Until we meet again somewhere, someday, take care of yourself, my love. You are more precious to me than you can even imagine.

Love forever,

Novac"

Faith fell asleep that night holding the envelope. Its presence had comforted her. However, the very words contained inside only reinforced the fact that Novac was truly gone. This had not been a bad dream, as Faith had hoped upon waking.

Cal was restless and eager to get out of his crib and begin his day, full speed ahead. Alice was happy to keep Cal for the day while Faith went to the cottage.

Faith's mind wasn't on her drive to 'Sconset, so all the familiar landmarks went unnoticed as she neared her destination. She turned down the narrow road to the cottage;

her eyes fixed on the gate seven houses down. As she approached the sidewalk in front of "House of Alvin", she half-expected to see him walk out the door to greet her, laughing and telling her it had all been a tasteless joke. But he did not appear in the doorway, with Doolittle bouncing excitedly next to him. Grief and nervous anticipation saturated Faith, body and soul. "I can't do this," she whispered as she sat in the car staring straight ahead. Out of the corner of her eye, she noticed someone watching her.

Mrs. Graham stood in her yard watering her potted begonias. She dropped her garden hose and walked across the street as Faith emerged from the car. No words were spoken as they embraced tightly, each understanding the pain the other felt.

"You'll be here now, won't you?" Mrs. Graham said as she took a couple of steps backwards, holding onto Faith's hands. "I just assumed that Novac—", Mrs. Graham stopped herself.

"I don't know what my plans are at the moment," Faith replied. "I need time to collect my thoughts. I still can't believe he's gone."

"I sure hope I'll see you around. I'll leave you alone now. Will you be okay?" Faith nodded and wiped the tears from her cheeks. Mrs. Graham went back across the street and resumed her watering as Faith pulled the keys from the envelope. She kept out the one she recognized as the house key and slipped the other two into her pocket.

She clutched the key in her sweaty hand as she inserted it into the lock. She turned the knob and slowly pushed the door open, taking a deep breath as she stepped inside. Stacks of papers rose up from nearly every flat surface she saw. Novac's bedroom scuffs sat in front of the couch exactly as he'd left them the last time he slipped them off his feet.

Faith flipped on a nearby lamp and walked into the kitchen, noticing that it looked cleaner than she had ever seen it before. *The nurse must have straightened it up,* she thought as she walked over to the back door and gazed at the deserted beach. *That's where he saw me the day I stepped on the thorn.* "My knight in shining armor," she whispered.

Faith felt uneasy as she walked through the remaining rooms. She had never been in the cottage without someone's—at least Doolittle's—presence around. She wished for the dog's happy company to break the solemn mood of the quiet house.

On Novac's bed sat the lap desk. She had always been forbidden to look inside and now approached it with trepidation. *What secrets are hidden inside? Novac wrote that he was eager for me to read his papers. Is this something that will make me happy or will I be upset over the words I read?*

Faith reached into her pocket and pulled out the small key. She sat down beside the lap desk and gently unlocked it. She rubbed its smooth surface and lifted the lid back, exposing the thick journal in which she had seen Novac write many times before. "My Love Story" the front cover had scrawled on it in black marker along with a hand-drawn smiley face. Funny, she'd never noticed those words written on it before. She opened the cover and read the first entry, dated May 3, 1989. "The day after I arrived on Nantucket," she whispered, as she read on:

"Tonight, I'm sitting down to write, although it is quite late, because I am unable to fall asleep. I just met someone. Faith is her name, and her voice is still dancing in my ears. I'm sure she hasn't given me another thought, but I can't help but believe my path will cross with hers again soon. I'll anxiously await that moment."

"May 4, 1994:
I've just taken a thorn out of the foot of the woman I'll marry someday. She would be completely appalled to read

my sentiments."

Faith felt confused. "You were in love with Venus then. Why were you writing these things about me?" she said to the journal. She noticed diary entries for each day they had been together. Hundreds of them. Some were only one line; several were many paragraphs long. A plain gold ring rolled around in the lap desk as she lifted the heavy journal out. She set the book down on the bed and held the ring up to the light. "Looks like some kind of wedding band," she mumbled. She squinted to read the inscription inside. "To the love of my life." The ring looked brand new. Faith held the ring up to her finger. "This would never fit a man's finger. No way. Maybe it belonged to his ex-wife." She set the ring back into the lap desk and continued to read the journal, flipping ahead to the final several entries.

"April 25, 1990:
"This will either be the beginning of the happiest period of my life or the most regret-filled time I'll ever encounter. Today, I purchased a ring for the woman I love more than life itself. Doolittle chewed up the box. Suppose I'll have to get him to apologize when I give the ring to her.
"I'll need to be in Boston for a while at the urging of my doctor. He will poke and prod me until he decides whether or not I'm having a recurrence of the big 'C,' and if it has spread throughout my body. I haven't been feeling very well lately. I'm not getting any younger and my old body has been working mighty hard lately getting ready for the baby's arrival. I'm hoping it's just a case of exhaustion taking its toll on me.
"On the lighter side, if I'm pronounced free and clear, I plan to ask Faith to become my wife after she comes home with the baby. It's a dream I've had almost since the moment I met her."

As Faith flipped the page over, she imagined Novac sitting at the desk, writing into the journal, spilling his heart out onto the pages. "Why didn't you tell me any of these things? I needed to hear them." She noticed that the next date was Cal's birthday.

"May 1, 1990:

"Today is a happy day! Calvin made his entrance into the world, speaking his mind, just like his mother has been known to do on many occasions! He's beautiful, just like his mother.

"As I held him, I longed to call him my son; to kiss his mother and tell her I'd take care of them forever. However, if my suspicions are correct, my time with them will be short. I will, in all probability, be the one needing to be taken care of. But enough of that! This is a time to celebrate the new life amongst us. I love him very much already. Almost as much as I love his mother, Faith."

"May 3, 1990:

"My doctor has just informed me of my fate. No longer can I keep my head in the sand, pretending the aches and pains in my body are merely exhaustion. The optimist in me hoped that if I kept my head buried in the sand long enough, I would emerge a whole and healthy man, like waking from a bad dream.

"With my doctor's fateful words, my hope of a future with Faith fled out to the water's edge, allowing the current to carry it far out into the sea. She has lost before and suffered greatly. I will never allow myself to be the reason for such pain in her life. Yes, she will have to endure more grief with my passing, but it will be sorrow over the loss of a dear friend, not the unbearable pain of losing one's spouse in the prime of life.

"I can only hope she forgives me someday for not being

totally truthful with her; for not disclosing the innermost desires of my heart. I love her so completely, but I've selfishly kept this love a secret from her.

"I have to wonder, however, is this indeed a selfish thing I have done or the most unselfish act humanly possible? I've struggled with this question and pray I've made the right decision. Oh, how I've come close to giving in every time I'm around her. How I long to hold her close as my wife. I stop myself from thinking these things when I realize I could never deceive her like that. To make her think we have a future together."

"Continue our story, Faith." The next entry read: "Keep an account of our lives for Cal's sake. I want him to know me and to always believe in love and the truth that love never ends, just as Faith taught me from the words of her Bible."

Faith closed the journal and reached for the box of tissues next to the bed as all the emotion she had held inside escaped in heaving sobs. She no longer needed to be brave for Novac's sake.

Faith finished straightening the room and sat on Novac's bed. She reached into the lap desk where the gold band lay amongst pens and small scraps of paper. She slid it onto her slender finger and whispered, "I understand, and I forgive you, Novac."

A small, familiar Bible lay under the journal and stack of papers in the lap desk. She opened the cover and saw the inscription she wrote before presenting it to him on his birthday. *"Read it and you'll better understand some of the things I've spoken of to you and a little more about my heart."* Faith remembered feeling somewhat pushy and preachy in choosing that gift for him, but he accepted it with grace and even seemed pleased that she cared about his soul. She had marked places she especially wanted him to take note of. The pages fell open to the book of John. Her eyes grew wide as she noticed the many verses that had been underlined in that crazy, green-inked pen Novac often used to edit his manuscripts. Faith flipped through the Bible and read several green notes written in the margins. *"Wish I'd known this before"* and *"I believe this with all my heart"* he had written a few times. *"Ask Faith about this,"* she read in Romans. *"Unequally yoked no more!"* Her heart filled with happiness and hope.

SEVEN YEARS LATER

Faith wrapped the last of the glassware in newspaper, put it in a box, and taped it closed. She glanced at her watch. Ten o'clock. *Time to be going to bed. It will be an early day tomorrow.*

Her fingers lovingly caressed the top of the old lap desk. In the morning, it would ride with her in a place of honor on the short trip to The Scrimshaw Inn. She lifted the lid and opened the journal to the next blank page. Her fingers gently twirled the simple gold band around and around her finger. She had remained true to Novac's request for her to continue the story. Nothing spectacular. Only a few scattered entries since she moved into the cottage seven years ago. It seemed only fitting to add another to the journal on this evening.

She scribbled a little to get the ink flowing and tapped the paper lightly as she tried to think of what to say:

"Well, it's almost time," She wrote. "Tomorrow I'll be leaving to take over full time duties at The Scrimshaw. I'm not deserting my little rose-covered cottage forever; only helping another dear old friend. Alice has left for Florida—a 'snow bird' she calls herself. The wintry weather was getting to be too much for her. She has asked me to move in and manage the inn until she makes the final decision to sell and stay where the weather's warm all year 'round. She has many emotional ties to The Scrimshaw. I can certainly understand that.

"In the meantime, a young fellow will be moving in here

to keep the home fires burning, so to speak. Someone from your old alma mater, Novac. A writer. He's excited about renting the cottage that once belonged to his hero. He'll take up residence here next weekend after his college graduation.

"I'm going to miss my precious rose-covered cottage. But I think it's only appropriate that just as the vines outside will soon be bursting into bloom, this cottage will, again, be inspiring someone else's imagination. May his stories of love and the sea touch as many hearts as yours do, my darling!

"I won't cry, Novac. This is a happy occasion. Cal and I won't be too far away from our home. And when I come back, it will be forever—my precious 'House of Alvin'. This is where I got to know my beloved friend. Where I have begun to raise my only child. Where I learned what love and devotion really are. Where dreams were tragically dashed only to come alive again for me and flourish . . . just like the roses that climb ever higher with each passing year.

"My dear Novac, this is our love story. It's not finished yet. It will continue in my heart as long as God allows me to roam this planet. You've given me a sweet gift, the gift of love, for which I will be forever grateful to you. Until we meet again, my love . . ."

The sun rose over the ocean as Faith sipped her cup of coffee at the kitchen table. Cal hid behind the large boxes stacked in the living room, pretending they were a fort.

It won't be long now, Faith thought as she looked at her watch. She rose and wandered one last time through each room of the tiny house, taking a mental photograph of the place that had been her home for the past seven years. In one last nurturing gesture, she raised her arm to the bathroom mirror and wiped away a spot with her sleeve.

"Mrs. St. John," she heard a low-pitched voice call through the open front door. "We're here to move some things for you."

The men were quick to load the boxes and furniture into the waiting truck. Faith took a glance around the inside of the house and locked the front door. Cal ran across the yard in hot pursuit of a lizard.

On the short walk down the sidewalk toward her car, Faith paused briefly to raise her hand and whisper, "See you later." A round, smooth stone lay embedded in soil next to the sidewalk; a circle of pansies surrounded it. The chiseled word "Doolittle" on top of the stone caught her eye in the bright morning sun and seemed to twinkle back in response to her, "All will be well, dear friend. All will be well."

END

Peggy Godson Mueller is an Atlanta-area native with a heart split between the charm of the South and the history and beauty of New England—two regions that often inspire the settings of her novels. Recently retired and newly married, Peggy now spends her days exploring new places and hole-in-the-wall restaurants with her husband Steve Beaupré, and crafting stories that speak to the soul.
Her writing style is rooted in creating lovable, relatable characters who are perfectly imperfect—just like the rest of us. Through her storytelling, Peggy aims to touch readers' hearts and leave them wishing they could spend just a little more time in the world she's created.